every visible thing

also by lisa carey

LOVE IN THE ASYLUM

IN THE COUNTRY OF THE YOUNG

THE MERMAIDS SINGING

Lisa Carey

WILLIAM MORROW
An Imprint of HarperCollins*Publishers*

every visible thing

This book is a work of fiction. The characters, incidents, and dia-
logue are drawn from the author's imagination and are not to be
construed as real. Any resemblance to actual events or persons,
living or dead, is entirely coincidental.

FIRST EDITION

Designed by Jennifer Ann Daddio

Printed on acid-free paper

Library of Congress Cataloging-in-Publication Data

Carey, Lisa.
    Every visible thing : a novel / Lisa Carey.—1st ed.
        p. cm.
    ISBN-13: 978-0-06-621289-0 (acid-free paper)
    ISBN-10: 0-06-621289-8 (acid-free paper)
        1. Separation (Psychology)—Fiction. 2. Domestic fiction.
    I. Title.

PS3553.A66876E84 2006
813'.6—dc22

                                                            2005044855

06 07 08 09 10 WBC/RRD 10 9 8 7 6 5 4 3 2 1

FOR TIM

contents

acknowledgments

Thanks to the MacDowell Colony for time, space, and pampering, and to my MacDowell friends, especially Erin Flanagan, for lunch breaks and laughter. Thanks to my editor, Jennifer Brehl, her assistant, Katherine Nintzel, Michael Morrison, Lisa Gallagher, Pam Jaffee, and all those at Harper-Collins who have been so wonderful through every step of the last three novels. Thanks to my agents, Christy Fletcher and Elizabeth Ziemska; to my favorite bookstores, Brookline Booksmith and Longfellow Books in Portland; to my family and friends—unpaid editors and therapists; to my grandfather, Thomas J. Carey, for selling my books to everyone he meets; to my husband, who must have thought being married to a writer would be more exciting; and to my three best friends, Sascha, Beth, and Marianne, who remember what I was like in high school and love me anyway.

every visible thing

prologue
the fureys, 1975

Lena's favorite part of kindergarten is the end, when her brother comes to pick her up. At two P.M. on the clock where she is learning to tell time, Hugh descends from the second floor where they keep the fifth-graders, and her class is let loose to gather coats and clean out their cubbies. The kindergarten is not a room with desks, but an open pit with massive red-carpeted stairs leading down, each one as high as Lena's waist. Her brother likes to run down to the center of the pit and back up again, because he remembers, when he was in kindergarten, climbing these stairs like she does now: as if they are mountains.

Hugh is a giant towering over toggle coats. He is as tall as the mothers, who arrive in dribbles, flushed and hair blown wild as if they have run all the way. Hugh helps Lena gather her projects, rolls up her finger paintings, and carefully stacks the macaroni sculptures on top of one delicate, official envelope, somehow making it all fit into her monogrammed canvas book bag. He refuses to carry her Spider-Man lunchbox, even though it was once his, a *boy's lunchbox,* a girl in her class has told her, as if this involves some sort of betrayal. Lena can't always remember which things belong to boys and which to girls; the distinctions are recent and make little sense to her.

Outside it is October. This morning she left her new sky-blue coat open, but now it is chilly, and Hugh helps her thread the imitation bone tusks through the loops. In her pockets she finds leaves ironed in the school's waxed paper—yesterday's project already forgotten. As soon as they are out of sight of the park, where eighth-graders run laps and the Extended Day kids form clusters by age in between the jungle gyms, Hugh accepts her backpack and lunchbox so she can run ahead unencumbered. She kicks through leaf piles, worries briefly about the new scuffs on her saddle shoes, skips a block to the intersection she is forbidden to cross alone, sprints back and asks her brother if he will play LEGOs with her when they get home. "Maybe," he says, refusing to promise. She pleads until he says he has homework, which silences her. Homework is serious, sacred. Lena doesn't have any because kindergarten, according to her brother, is merely a practice year before real school begins.

On these walks home Hugh is quiet. Lena doesn't mind because she knows once they're home they'll have to tell their mother and then their father all about their days, and on the way there he likes to stay in his head. Hugh is very smart. There is talk of him skipping the sixth grade, going directly to the third floor where there is a separate teacher for every subject. He will get annoyed if she interrupts his thinking, so she thinks with him. She thinks about her birthday, which is the day after the day after tomorrow, wonders whether her mother will make a bunny-shaped cake with coconut fur, or if she's old enough now to have an ice-cream cake from Carvel. She thinks about Halloween and the angel costume her father made for Hugh that she is now big enough to wear without toppling over from the heavy wings. She thinks about Thanksgiving at her grandmother's house where she will play unsupervised with children called her second cousins, as if the first batch has been misplaced. She thinks about her snowsuit with the clip-on mittens and igloos and Christmas and smelling the tree and new pajamas and her mother's reindeer cookies and the baby doll at church and the Charlie Brown Special about the tiny tree that nobody wants. She knows as she march-swish-march-swishes through the leaves that all these things are coming because of the smell of the cold and the apples in her lunchbox and the darkness that ends her day too early and seals her inside.

Their house, a brown-shingled two-family, is at the end of a dead-end street. Lena's family lives on the first floor and a group of nursing students live on the second, in an apartment that is both identical and completely different from theirs, because of the furniture and photos and strange smells. The nursing students change every year, except for Joyce, who is already a nurse, and needs roommates to pay the rent. They all adore Hugh, call him a ladies' man, and let him try their stethoscopes. Lena doesn't know what to say to them. With their bickering perfumes and starched uniforms and pristine white clogs, they seem like a different kind of woman than her mother.

Once home Lena will tack her projects—they mean nothing to her, she has moved on, but this is expected—on the wall-sized corkboard in the kitchen. She will present her mother with a white envelope: her first school photo back from the printer. There is one eight-by-ten framed in the plastic window, behind it are two five-by-sevens, four three-and-a-half-by-fives, and twenty-four wallet-sized. On photo day her mother dressed her in a patchwork blouse, far more girly than what she usually wears, and pink plastic barrettes shaped like butterflies. She does not look like herself; the blue background makes her pasty, and her smile seems on the edge of tears. Her hair is tangled as usual, past the help of the small plastic comb given to her by the photographer's assistant. When her mother looks at these photos she will sigh a little, then smile and praise and immediately cut along the white bars and release one of the wallet-sizes to tack onto the corkboard. The eight-by-ten will be framed and set next to the series of Hugh's photos that crowd the built-in bookshelves in the living room. The rest will be sent in cards to her relatives, on which she will be asked to write her name under a note composed by her mother. This will happen on a sunny Saturday morning when she'd rather be outside, long past the time she has forgotten both her pride and her embarrassment over the photo.

Lena prefers the photos her brother takes with his Polaroid Instamatic—given to him on his last birthday. He encourages her goofy poses, doesn't care what she wears, and gives her the smelly piece of film that the camera spits out. She holds it carefully by its edges, and watches as it slowly develops into her. She likes seeing herself the very next moment, rather than weeks or months later, when so much has happened that she feels like a different girl.

While her mother makes dinner, Lena will play with her baby brother, Owen, spinning, squeaking, and rattling the objects on an activity center that was once hers, the white plastic edges spoiled by tiny teeth marks. She will watch her mother chop vegetables at the kitchen counter, pausing every few seconds to lift her cigarette from the orange plastic ashtray, laughing at everything Hugh says. Lena will run to answer the door for her father, who thinks it's funny to ring the bell as if he is a visitor, then watch Hugh play chess with him at the same time as he does his math homework. When Lena whines over the injustice of this, Hugh will help her build another complex in the LEGO city that he started when he was six, and has recently bestowed to her. They will all have dinner together, salad and steak for the grown-ups, mac and cheese with cut-up hot dogs for what they call their "two-point-three children." Except Owen doesn't really eat, just sits in his mother's lap and sucks a bottle.

After dinner will be her bath, a lonely affair as she is now trusted to clean herself as long as the door remains open and she calls out every few minutes to say she is okay. Her mother will put Owen down in his crib, installed in a curtained-off corner of Lena's room, and her father will grade papers while Hugh watches the news. Once in her pajamas she might get a few precious minutes with her father, who has recently begun to talk to her the way he talks to Hugh. He asks her what she is learning in school, and she knows instinctively that she must give an interesting, nonbabyish answer. Occasionally, when stumped (most of what she does in school is play games), she makes something up, and she can see, even before her father's frown, something like a curtain pass across his eyes. Then she will ask him if God is a man, or where heaven is, or what her guardian angel looks like, because these questions are sure to light his eyes and distract him from her childishness. His answers are long and convoluted; he peppers them with phrases like "the Jews believe," "the Christians think," and "in the Muslim tradition," until Lena is completely lost and has forgotten what she asked in the first place. But she nods along, because anything is better than being alone in bed.

Eventually, her mother will come in and say "Lena, bedtime," though she will look pointedly at her husband, in that way that Hugh once told her means they are teaming up. Her father will tuck her in, tight down to her ankles like a mummy. Hugh is allowed up for another hour, so she will hear his voice, along with her parents', murmuring importantly in the living room. She will hold her eyes wide open, determined to stay awake as long as everyone else. And she will fall asleep until another day when she will start school—she still does not quite understand this—at the same hour she went to bed.

But home and all that it encompasses are a few minutes away. Right now she is still walking with her brother, the tallest boy in the fifth grade, who, despite his deep thoughts, takes her hand and march-swishes for a few squares of the sidewalk. For the moment all that matters is his slightly sweaty palm around hers, and she wonders, as the leaves fall, laying the path before them, what it is like to stride at the height of a grown-up, to be a boy, to dwell on things that are more complicated and farther-reaching than the games you will play in the next hour or day or season. She wonders what her big brother thinks about.

1. camera

1985

The first time I tried killing myself, nobody noticed. This was last year, when I was in the ninth
grade. I took a whole package of Actifed, tiny
white pills I had to push one at a time through the
tinfoil backing. It was the only drug I could find in
the medicine cabinet besides vitamins and Owen's
inhaler. The thing is, I'm not sure why I did it, except that I had a test the next day in Ancient Civilizations that I hadn't studied for. It was an honors

class. I used to get all As in grammar school, which was why I was allowed to take it. I'd never failed a test in my life. But I hadn't been doing my homework, and I'd barely taken notes in class. It had gotten to the point where just seeing the textbook in my bag made me chant *you're dead you're dead you're dead,* over and over in my mind, until I barely knew what the words meant, but they scared the shit out of me anyway. I took the pills at three in the morning with a bottle of ginger ale. All that happened was my vision went a little funny and then I threw up. By the time my parents woke up I was green and pasty-mouthed and still heaving. I didn't exactly announce what I'd done, so they thought I had the flu and let me stay home. My mother is in medical school, where she gets to pretend to be a doctor and has to stay over at the hospital about every other night. My dad used to be a theology professor at Boston College, where I was supposed to go someday because it would be half-free, but they fired him. Now he works for a publishing house downtown, editing religious books written by other people. It must be boring because he never talks about it. When Owen and I stay home sick, we do it alone.

For some reason that day, when they were gone, after my stomach settled and I had some toast, I decided to go through Hugh's stuff. I inherited his room. It's in the back of the house, far from my parents and Owen, near the sun porch and the back door and the kitchen. They gave me Hugh's room when I started high school, making a big show out of cleaning him out, not wanting me to feel like I was living with a ghost. They couldn't go all the way, though, and I found everything in the basement, in banker's boxes with his name written in black Magic Marker on the contents line.

I took a few things at a time, so they wouldn't notice. First it was his turntable and his records, which I listened to when the rest of them were asleep. My favorites were the Beatles and Prince, much easier to listen to than the Clash or the Sex Pistols. My brother's tastes seemed divided between normal music and the loud, scream-ing, unbearable stuff he must have thought was cool. I tried but couldn't stand those. Only boys, and the occasional tough, disturbed girl, listen to punk as if it is music.

I brought his books up next, sliding in between my *Anne of Green Gables* series and *Gone with the Wind,* Hugh's mauled copies of *The Catcher in the Rye, Invisible Man, The Brothers Karamazov.* His Snoopy, with its loose neck and the fur gone gray. I even sneaked a few items of his clothing: a flannel shirt, black fatigues from the army-navy store, the leather jacket with snaps and a dozen zippers, unfathom-ably left behind. I couldn't wear these things without my parents recognizing them, so I kept them in my closet, hidden at the far edges behind the confirmation dress I never wore and my old blue toggle coat, which for some reason I refuse to let my mother send to Goodwill. At night, after my parents went to sleep, I would take out the jacket, slip it on over my flannel pajamas, and finish my home-work with leather heavy as a warning on my shoulders. (I made up all my work for Ancient Civilizations. I didn't want things to get so out of control again.) In the tiny zippered breast pocket, I found a smashed, brittle plastic square with one squishy condom inside. This was disgusting, the thought of my brother stashing it in there. He had a girlfriend in the ninth grade, and I wondered if the condom was something he would have actually used, or just wishful think-ing. It was kind of exciting after I got over the shock. No one had ever found this before; it was something only I knew. That my brother, at the age of fifteen, had walked around with the promise—or hope—of sex in his pocket. Though the date stamped on the edge of the plastic was from three years ago—apparently condoms expire, just like milk—I left it in there. I liked the idea of it wrapped in the satin lining, still waiting to be used.

It wasn't until this past summer that I found the film. It was in a box with other photo supplies—printing paper, bottles of chemicals, a metal can of compressed air. Hugh was obsessed with photography. He was the one who took pictures when I was little; my parents only ordered the school photos and took half a roll on Christmas and birthdays. When he was in high school, they let him convert the back bathroom with the broken toilet into a darkroom. He spent his weekends locked in a cube of red light, printing his photos onto eight-by-ten paper, hanging them on a clothesline to dry. There were only a few old photos in the box, mostly rolls of unprocessed film and envelopes full of plastic strips of negatives. It was hard to tell what the pictures were of, except that they involved people. When I held the strips up to the window, the dark and light areas were reversed, so faces looked like black holes and trees like lollipop sticks.

I used to think the police took Hugh's photos, along with all the other evidence they eventually returned. Besides the few pictures framed in the dining room, all of Hugh's photos seemed to have disappeared with him. But then I remembered my parents looking for them, asking me if I knew where they were. Maybe they wanted to find out who he was hanging out with, something they weren't so sure about near the end. Now I think they never even came across this box. It was mislabeled, in Hugh's writing, with the words "Old Stuffies." I am the only one who knows about it.

I signed up for Photography this year. I could have brought the film to CVS, but that seemed wrong. I want to develop them myself. It will be like searching for him, long after everyone else has given up.

My last class before Photography is always Honors Geometry, F block, room 247. On the first day of class, while taking attendance, Mr. Herman looked up after my name and asked if I was Hugh's sister. I didn't study for the first test and a received a 47. He hasn't looked at me since.

Every day in Geometry I keep a record of the minutes left in class along the margins of my notebook. It's the only way I can get through it without screaming. I write each minute down and cross it out when it has passed. In between, I write notes to Tracy, who sits behind me. Tracy is my only friend. After being tortured by all the popular girls in grammar school, I never thought I'd have a girl as a friend. But it's too complicated to be friends with boys in high school. Most of last year I had no friends at all, besides the desperate-to-sit-with-anyone lunch partners my first month. Because I didn't act as eager as they did to have a shadow, I got a reputation for being a loner, and it made people assume I didn't want any friends at all. Sometimes I don't.

Tracy and I both have classes in the Unified Arts Building after Geometry. We walk there together. That's pretty much the extent of our relationship, besides the notes I write her, which she refuses to answer, because she doesn't think I should write them in the first place. Not that she cares about Geometry, she doesn't, she just respects rules. Tracy is a horse fiend. She spends every afternoon and all weekend working at a barn an hour outside of the city, to pay for the board of her own horse, Cecil. Which is why we never do anything outside of school. She wears dirty jeans that smell slightly of barn and worn T-shirts over her totally flat chest. Her brown hair is always pulled into a neat, low ponytail. She's not interested in boys and reads while eating her lunch. It takes a lot, usually something weird, to make her laugh. I'm not even sure she likes me very much.

The main building of the high school has four floors and is shaped like a square with a landscaped quadrangle in the middle. On our way from Geometry, Tracy and I cut through the Quad. There is no major popular crowd here like there was in my grammar school.

Now there are different groups, named for the places they choose to hang out. There are two red-brick stairways leading up to first-floor classrooms, labeled the Punk Stairs, where kids with Mohawks keep pet rats hidden in the hoods of their sweatshirts, and the New School Stairs. The New School is a probation program for extreme fuckups, delinquents who are starting over after some tragedy, who take non-taxing classes and spend a lot of time "cooling off" in the social work office. There are other groups who hang out inside: drama kids, science geeks, socially conscious rally organizers. Jocks sit along the benches in front of the sports building that has the gym and the community pool. The Quad is mostly for the bad kids, the ones who smoke, who drop acid, who look world-weary one minute and like excited toddlers the next. Half the classrooms overlook it, so normal kids, whose lives have never fallen apart, can look out of the windows to see what they are missing.

Tracy would rather not walk through the Quad. She's always trying to get me to go around the hallways and out the front entrance. I'm the one who insists we walk this way. Sometimes I torture her by stopping to lean on a stone wall, turning my face to absorb the sun.

"Lena, let's go," she says when I linger today, looking around and pinching her mouth.

"I think I'll start smoking," I say, watching a New School girl hold her long hair out of the way as a shirtless boy lights her clove cigarette with a match.

"Don't be stupid," Tracy says. "Why would you want to smoke?"

"Why not?" I say.

"Lung cancer, for one thing. Plus, it smells gross."

"Teenagers don't get lung cancer," I say. She has no answer to this except her superior shrug.

The heavy blue door to the right of us bursts open and out pours a group of sophomore girls. They wear sweatpants twisted in toward the ankle, white Gap socks, L.L. Bean shoes with laces spiraled at the eyelets, and huge polo oxfords in pastel colors. They march past us, ringlets swinging, flavored gloss oiling their lips. Two of them were popular girls in my grammar school. They pretended to be my friends for about two weeks in the fifth grade, after Hugh disappeared and I was briefly interesting. In grammar school I had to endure them every day, but here I can go a week without seeing them at all. They stare at me and snicker, as they always do now, like they can't be bothered to insult me outright. Tracy doesn't notice, rummaging in her backpack for a book.

I look toward the Punk Stairs, where a guy with spiked green hair keeps the attention of a group of girls by burning his arm hairs off with sweeps of his Zippo.

"Tracy, don't you ever get bored of yourself?" I say. This doesn't come out the way I mean it, and I'm afraid she might feel insulted. But she doesn't really hear me. She shuts her paperback, tucks a strand of frizzing hair back where it belongs.

"I'm bored now," she says. "Can we go? I'll be late for class."

Arch kids, in the darker of the two tunnels that lead from the Quad to the front of the building, are tough, from the poorest neighborhood in town, Whiskey Point, where I once went to church and Sunday school. When Tracy and I walk through, girls with bangs that defy gravity glare at us and blow smoke out their nostrils. We part on the first floor of the Unified Arts Building without goodbyes, she to her drawing class, me to Beginning Photography. I've seen her portfolio in her bag. All she ever draws is horses.

The photography lab is on the third floor, at the end of a long linoleum hallway that smells more like a science lab than an arts building. The first part you see when you walk in is a normal classroom, with writing desks and a rolling blackboard and a projector. Behind this is a galley of sinks and cabinets stocked with white plastic bottles of chemicals, a tall drying rack where we can peek at the advanced classes' photos. Most of them are of trees or of people's feet. There is a closet-sized room for developing negatives, which you have to do in pitch-blackness. At the end of the sinks is a doorway covered with a black curtain. This is the darkroom, where the entrance breaks off and turns three times, like a maze, to keep the light from getting inside. The walls are lined with soft black fabric. The darkroom is huge, with machines on the counters and a long deep sink down the middle with constantly running water and dishpans full of chemicals. The whole place is barely lit by red bulbs, making everything lose its color to shades of pink and red. It gives me this weird feeling, like I'm camouflaged, and though I can see everything, no one can see me.

There was a tour of all this on the first day, but so far we've only been in the classroom part, learning how to use our cameras. Our teacher, Mr. Allen, is new this year. He smiles too much, and on the first day his hands shook when he wrote on the board. If this were History, he'd be eaten alive, but since Photography is an elective, we all feel sort of sorry for him, and are well behaved. There are ten kids taking the class, three other girls, who know one another already and won't talk to me, and six boys. One of the boys, Jonah Baskin, is in New School. The rumor is he slit his wrists and missed most of sophomore year, first in a hospital, then with his mother in London. The girls in class must think he's cute, because they whisper and stare at him and ask him to say things with an English accent. Jonah pays no attention to them, or to any of us, just takes notes and fiddles with his camera, greasy hair like curtains closing over his face. He never pushes up his sleeves.

I had to ask my parents for Hugh's camera. It's valuable, a Leica given to him by my grandmother, and has been living in my parents' closet in a camera bag with a Clash sticker on it. No one knows why Hugh didn't have it with him that night, since he never went anywhere without it. But he left it behind, and now I carry it like he did, slung around my neck and under one arm by the frayed yellow strap. Though I have learned to load and rewind the film, set f-stops and focus and the light meter and depth of field, I haven't taken any pictures. That's not what I'm here for.

Today is our first day not spent at our desks. In the kitchen galley, Mr. Allen shows us what we will do in the developing closet. Break open our finished roll of film and wind it onto a metal wheel, which we put into a matching canister with two lids, a large one to seal it into darkness, and another smaller one to pour the chemicals into. Once the film is safely in there, we can come out and do the chemical part.

It seems easy enough, but once locked in the room, a bunch of kids freak out and ruin their film. One boy gets claustrophobic, another one opens the door to ask Mr. Allen a question, exposing his film. The girls are better at it, winding their film in record time, making the boys sneer from where they wait their turns, sitting up on counters at the end of the room. Jonah and I practice on blank rolls of film with our eyes closed.

When it's my turn, Mr. Allen gives me a brief tour with the light shining through the door; all that's in there are a counter, a sink, and a light switch taped down in the off position. He hands me the scissors and tells me to take one last look at everything, then shuts the door.

It's like I never knew what the word *dark* meant before now. I have no sense of myself, let alone what's around me; like I've disappeared instead of the light. I manage to get the scissors under the lip of the film roll and cut a line into the hard plastic. I break the shell and am careful not to smear the film with fingerprints. Winding it on the metal roll was simple outside in the light, but now I can't find the little groove I'm supposed to anchor the end of the film on. I think I've got it four times, but when I roll the film it flops loosely away. Then I drop the ring and have to squat and feel around with one hand while I hold the unraveled film above my head with the other. The dark is really getting to me now, and I can understand why that boy started screaming to be let out. It's almost like it gets deeper inside you with every breath. And even though there's no time limit, the dark makes me feel like if I don't hurry up something awful will happen. Like my chance at getting out will slip by.

By the time I find the ring on the floor and miss twice more at winding the film, the dark seems to be getting thicker, like I have to fight to move through it. I'm kind of dizzy and my breath is quick and shallow, like Owen having an asthma attack. It occurs to me that I can't do this, that I will have to open the door and expose every one of Hugh's unseen photos on this roll of film. I try one more time, and even with my shaking hands and having already half given up, it works, so easily I don't understand how I missed it before. I quickly wind the film and slip the ring into the canister, sealing the top with a few twists.

"Ready!" I call out, because by this point I've forgotten where the door is. I stumble out and someone steadies me by grabbing my arms.

"Are you all right?" Mr. Allen asks. He's not the one holding me, though, it's Jonah, which I don't like, so I wriggle free.

"I'm fine," I say. Jonah backs away.

"We were wondering what happened to you in there," Mr. Allen says. I think he's referring to how long I took, but it turns out that he's been calling my name for a few minutes, and was close to breaking the door down. I didn't hear a word.

I follow the laminated instructions taped above the sink, adding developer, swirling it every thirty seconds, pouring it out, adding stop bath, then fixer, then fixer remover, then rinsing with water. Just before the bell rings I take off the top of the canister and pull out my negatives. I hang them on a line with a clothespin, taping a small label with my name on it to the bottom edge. They hang in a curl like flypaper. With the light from the window I can make out a few images, human figures, stone stairs, a graffiti-covered brick wall. The Quad. It doesn't look very different from how it looked today.

The difference is that Hugh took these pictures. First of our family, but then of his friends, his places, what he blinked his eyes open and shut upon. Besides books and albums, a leather jacket, and the stiff, averted faces of my parents, these pictures are all I have left of him.

2. stopwatch

Fridays are Owen Furey's worst days, because of the time tests. After lunch, while the students are still sluggish with peanut butter, Mr. Gabriel passes out mimeographed sheets of numbers, facedown, with the solemn expression of an Olympic coach. They are given four minutes to solve twenty multiplication problems. Mr. Gabriel holds a stopwatch, interrupting their concentration to announce the close of each minute. The same four students compete for the record, the rest are left hoping only for a respectable time. Owen—skinny, fidgeting, purple-eyed with sleep deprivation and self-criticism—has yet to finish within the time window. The last rows are always eights and nines, his doom. There is only one other student so pathetic, Mindy Turner, who is rumored to be slightly retarded. It doesn't help that the fast kids shoot their hands up when finished, and that Mr. Gabriel bellows out their time as if they are running the fifty-yard dash. *Two minutes ten seconds, new record!* Owen wastes his math energy on calculating minutes gone by against problems left, convinced he'll never make it.

The desks, normally grouped together in clusters of four, are rearranged in a circle for time tests, to discourage cheating. Owen normally sits with his desk diagonal to Danny Gray, the new arrival of Indian summer, a year and a half older than the fifth-graders (a fact that hushes them, the horror of being "kept back") and Owen's best friend. Even Danny does better than Owen on the time tests. He regularly finishes somewhere around the three-minute mark, but writes his answers slowly, pausing to glance around the circle, eyes too white from his recess application of Visine, making the record-holders, who hunch in concentration over their desks, look paranoid. As if he could beat their best time if he bothered to try.

Danny Gray has moved from New York and calls Owen's town "the country" even though they are walking distance from Boston. During recess he leads Owen behind the tennis courts to the deserted merry-go-round, hunches in a little archway of fallen brick wall, and lights a joint. The first time he offers it to Owen, he closes the glowing end in his mouth and gestures for Owen to lean forward. He blows the smoke in one thick billow that Owen inhales with his whole face, not just his lips which, for the briefest instant, touch Danny Gray's. Owen is shamed by his embarrassment; clearly this is a normal practice that causes no one but him to linger on the memory of their best friend's lips. Danny's are full, darker than Owen's, as is his skin and his thick glossy hair. He is part American Indian, though the person who planted this in him, his father, has long disappeared. This makes him the smallest ethnic minority in their class. The majority seesaws between Jews and Wasps, followed by the Asians, lumped together by others if not by themselves, then six African-Americans, four of whom come from mixed marriages, three children who speak Spanish at home, and two Irish Catholics including Owen. Danny stands alone, though some kids lump him with Rohit, a boy who missed the entire fourth grade visiting family in Calcutta.

Danny is fascinated by Owen's family. He is amazed that Owen's parents are still married, and asks questions Owen either finds insulting or doesn't know the answer to, such as does his dad hit his mom and do they still fuck. "Have you got any sibs?" Danny asks, and Owen's chest tightens. "A sister," he says. "Is she hot?" Danny asks, and Owen shrugs and says, "She's fifteen." Danny nods, as if this is explanation enough. When he meets Lena, or at least glimpses her storming through the living room to the back of the house, he informs Owen that she has no tits but a cute ass. Owen suffers such a variety of reactions to this statement, he ends up saying nothing. He is embarrassed for his sister, leered at in this way, suspects he should defend her. He is also furious, as if Lena has walked into his room uninvited. Mostly, the emotion he feels is one he doesn't dare name, but it's familiar. It's the same way he feels about the attention Danny attracts from girls in their class. Danny, with all his talk of tits and ass, is unimpressed by these girls, though occasionally he will exchange a series of notes with one of them, plummeting the girl and her friends into turmoil. While they giggle and whisper and sigh, Owen likes to imagine different ways of inflicting pain and shock on them: hair pulling, biting, comments about imaginary B.O.

The boys spend most afternoons skulking around Coolidge Corner, trading stacks of coins for candy bars and McDonald's fries, occasionally shoplifting random items from Woolworth's—shoelaces, pink disposable razors, badminton birdies—which they then toss into public trash cans. They ride on the backs of green MBTA trains, planting their sneaker soles on the metal prong used to connect one car to the next, holding on to windshield wipers with fingers numbed by cold. The first time, Owen almost loses his grip when a train passes them going the other direction, the suck of air and the surprise startling him off balance. Danny grabs onto his collar and pulls him back, and for an instant, the seriousness of the near-fall allows Owen to press his face into the greasy shoulder of Danny's jean jacket. At the next stop, the driver, tipped off via radio by his passing colleague, comes running to the back of the train to curse at them. Danny has to pull Owen away, laughing at the way he holds on for dear life even while the train is standing still.

On rainy days they go to Danny's house, so far from Owen's he thinks of it as a different town. Danny lives on the outskirts of Whiskey Point—named for its blue-collar Irish population, most of whom send their children to the Catholic school—on the top floor of a beige three-family house with chipped, decrepit balconies. His mother, a waitress home most afternoons, serves them grilled-cheese sandwiches and root beer. When Owen calls her Mrs. Gray she laughs, insisting that he call her Sylvie. He can't bring himself to do this and so avoids her name altogether. She also asks about his family as if they are fascinating, tells him it is a blessing his parents are still married. She wants to know if his mother works, and he has to explain, mumbling because he finds this fact too weird to be proud of, that his mother is in medical school. "Wow," Mrs. Gray says, prying the top off a Seagram's wine cooler. "She must be smart." Owen shrugs. His mother's intelligence is not something he thinks about. He measures her in other ways. He can't remember, for instance, the last time she made him a grilled cheese.

Owen prefers to sleep over at Danny's. Their parents make them switch off, one weekend at Owen's, the other across town. Sleepovers at Danny's are long, luscious nights of unsupervised boredom. Danny's mother leaves for work as it's getting dark and doesn't come home until after two A.M., a fact that hasn't been mentioned to Owen's parents. Owen believes his father, who is still new at being in charge of such things, hasn't thought to ask. The boys are instructed by Danny's mother to go to Mrs. Curran downstairs if there's an emergency. They stay up until they hear her key in the door, gorging themselves on Jiffy Pop, Hostess cakes, and reruns of *Hawaii Five-0* and *The Twilight Zone*. Sometimes they share one of the wine coolers, staining their tongues with berry. Danny has a futon mattress on the floor of his room, and Owen secretly prefers this to the twin bed setup at his house. It's easier to watch his friend sleeping, savor the moment his eyebrows relax their normal furrow, when Danny is right next to him. Danny's eyelashes seem to grow longer when he's asleep, like the hair of vampires in the Anne Rice books Owen loves. On the futon, Owen can get close enough to smell his best friend's unbrushed breath.

On their third night at Danny's they go through his mother's dresser, shaving off from the piles of change on the surface, pushing aside alarmingly large bras to look for her stash of pot and pills. Mrs. Gray's underwear drawer resembles the junk drawer in Owen's kitchen—a collection of essential and nonessential items without clearly defined categories. The same sandpaper sticks Owen's mom uses to file her nails jostle against uncashed WIC coupons for the two-gallon jugs of milk that bow the top shelf of their refrigerator. Underneath a sixteen-tool Swiss army knife, there is a round plastic case with a rubber disk inside that looks like a cross between a miniature Frisbee and an internal organ. After encouraging Owen to whip it across the room, Danny informs him that it is a diaphragm. He is unable to tell Owen what this is exactly, except that it is involved in sex. "So's this," Danny says, removing a battery-operated dildo the size of Owen's forearm. Owen, watching Danny switch the vibrator between its various humming speeds, wonders if the diaphragm and the dildo need to be used together. At the back of her drawer, wrapped in a pair of men's flannel boxers, is a small, heavy, block-shaped handgun.

"It's never loaded," Danny says, pointing it at Owen and spreading his legs in a *Miami Vice* pose.

"What's it there for, then?" Owen asks, trying not to flinch when Danny makes explosive noises, mimicking the kickback of a fired gun. He wonders if Danny can hear the tiny wheeze beginning to form in his breath.

"She keeps all the shit my old man left." Danny shrugs. "In case he comes back or something, I don't know. What a sucker, right?"

Owen nods. The thought of Mrs. Gray hoarding things in expectation of Danny's father's return makes him sad, but, since this is clearly not the reaction he is supposed to have, he looks away. He has an urge to wipe his hands—microscopically soiled by her slippery underwear—on his Thunderbird pajama bottoms. He says he has to piss and goes to the bathroom for a quick restorative hit from his inhaler.

During Danny's first sleepover at the Fureys', Owen's father makes an embarrassing deal out of ordering pizza and letting them rent horror tapes from Videosmith. Danny follows Owen's father's every move with eager eyes for the first hour, then sums up and dismisses him with one phrase.

"Your dad's a mom," he says, sounding disappointed.

Later, sent too early to the twin beds in the room Owen once shared with his sister, Danny asks who the extra guy is in the one family picture in the hall.

"My uncle," Owen lies easily. He does not want to juggle the sort of tactless questions most friends ask about Hugh. He doesn't have the answers. He can't even remember him.

It was the picture that made him forget. One picture of his big brother replicated a thousand times, posted on telephone poles, in the newspaper, the playground, said to be on milk cartons though Owen never saw one. The picture was Hugh's school photo from the ninth grade. His hair was still brown and feathered, his shirt had a turned up collar and a tiny alligator on the breast. It was the last formal photo he posed for—his tenth-grade photo, despite the check their mother sent to school, was never taken, so no one could find a picture of his dyed black spiky hair. Hugh was the only one of them who really took pictures.

Owen's memory, apart from the occasional flash from toddlerhood, begins when his brother is gone. He remembers vividly what came afterward, mostly his sister not sleeping. Blurry recollections of Lena upright against her headboard, clip-on lamp shining so harshly it looked like it might singe her hair. Sometimes, she was closer, leaning over his bed with an expression so unreadable he wasn't sure if she were about to kiss him good night or smack him. Once, when he woke to her huge eyes practically touching his face, and they both yelped, he asked her what she was doing.

"I wanted to see if you were breathing," she said.

Back then, his sister took care of putting him to bed, reading *Where the Wild Things Are* and tucking him in. The tucking was all wrong—she bound him so tightly he had to kick himself free as soon as she left the room. She was in charge of his bath, his tooth-brushing, the clean underwear and shirt draped on a chair for the morning.

Owen resented this; she wasn't supposed to be in charge. He gave her a hard time, whining and delaying more than he would have dared with his mother, who now went to bed in the middle of the afternoon, which was why she was not there to tuck him in. His father spent most of his time in his basement office, which was usual enough, except that his piles of papers and books had been replaced with that photograph, box upon box of it from Copy Cop, with the first long word Owen had ever learned to spell printed in capitals beneath. His father had once tacked the pages of the book he was writing on the wall; now that same wall was covered with newspaper articles, police reports, lists of words hastily crossed out, his brother's name glaring out from every page. In the middle of this collage was the original picture, enlarged and copied so many times it obliterated Owen's real brother, wallet-sized, backed by a heaven-blue sky. The same sky appeared in Owen's kindergarten photo, which, when presented to his parents in a package of descending sizes, made both of them leave the room, their mouths tight, white lines slashed into yielding faces.

For Halloween, Owen wants them to be Louis and Lestat, from *Interview with the Vampire,* and dress in period costumes. Danny declares this idea is gay, and insists on darkened eye sockets and fake blood dripping from plastic fangs. They wear black hooded sweatshirts and dark corduroys, dress shoes so their bright Nikes won't show up in the shadows. After an initial hour of pushing their way ahead of toddlers to fill their pillowcases with miniature candy bars, they abandon trick-or-treating for the more respectable activity of vandalism. They have prepared by raiding the hair product aisle of CVS, plucking the aerosol tips from cans of Final Net and transplanting them onto cans of Barbasol. The aerosol makes the shaving cream emerge in a thin, powerful stream perfect for outlining bushes with the obscenities Owen has just begun saying out loud. Danny is an Olympic swearer; outside of the classroom and his mother's hearing he uses *fuck* in every other sentence. He calls people cunts, even boys, a habit he has picked up from the construction workers from County Cork who live on the second floor, between his apartment and Mrs. Curran's. His favorite insult, however, is to call someone a fag. He refused to watch *It's the Great Pumpkin, Charlie Brown,* because Linus and Charlie Brown are fags. Mr. Gabriel is a fag, as are the fathers of most of their classmates who holler encouragement at soccer games. "I'll bet he fucks guys up the ass," Danny will say about a store clerk or a lone male driver waiting at a stoplight. Owen is confused by the violence of this image, adds it to his growing list of the perverted behavior of fags, wonders if it is a friendly form of punishment among them, an adult version of Indian arm burns or wedgies.

When Owen swears, he doesn't sound as natural as his best friend. But he likes practicing, repeating phrases that would make his parents, if they heard him, blush with astonishment.

While Danny is spraying SUCK MY DICK onto someone's garage, a side door opens and the outside light is switched on. A man in a T-shirt so thin you can see smudges of dark hair around his nipples yells to them that he has called the police. "Little faggots," he hisses, and this makes Danny laugh so hard that Owen must pull him away from the crime scene, boosting him over the stone wall that borders the Muddy River Cemetery.

When they're a safe distance away, Danny collapses in laughter on a grave, holding his stomach and rolling in the leaves. Owen is still frightened, mostly from the running and getting out of breath, but pretends to be mad. "What the fuck is wrong with you?" he says, his voice squeaking on the *fuck,* which makes Danny whoop. They lie there, Owen fuming and Danny giggling, until the night begins to soothe them toward silence. Owen turns his head toward Danny, who is watching him, his full mouth already hanging open with the question.

"How come you didn't tell me about your brother?" Danny asks. Owen is grateful for the gravestone behind them, which cuts the stream of moonlight that would otherwise illuminate his face.

"I dunno," Owen mumbles. He knew this would happen eventually. The thought of someone in school, probably a girl, taking Danny aside and telling him the story of Hugh—the statewide searches, the trained dogs, the news coverage, and the milk cartons—makes Owen both furious and piercingly lonely.

Danny is still staring, waiting for a better explanation.

"We don't talk about it," Owen says finally. Though this is vague, Danny nods as if it explains everything. He once told Owen that if he mentions his father, his mother will cry for hours. He made it sound as if he were bragging.

Owen cranes his head back, looking at the stone that sags unevenly into the earth. He can see the worn outline of a skull with wings, and a name, CHRISTOPHER HAVENS, carved above an epitaph. He considers briefly telling Danny everything. About how Hugh's name is never mentioned in the house, but his things are still kept in banker's boxes in the basement. That though he can't remember him alive, he has an idea about what his brother has become, an idea he has never admitted to anyone, for fear that they will tell him it is impossible. But Danny speaks up first.

"I used to want a big brother," he says aggressively, as if this wish needs to be defended.

"Me, too," Owen says. This starts Danny laughing again. Deep, husky laughter that doubles him over and makes him moan to catch his breath. It occurs to Owen that his friend is stoned; which means he would have had to smoke before they met up, all by himself.

"Fuck off," Owen says, but Danny laughs even harder.

Owen attacks, straddling him, squeezing him immobile with his knees and delivering a series of fake punches, making explosive sound effects in his cheeks. Danny snaps his head back and forth in mock impact, then rears up and knocks Owen over, pinning him down instead. Danny is the stronger one, and always ends up on top, demanding uncle. He holds Owen's wrists together, pinning them above his head. With his free hand, he slaps Owen's cheeks lightly, barely enough to sting. Owen is laughing now, too, his stomach heaving against the arc between Danny's legs. Danny stops hitting and continues to laugh in exhausted, intermittent huffs, his face so close Owen can feel every exhalation brushing his lips.

In that moment before Danny climbs away, Owen wishes for Mr. Gabriel's stopwatch, so he can keep a record of it all: their breathing ragged with laughter, their thin, black-clad bodies pressed into moldering leaves and against each other, creating an urgency that is as unfamiliar and as welcome as the foul words he has recently learned to sing.

3. zippo

Photography is only forty-five minutes long, and
Mr. Allen has to show us every stupid step about
sixteen times, so we never get much done. So far,
we've only printed contact sheets, cutting our negatives into strips of five and lining them up together, burning the images onto eight-by-ten
sheets of photo paper. These make rows of tiny
photos, so we can choose the best ones to print
later. I was getting impatient, so I asked Mr. Allen

if I could stay after school a couple of days, and he gave me a key to lock up. I've printed a dozen of Hugh's photos, all taken in the Quad, of punk kids loitering on the stairs. I don't recognize any of these kids, but I can picture Hugh there, the center of a cluster of dyed hair and heavy boots, the sort of boy who gives out nods rather than one who feels relieved by them. My brother was always popular. I once asked him, when I was in the fifth grade and my class was dividing into cool and uncool as cleanly as a cell under a microscope, how to be popular. He had shrugged and told me to be myself. I didn't tell him that I thought it was myself that was the problem. Popular kids were always really normal or extra special. I was neither one.

In grammar school, my brother's best friend was Jeremy Lispet, whose yard was behind ours, separated by a low, rotting fence. Jeremy was the opposite of my brother. He wasn't cute, or popular, or even on speaking terms with any of Hugh's other friends. Their friendship was limited to after-school computer programming sessions or D&D games. These were the hobbies of greasy-haired, genius boys who were picked on by the sort of kids Hugh hung out with. Hugh's friendship with Jeremy was a secret, just like I was if I passed by him and his friends in the park. Talking to your little sister and programming text adventures was not cool, not like leather jackets and chain-smoking and music played at a deafening volume and the hair gel Hugh emptied, half a tube at a time, into his dark, spiked hair. I never wondered why Jeremy Lispet put up with Hugh's part-time treatment. Hugh was the sort of person who got away with stuff like that, because people felt lucky to be around him.

One afternoon in the darkroom, while waiting for prints to dry, I make a new contact sheet from some negatives I found in Hugh's box. The pictures are from a long time ago. Owen as a baby, standing up and holding on to the arm of the sectional couch, his legs looking fat and unsteady in their little gray sweatpants. My parents at the dinner table, laughing and trying to hold their cigarettes outside the frame. Jeremy Lispet turning his eyelids inside out. And me by the community pool, my hair dripping onto my striped shirt and the cement steps, where we are waiting for our mother to pick us up. I remember that day. Hugh was supposed to bring me swimming, but instead he left me alone and ran off with Jeremy. He told the pool lady I was seven, the age children were allowed to swim unsupervised, when I was really only six. I was so paranoid about being found out that I burst into tears halfway through the swim session and admitted the lie to one of the lifeguards. The pool lady, so fat that her arms didn't fall straight to her sides but splayed out, yelled at Hugh when he came back for me. I'm not smiling in this picture. My eyes are swollen from chlorine and crying, and I'm glaring at the camera. Hugh was trying to cheer me up before my mother came, but I knew it was all a bribe, because he didn't want me to tell on him. I had no intention of telling, but I let him think I would. It was the first time I can remember ever being mad at him. It was such a strange feeling, and I didn't know how to tell him about it, so I kept quiet and tried to look mean. It's weird looking at the picture now. I look like some other kid. Sort of bratty and smaller than I thought I was at the time.

In class, I print a new contact sheet of Hugh's high school photos. These were taken outside, but not of the Quad. While I'm using plastic tongs to move the paper from one tray of chemicals to another, Jonah, in line behind me, peers over my shoulder at the blooming images.

"You don't seem like the type," he says. His voice is soft and low, and at first I don't understand him, but after a delay the words repeat back to me like a whisper in my head.

"Type for what?" I say rudely. I don't like Jonah; he seems like a freak and I didn't appreciate the groping the other day. Sometimes I think he's trying to be friends, but most of the time he ignores me just like he ignores everyone else. I always end up acting defensive when I should be casual like I don't give a shit.

"Type who hangs around the Pit," he says.

"What pit?" I snap. I don't like how superior he sounds. Like he knows so much about me, when the truth is, everyone knows his darkest secret even if he keeps his sleeves down.

"The Pit," he says, pointing at my photo. In it punk boys with skateboards are hanging around a cement circle, a plank of wood laid against the stairs that lead down into it.

"Harvard Square?" Jonah says. That's when I recognize the brick, the line of pay phones, the edge of the round hut that is an information booth for tourists. I've only ever been to Harvard Square to go out to dinner with my parents, at a loud Tex-Mex restaurant where the soda comes in plastic glasses the size of my thigh. I didn't know my brother hung out there. He'd wanted to go to Harvard, but my father said he'd probably end up at BC, because of the price break.

"Develop your own pictures," I say to Jonah, and he shrugs, retreating beneath his hair, looking like he never cared enough to peek over my shoulder in the first place. I rinse the chemicals from the photo, studying a handsome, older teenager with spiked blond hair and a plaid jacket. He is at the very edge of the photo, the only one looking at the camera, and he is giving it the finger. He looks mischievous, the type of kid whose job it is to teach other kids how to get in trouble. I hang him up to dry.

Just before the bell rings, one of the girls in my class asks me in a whisper if I have any tampons. I must look at her blankly, because she screws her face up.

"What, do you still use *pads*?" she says.

"No," I say. When I don't explain, she storms off, shaking her head to her friends to say that I'm as hopeless as they suspected.

When we started school this year, all the sophomores were given welcome kits, like party favors—the boys got blue cardboard boxes, the girls, pink. Inside the girls' kits were pamphlets on depression, rape, and birth control, a sample size of Secret roll-on deodorant, a box of o.b. tampons, and Tic Tacs. Some people said the boys' boxes had condoms in them. I threw my box out, saving only the Tic Tacs. I haven't gotten my period yet even though I turned fifteen the week before Halloween. My mother thought something might be wrong with me, since she got hers when she was twelve, but Dr. Cloherty, our pediatrician, said I was just a late bloomer. He's been saying that my whole life, as if it's something to be proud of.

I go to the Pit on Friday night. I tell my parents I'm going to the movies with Tracy. They don't bat an eye at this, although I've never been anywhere with Tracy before. You'd think, after Hugh, that my parents would be overprotective, but they're not. They even let Owen walk to and from school alone.

I take the T from Longwood, changing at Park Street to the Red Line, which goes aboveground to cross the river, then dives again and squeals along the third rail to Cambridge. In the Harvard Square station, I'm not sure which exit to take. I decide against Church Street and choose the larger exit on the left, next to carts selling Mexican ponchos and maroon Harvard sweatshirts. I have to breathe through my mouth on the escalator because it smells like pee.

Aboveground I am bombarded by people. The intersection in front of the Harvard Coop is packed with pedestrians strolling across a brick crosswalk, ignoring the cars that honk on both sides. Along the opposite curb is a long line of orange cabs. The drivers stand around drinking coffee until the front one gets a customer, when they have to start their engines and move forward the length of one car. Behind the T station is the Pit, a depressed circle of sidewalk with stairs on all sides, like a concrete version of my kindergarten. Kids are sitting on all available surfaces, including the slanted back of the subway entrance where they are perched almost on top of one another's shoulders. They are clustered into groups, and their faces have the same combination of boredom and barely contained mischief as the kids in the Quad. As if something melodramatic and possibly life-changing is about to happen, and everyone is ready for it. A few boys with skateboards have slanted a plank down against the stairs, like in Hugh's photo, and ride around in loops, skateboard wheels rattling, the wood plank scraping against the concrete. The style here is punk, fluorescent Mohawks and multiple earrings, girls barely distinguishable from boys. Everyone seems plastered with accessories, zippers and leather and layers of different fabric patterns. The more an outfit clashes, the more authentic it seems, though I do see a few people with pet rats dyed to match their hair.

I wish I'd brought Tracy with me. She'd be annoying, but at least she looks like me. I'm sure I stand out in my outfit. I'm wearing red Converse high-tops, Guess jeans, a black hooded sweatshirt, and Hugh's leather jacket. At home I'd imagined I looked sloppy and tough. Now I know it's all wrong, not the pieces themselves but the overall effect. It looks too clean, unoriginal, like a costume bought in a bag at Woolworth's the day before Halloween. I have zero accessories, only my green JanSport backpack over one shoulder, which suddenly seems childish.

I lean against a pay phone and take a pack of cigarettes out of my bag. Smoking, I know from the Quad, makes you look occupied, like you belong. I light one and inhale deeply, exhaling with an addict's sigh.

It used to terrify me that my parents smoked. I'd stay up at night imagining their funerals. Our house smelled stale and dirty compared to the houses of my friends. When Hugh started smoking, I photocopied a picture of lung cancer from the encyclopedia in the library and gave it to him. He laughed and hung it up in his room. Now that I've started, I understand why they all ignored my begging for them to stop.

I tried smoking occasionally last year, but couldn't get the hang of it. A week ago, I inhaled for the first time, accidentally, and already I'm up to a pack a day. I love everything about it—the smell the smoke leaves on my jacket collar, the bruised feeling of my lungs, and the rituals: thumping a new pack on the heel of my hand, removing only half of the tinfoil wrapping, turning one cigarette, middle row, second from the right, upside down and leaving it to smoke last, making a wish like it's a birthday candle. I learned all of this in the Quad, where I now stop for a smoke before Photography. Tracy sits beside me coughing and waving her hand in front of her face. I'm saving the empty boxes of Marlboro Lights, which I buy at the convenience store on the way to school for $1.10, and taping them on the wall behind my bed. I plan to smoke enough to cover every inch of the walls of my room. My mother quit smoking when Owen was diagnosed with asthma, so I recently dug out the orange plastic ashtray she used to carry around the house. I keep it in my room, emptying it only when it gets so overcrowded it starts to smolder. I cover the smell by burning pine incense in a long wooden tray. As for my dad, he still smokes, mostly at the office and never around Owen. I can't even stand it when he tries to talk to me, so I don't worry about him dying anymore. I just find his smoking convenient. When I run out of cigarettes, there is always his carton in the pantry, extra long menthols that feel medicinal when I inhale, like Vicks VapoRub.

After three cigarettes in a row, a small corner of a cement stair clears of people, and I settle there, taking out the binder where I store Hugh's photos and negatives in three-ring plastic sleeves. I have the camera with me, but I feel like I'll draw too much attention to myself if I start snapping photos. Instead, I work on my photo lists. I'm matching the numbers on the negatives to memories, figuring out the year they were taken and writing down what I can remember. His later photos, of the Quad and his friends I never met, have big question marks next to them. Writing stuff down has always made me feel better. That's why I keep track of the time in class. When I was little I kept lists of everything, like my stuffed animals by name and birth date, or my Christmas presents in the order I opened them.

It starts to drizzle, and I tuck my hair into the neck of my sweat-shirt, pulling the hood like a visor over my forehead. When I next look up, someone is standing in front of me.

"Pick a hand," a voice says, and I squint up, focusing on him. A boy a little older than me, hair sculpted sharply into black spikes, a dia-mond stud in one ear. His outfit is similar to mine, jeans and a leather jacket, but he has great accessories. Black combat boots that lace half-way up his calves, a thick chain leading from his back pocket to his metal-studded belt, a red plaid shirt, the flannel so worn it looks like it has a history, black waffled long underwear peeking at the collar. His jeans are dark with graffiti, cartoons fighting for space with what looks like poetry. His nose is small, slightly turned up, the same little-boy nose as Owen, like it's his only feature that survived pu-berty. I think he's wearing eyeliner.

"Go on," he says. "Pick a hand. They don't bite." He's holding two closed fists in front of me. One hand is in a fingerless gray glove, the other is bare, scabbed, and dirty.

I try to look bored as I tap his fist with my pen. I pick the gloved one, avoiding the scabs.

He turns the hand over, opening an empty palm.

"Sorry." He grins. "Better luck next time." Though I'm annoyed, I figure I can't afford not to be nice to him. So I shrug and fake a smile.

"Can I bum a cigarette?" he says, and I take the pack of Marlboro Lights from my pocket. I have three left, and hesitate before grabbing two, leaving the lucky cigarette rolling alone inside the cardboard. I hand him one, and he wrinkles his boyish nose.

"Chick cigarettes," he complains, but accepts it anyway. He sits down next to me and takes a metal Zippo from his pocket. He drags it across his thigh, opening and lighting it in two swift motions. He lights his cigarette with the sloppy flame first before offering to do mine. The lighter smells of gas, which I taste in the back of my throat on the first drag. On the thigh of his jeans, smearing the graffiti, is a dark mark from dragging that lighter over and over again. He holds the cigarette with his thumb and two fingers, drags deeply and looks around, bouncing his knee up and down like he can't bear to sit still. At the nape of his neck is a braid so small and delicate it is like the hair of a doll.

"Whatcha writing?" he says, peering rudely at my binder. I shut it and cap my pen.

"Nothing," I say, and he chuckles.

"You're new here."

"How do you know?"

"Because I know everyone in Harvard Square and I don't know you."

"You can't know everyone," I argue. "That's impossible."

"Ev-er-y-one," he repeats, dragging each syllable out with a tired emphasis.

"I'm from Brookline," I say. After I say it, it occurs to me that I could have lied.

"You run away?" he asks casually.

"No," I say, too loud, making it sound impossible, when actually I liked him thinking it.

"Why'd you come all the way here to sit alone and write in a notebook, then? Don't they let you loiter in Brookline?"

I shrug, not meeting his eyes. I can remember when it was effortless, talking to boys, I rarely thought before I opened my mouth. Now I am some sort of social retard.

"Oh, come on," he says. "Is it a secret? You can tell me. I keep everyone's secrets. Can't get them out of me. I'm like a lawyer, or, what's the other one?"

"A priest?" I can't help but smile.

"Exactly. Tell Father Sebastian what's troubling you, my child."

"Nothing's *troubling* me. I'm just looking for someone, that's all."

"Who? I told you I know everyone."

"You don't know this one," I say.

"Try me," he says.

I shake my head, my brother's easy smile intruding into my mind. Then I think of something. I pull the picture of the Pit out of my folder, pointing to the boy with the spiked blond hair. "Do you know this guy?" I say.

"Sure, that's Lionel," he says, looking less amused. "But I can score for you without going to him." It takes me a minute to get this.

"He's a *drug* dealer?" I squeak before I can stop myself. Sebastian's eyes had gone kind of cold and professional when I showed him the picture, but they flicker at this.

"Did I say that? I don't think I did."

"I just want to talk to him," I say.

"Lionel's not much of a talker."

"Is he here?"

"Nope. Haven't seen him today. Why are you looking for Lionel if you don't want to score?"

"I just . . . I want to ask him something." I have no idea what I might say to Lionel. *Did you murder my brother? If not, do you know who did?*

"Well, be careful. Guys like Lionel don't like questions."

"Forget it," I say, feeling foolish. I've given too much away, too quickly. "It doesn't matter," I add. "I know a friend of his, that's all."

The drizzle that chased half the crowd into Au Bon Pain has cleared and people are now collecting around us again.

"Me, on the other hand, you can ask me anything you want. Go ahead. Ask me something."

"Okay," I say. "What are you doing here?"

He laughs. "I'm always here," he says. "Twenty-four seven."

"Are you homeless or something?"

"Not yet. They do kick me out periodically. Keeps life interesting."

"Who does?"

"The 'rents," he says.

"Your *parents* kick you out?" I've never even been grounded, and can't imagine my parents ever getting mad enough to do such a thing. "Where do you sleep?"

"There's lots of places I can crash."

"Your parents must be horrible."

"Aren't yours?"

I shrug. I complain about my parents all the time, but it's automatic. They are annoying, but have never done anything truly awful like hit me or molest me or send me away to a school for delinquents like other parents I know. They're just generally disappointing, in ways that are hard to explain.

"Want to get high?" Sebastian asks me suddenly.

"No," I say, trying to sound casual. "Not right now."

He looks at me as if I'm about ten years old.

"Give me your lucky cigarette," he says.

"It's my last one," I say.

"I know it's your last one. Sheesh. I'm not gonna smoke it, I'm going to do something to cheer you up."

"What, do I look sad or something?" I say, taking out the pack.

"Yeah, you do," he says. He makes this observation quietly, without looking at me, as if he's not expecting me to protest. He takes the Marlboro Lights box from me and digs in his pocket for a lighter—a yellow plastic Bic this time. He tells me to lay my binder flat on my knees, and he leans over it, grinding the flint wheel of the lighter back and forth without pressing on the lever. He does this for a minute or two, raining little black specks onto the marbled orange cover of my binder. He is so close I can smell the damp of his leather, stale cigarettes, and jeans worn too many times without a wash. I can see the white flakes of dried hair gel glittering at his scalp.

When my notebook has a fine layer of flint, he takes my lucky cigarette from the pack and runs it quickly over his tongue. Seeing inside his mouth startles me, and I blush, but he is too absorbed to notice.

He sweeps both sides of the damp cigarette across the notebook, collecting the flint. He blows on the paper, drying it, and replaces the cigarette, still upside down, into my empty package.

"For later," he says, and he smiles. His eyes are mossy green with a star of gold around the pupil.

"I'm not," I say.

"Not what?" he says, staring at me. He has annoyingly steady eye contact.

"Not sad," I say.

"If you say so," he says.

Two older boys come up to us, one with an orange Mohawk, the other with a wool hat pulled low over his ears.

"Let's go, Sebastian," the Mohawk says. "College kids need their fix."

"Who's this dude?" the other one says, gesturing at me.

I haven't bothered to remove the hood of my sweatshirt. They snort in apology when Sebastian tells them I'm a girl. When I was younger, with my short hair and scraped knees, lots of people thought I was a boy. I always took it as a compliment, and though I know it should be insulting now that I'm older, I can't bring myself to care.

"Want to come?" Sebastian says. I don't get a chance to answer.

"No way," the Mohawk says. "None of your girlfriends tonight. Slow us down."

Sebastian looks as if he may argue, but I stop him.

"It's okay," I say. "I'm going home soon anyway." I feel silly and kind of mad at the mention of his girlfriends. I don't want to be added to a list of conquests. At the same time, I'm kind of disappointed that he was about to deny that I was one of them.

"See you later," he says, and he lopes off, leaving me so abruptly I feel conspicuously alone. I open my notebook and write *Lionel* next to all the numbered negatives he appears in. I push away the hood of my sweatshirt to let the cool air tickle my scalp, and take out my lighter and the last cigarette.

"Lena?" a voice says, and I turn my head, looking up. It takes me a moment to realize that the preppy guy staring at me is Jeremy Lispet, who is twenty now and a student at Harvard. He's with a girl, a short, chubby girl with glasses and bright red cheeks.

"Hi, Jeremy," I say, standing up. He's wearing a blazer and a maroon scarf over a white shirt and khakis. He's looking around at the Pit as if he has just turned over a rock. He squints at my jacket, wondering.

"Do your parents know you're here?" he says, and I force a smile.

"Sure," I say. "I'm meeting friends to go see *Back to the Future,* but I was early."

"Which theater?" Jeremy says. I had no idea there was more than one, and I open my mouth without planning an answer.

"Do you want us to walk you there?" Jeremy says.

"No, I'm okay," I say. He is looking at me in a way I can't stand. A way that has made me avoid talking to him for the last five years. My mother hears all about him when she sees Mrs. Lispet, and it always makes her lock herself in her bedroom like the old days.

"All right," he says. "Be careful. Oh," he says, when the girl next to him takes hold of his arm. "This is Sarah. My girlfriend."

"Nice to meet you," Sarah says. When she smiles she is suddenly pretty. I can't help but grin back. That's funny—Jeremy Lispet with a girlfriend.

"You really shouldn't hang out here all alone," Jeremy says, and that's when I know my mother will hear about this. Sarah rolls her eyes.

"Give her a break, honey, this is Cambridge. What could happen to her in Cambridge?" Jeremy smiles stiffly, and they say good-bye. But he gives me a quick look back, as if to say: *You know what can happen. We both know.*

When they're out of sight, I sit back down, lighting the cigarette I've been hiding in my palm. White stars explode from the tip, like the sparklers Hugh and I used to light on the Fourth of July. They'd always seemed dangerous to me, and I'd held them at arm's length, turning my head and flinching. Now the sparks are closer, spiraling out with every drag of my cigarette, and I sit still, letting them almost touch my face before they disappear.

4. light bulb

The permission slip Mr. Gabriel sends home calls the class Human Development, but Danny says it's sex ed. There is a check box on the bottom for religious parents who want their children to go to the library instead. Owen gives the form to his father, who blinks at it in the dim light of the living room.

"You're doing this already?" he says, but doesn't wait for an answer. "Come to me with any questions, okay?" he adds. Owen nods. His father has already told him how babies are made, warned him about wet dreams, alluded to and vaguely excused masturbation. Owen knows that Lena took Human Development, but wonders if, ten years ago, when the Fureys were still Catholic, and Hugh was in the fifth grade, his father would have described masturbation as a sin and checked the library box. Now Owen's father signs the permission form with a quick, uninterested scrawl, barely forming the separate letters of his name.

On Friday after lunch, instead of the math time tests, all the girls go across the hall to Ms. Lieberman's room, and her boys come over to fill the empty desks. The boys are strung tight, shooting crude phrases across the room like rubber bands. Their eruptions of laughter startle Mr. Gabriel, who, normally impenetrable, now looks pale and in pain.

"Settle down," he calls out meekly, unrolling two posters that he tacks to the same corkboard he wheels out for geography. When he turns the board toward them, they explode again.

"That's enough," Mr. Gabriel barks, with more authority this time. They fall silent, but continue to grin and poke at one another.

On the corkboard are two naked figures—one male, one female. To the right of each figure are detailed genital and internal diagrams. The woman's poster has more diagrams than the man's.

Mr. Gabriel goes through the diagrams abruptly, pelting them with terms: *scrotum, vas deferens, epididymis, seminiferous tubule, Cowper's gland, urethra, ovary, fimbria, fallopian tube, cervix, clitoris, hymen, perineum.* Ethan Fine, the class brain, sketches furiously and records definitions until Mr. Gabriel tells him they won't be tested on it. He lectures in detail about what happens to the penis and testicles from arousal to ejaculation, and takes them through the cycle of menstruation. He informs them that if a boy can ejaculate he can get a girl pregnant, and that girls ovulate before their first period. He announces that the discomfort that results from not ejaculating (*blue balls,* someone whispers) is not physically harmful and it is no reason to pressure a girl into having sex. He warns them that comments about a girl's developing body, or jokes about late bloomers, will end in a visit to the principal's office. He lists venereal diseases and their symptoms until a few of the boys turn green at the repetition of the word *discharge.*

This is not what Owen expected, and he can tell by the stunned expressions of his classmates—a few of them look on the edge of tears—that it is not what they expected, either. From his browsing of a book at home—*Changing Bodies, Changing Lives,* which once belonged to his sister but was left behind when she moved into her own room—Owen assumed that they would all sit in a circle and discuss their feelings about adolescence. That's what the boys and girls in the book did. Mr. Gabriel is giving them too much information. As Owen's body has yet to change—he still has the soft, hairless testicles of a boy and a voice mistaken on the phone for his mother's—he is not interested in the anatomy lesson. He doesn't really need to know how semen is produced when he hasn't produced any semen. It is like learning what is going to happen when he dies of old age. What Owen wants to know he is clearly not going to be able to ask. Not even via the anonymous question box, which Mr. Gabriel says he will set up by the watercooler. That is for sex questions, and sex is not what Owen's worried about. Not exactly.

Mr. Gabriel is now talking about AIDS. They have all heard of Ryan White, and are told that they attend a public school that would not discriminate against a dying boy. The class thaws a bit and starts asking questions. AIDS is in their parents' newspapers, in magazines, on television, and it is more controversial, more interesting, than the anatomy of the reproductive system.

"Is it true you can get it from kissing?" one boy from Ms. Lieberman's class asks, and Mr. Gabriel says it is transmitted through blood and semen.

"What if you have a cut in your mouth?" the boy says. Mr. Gabriel admits that he is not sure, but that there are no documented cases of contracting AIDS from kissing.

"Can a boy get it from a girl?" they want to know, and Mr. Gabriel tells them yes, though it's less common.

"My dad says only fags and Haitians get it," Brian Dowd pipes up, and Mr. Gabriel, his teeth clenched, tells Brian his father is wrong. He says that though the largest group of victims seems to be homosexual men, it is a virus that has no prejudices.

He goes on to talk about homosexuality, and how it is normal for children to have sexual feelings for both boys and girls and to experiment. "Don't worry if you are attracted to other boys," he says, and a number of boys make retching noises until he glares them quiet. "It doesn't necessarily mean that you're gay." There is a silence of disbelief.

"If you're confused, though, it's important to find someone you can talk to," he says. He doesn't seem to be volunteering.

"Are you gay?" Danny says suddenly, and the room gasps at his boldness. Mr. Gabriel looks confused, then angry, then mortified.

"That's none of your business," he says. He turns around and begins to erase the blackboard which he has filled with a list of terms none of them will remember tomorrow. "But I'm not," he adds.

He launches into pregnancy, warning them that they'll be watching a video on childbirth next Friday. His knuckles are as white as the chalk he's holding, and he's talking too fast. The boys have stopped fidgeting, exchanging looks, and whispering *smegma* to one another. Even Danny, who looked so defiant when asking, is subdued, hunched forward, his face burning under the cover of his bangs. He knows he has gone too far.

The next Friday, there is a television in the classroom when they return from lunch. They watch sperm swim their way through tubes
and valleys to meet up with a massive egg. They see a jellied baby
grow, curled up tight as though it has no intention of ever testing its
sprouting limbs. Then a starkly lit shot of a woman giving birth. The
woman is moaning in a way that sounds more like sex in movies
than something painful, causing the boys to shift positions to hide
their spontaneous erections. There is an outburst of disgusted
"eeews" at the close-up of a mucous-covered baby head between fat,
sweaty thighs. The birth doesn't seem miraculous to Owen, as the
voice-over on the film suggests. It's not even as gross as he thought it
would be, although he is a bit startled by all the hair, both baby and
pubic. The rest of the class is disgusted, and Mr. Gabriel gives up trying to control their noise. Owen feels sorry for the baby, who slips
out amphibious and cold, who will be made to watch this video over
and over the way Owen once suffered through the silent, sped-up
films of his toddler years projected onto his grandmother's wall. The
whole family always hushed when the grainy, insubstantial image
of Hugh passed over the molding.

After the movie, Mr. Gabriel answers questions from the box.
Owen tries to guess who asked what by the way they either beam
with pride or stiffen up and try to look uninterested. Most of the
questions are about girls. Do they think about sex as much as boys
do? Does it mean a girl has her period if a dog smells her crotch? Is it
true that the bump which makes them excited is really a tiny penis?

Mr. Gabriel seems annoyed at the majority of questions, some of
which he won't even read out loud.

The final question of the day is: How do you convince a girl to
have sex with you?

"Tie her down?" Brian Dowd whispers, and a few boys snort in appreciation. Luckily, Mr. Gabriel doesn't hear and merely gestures for them all to be quiet.

"You shouldn't pressure anyone to fool around or have sex," he says. "It's a decision that girls and boys need to make when they're ready. Sex comes with a lot of responsibility. It requires maturity and compassion, and bullying or cajoling someone into it is wrong. If someone tells you no, it means no, and you should back off. If you force someone to have sex with you, it's rape, and you can go to jail for that."

Rape has been treated with similar gravity by Owen's book. Though the chapters about sex offered vivid detail, Owen barely skimmed them; he retains his idea of sex as uninspiring from what he has witnessed in movies and on TV. Sex appears to involve mostly the frenetic removal of clothing, then a brief mashing together of torsos followed by exhaustion; it doesn't seem to require any more thought or maturity than taking a bath. Except for the baby part, and everyone knows that girls can have abortions.

Owen worries briefly that Mr. Gabriel has noticed that none of the questions are in his handwriting. He'll have to make up a question for next week. Perhaps he can find one in the female section of Lena's book. He hasn't cracked this yet. He is even less interested in girls' bodies than he is in his own. The questions Owen would like to ask are not things he can phrase, and even if he could, he suspects Mr. Gabriel would not have the answers.

After school, when they're getting their coats and boots on, Owen hears Danny tell Mike Bisbee, who had blushed and looked at his lap during the last question, that there are guaranteed ways to get in a girl's pants. And that he'll tell him five for ten bucks.

Owen and Danny start going straight from school to Amanda Peters's house—a sixth-grader who sells glimpses of her crotch for a dollar, but lets Danny see for free because she's in love with him. While Danny and Amanda disappear to her bedroom, Owen is left with Amanda's sister, Chrissy, who is in the fourth grade but already wears a training bra and braces. Owen doesn't mind Chrissy, who seems to expect little from him. They make Ellio's pizza in the toaster oven, play Super Mario Brothers, and listen to Prince on her parents' cassette deck. One afternoon, Chrissy starts hitting Owen with couch pillows until he grabs one of his own and hits back. Though he can't say how, he's sure she maneuvers the pillow fight so she ends up pinned underneath him. Owen scrambles off; the friction of his jeans combined with an hour's worth of wondering what Danny and Amanda are doing, plus the lyrics of Prince's "Erotic City," leave him with a hard-on that he must hide beneath his rugby shirt.

"Owen, do you like me?" Chrissy says, and Owen shrugs, wishing he could disappear.

"How come you never kiss me?" she asks, and Owen imagines it briefly, a sudden, violent motion that has more anger in it than curiosity, as if he could press all his frustration at that closed bedroom door against her mouth.

"I'm only ten," Owen mumbles, and Chrissy, with a flip of her blond braids, storms off to her bedroom, slamming the door.

The next day, when Owen refuses to go to Amanda's, Danny replies "Whatever," and they go to McDonald's instead. Owen takes sharp, vicious joy in the knowledge of how quickly and thoughtlessly Danny gives her up.

In Human Development they talk about divorce. More than half the kids in Owen's class have two sets of parents, but this doesn't seem like a tragedy to Owen. Though girls often cry about it, they seem to do it on cue to get out of gym class, and the boys barely mind at all. Two boys in their class, Chris and Noah, have recently become step-brothers after knowing each other since kindergarten. Chris's mother and Noah's father, who met at a soccer game, had an affair and ended up divorcing their spouses and marrying each other. Now the boys share a room during the week and go off to live with their other parents on the weekends. Though they are famous for their merciless fistfights, they like living together, and were spoiled with gifts during their parents' guilty transition. Owen secretly wishes his own parents would get a divorce. When he is picked up at Danny's, Owen pretends not to hear the car horn, so his father will be forced to come inside and talk to Danny's mom. Mrs. Gray fusses over him, and though Owen's father avoids looking at her cleavage, Owen still holds out hope.

It seems like at least once a week, some kid goes to the social worker's office to discuss his parents' announcement of divorce or remarriage or both. Owen's house, where no one fights or threatens or uses children to get back at each other, is abnormal in comparison.

On a rare morning in which his sister stops in the kitchen, leaning against the counter to eat a banana, Owen looks at her from behind his cereal box. His mother left before they woke up, his father's low, melancholy whistling can be heard from the shower. He has the only whistle Owen has ever heard that sounds miserable rather than cheery.

"Do you think Mom and Dad are going to get a divorce?" Owen says. Lena digs a brown spot out of her banana, making a face as she drops it in the sink.

"Not a chance," she says, and though she doesn't look up, it seems like a rare moment of understanding between them. As if she, too, would like their nonfamily to become more like the fractured families of their friends.

He almost asks why not, but decides not to push it. He suspects that Lena would tell him that their parents are still married, not because of her and Owen, but because of Hugh.

What would they say if he ever came back?

Owen is the only one of them who knows that Hugh is dead. He came to this conclusion easily, between the ages of six, when his family was still Catholic, and eight, when he almost died himself.

The year after Hugh disappeared, Owen began the first grade and, along with it, CCD, which met every Monday afternoon at the Catholic school across town. Lena walked him there, leaving him at the door of his classroom. Inside were old-fashioned open-topped desks and a picture of Jesus with a see-through chest, his heart choked in thorns, like some science class dissection project gone awry, over the blackboard. The walls were thumbtacked with vocabulary words written in a teacher's perfect cursive, with notions weightier than the cardboard they were cut out of: GRACE, PENANCE, FAITH, HOPE, DEATH, RESURRECTION.

Owen's teacher was not a nun, but a pretty woman named Ms. Winter who smiled all the time and spoke to them in a high voice that made even the subjects of original sin and hell seem about as grave as sugared cereal. Owen was in love with her by the end of the first class, ready to believe anything she told him. In his painstakingly perfect handwriting, he copied down the Ten Commandments and filled out the weekly quiz testing his interpretation of them. His workbook, a purple paperback with pictures of happy Catholic children, dressed-down priests, and fields of wildflowers, laid out the year ahead of him, lots of blank space on which to record easy answers to weighty questions.

One afternoon, Lena was home with strep throat, so Owen's father had to pick him up after class. His father was late, so Ms. Winter sat with Owen on the wide marble steps of the school's foyer. The subject of class that day had been angels, something Owen should have known too much about, except that his father no longer discussed his former obsession. Owen knew that his father had once studied to be a priest, and later, after meeting his mother, became a divinity scholar. The book he'd been writing had been about angels. Owen could remember paintings that once covered his father's office, men with sorrowful expressions and massive wings sprouting almost painfully from muscular torsos. Everything was taken down to make room for the search for Hugh.

Ms. Winter's lesson that day had been about guardian angels, who, she said, were with you from birth, sitting on your right shoulder, whispering encouragement for good in your ear. Though he had long ago decided to believe everything Ms. Winter said, he found this one difficult. He couldn't imagine angels sticking by some of the bullies he knew; surely they'd give up after being ignored for years. And what about truly evil people? Did Hitler have the withered, resigned shell of an angel barely breathing on his shoulder? He didn't ask these questions out loud, deciding that the belief of his beautiful teacher was more important than his own hungry suspicions.

As he sat with Ms. Winter, the silence began to grow uncomfortable, so he asked her, more out of a desire to appear intelligent and devout than any real interest in the subject, if people became guardian angels after they died. Ms. Winter sighed.

"You must miss your brother," she said.

Owen was flustered. His question had not meant to refer to Hugh.

He rarely thought about his brother anymore, it was the space left behind that concerned him.

"I don't know," he said.

"Have you tried praying to him?" Ms. Winter said.

"My brother's gone," Owen explained. He never used the word *missing*. This word, still plastered all over his father's office, had too much weight for Owen to pronounce it comfortably.

"I believe that those who have gone watch over us from heaven, Owen," Ms. Winter said. "Your brother has not really left you."

Owen didn't try to correct her, mostly because that was the moment that Ms. Winter put her arm around him, and he didn't want to say anything that might have caused her to recoil. Just after Hugh's disappearance, his mother had sometimes clutched him with frightening force, but lately, entombed in her dark bedroom, she rarely touched him. His father, rather than draping an arm around him, was more likely to grip the back of Owen's neck, as if pulling him back from some abyss. More than anything, Owen was desperate for a hug.

Flushed and brave with such intimacy, Owen made the mistake of telling his father what Ms. Winter said on the ride home. By the time they pulled into the driveway, his father was muttering incoherently. He called the rectory, screamed at the secretary and then at one of the priests. Owen was not sure which one because his father addressed him as Jack, which in itself, Owen thought, must qualify as some sort of sin. After a few minutes, Owen's mother emerged from her bedroom, hair lank, the imprint of pillowcase creases on one cheek.

"What is it?" she said hysterically. "Oh, God, what is it?" Owen's father ignored her.

"My son is not dead," he yelled, more than once, and the final time, his voice broke and there was a frightening stretch of muffled, gasping sobs. Finally, when he had control again, Owen's father spoke three words, clear and cold and alien, into the beige receiver, before hanging it up with such force, the base let out a pale, false ring.

"Fuck you all," was what he said.

Owen and Lena were taken out of CCD. The Furey family stopped going to church on Sundays, no longer mailed in the preaddressed envelopes for the Cardinal's Annual Appeal. Phone calls from concerned parishioners and priests went unanswered. Lena skipped her Confirmation, which seemed to delight her. There were arguments with their devout grandparents. Henry Furey's parents had helped build their town's church, his mother was the rectory secretary, his father in charge of collection. They went to mass every morning at eight A.M. Owen's grandmother said that if Owen's father had kept his commitment to becoming a priest, none of this ever would have happened. They stopped going there for holidays. Owen still received a birthday card from his grandmother every year, but now it came with a check instead of a present.

Owen never made the First Confession and Communion Ms. Winter had been preparing him for. Initially he missed her, but he got over it. He was relieved not to be Catholic anymore. When he brought Noah Wasserman home from school one day, Noah laughed at his sister's First Communion photo, asking if she'd gotten married at the age of seven. It all seemed weird to Owen—the kitschy church, the saints, angels, and prophets, the sacrifice of a single skinny man to save everyone else—once he was away from it.

Two years later, when Owen's mother entered medical school at the start of summer vacation, Owen woke one Saturday morning to a quiet house. His sister and father were sleeping late, his mother gone to a morning class. Owen, encouraged by the warm sun and clear lungs, decided to ride his bike for an hour before his baseball game. Looking in his drawer for his Brookline Little League T-shirt, he remembered his mother had collected it for the wash the night before. He couldn't find the laundry basket in its usual spot by the linen closet, and, scowling at his mother's neglect, decided that it must still be downstairs. Wearing only his baseball pants and cleats, he descended the dimly lit stairwell to the basement, passing by the door to his father's office, all the way down a cement-floored hallway to the laundry room. The overhead light was broken, the cave-like room lit only by an ancient standing lamp with a bare light bulb, which had been left on. Even with the lamp, the room was harshly shadowed, dank and frightening, and the mold made him wheeze.

He checked the dryer but found it empty. He opened the washer door and stood on tiptoes to reach down; his hand plunged into water and sopping clothes. Suddenly, Owen realized his cleats were also wet, and that beyond the normal damp sweat of the basement floor there was the glimmer of a puddle. The washer had overflowed before, and Owen felt a surge of temper that his mother was not there to deal with it.

Owen turned around so fast he bumped into the lamp, which stood on the same platform as the washer. In a slow-motion trip and tumble that he would re-create over and over in the weeks to come, both the lamp and Owen fell to the floor, the lamp first and Owen on top, right into the puddle of soapy water.

Owen would never know how long the next part took. Though there was pain, pain unlike any he had ever experienced, pulsing and massive, and paralysis, he lived through it all like he was in a dream, floating above and watching it happen. Watching his half-naked body convulse on the floor, watching his legs not move even though he was making every effort to stand up, watching himself open his mouth to scream and nothing coming out except the dull hum of deadly voltage. Though his asthma made him wheeze, this was the first time he had ever been completely unable to breathe. He even saw the realization come over his face, the moment where it occurred to him that he could die. Then, with nothing but a ripple in the air above him, a slight change in the angle of shadows in the room, he was lifted from the charged floor and catapulted out into the small hallway, where his shoulder smashed against the cement wall. It was only then, after he was released from the current, that he was able to scream.

Later, there were different stories. The story of how Lena woke to his screaming, and when their father came bursting into her room and asked where her brother was, she said the laundry room, with no idea how she knew. The story of his father running downstairs and pulling him away from the still popping electricity, so that he felt the shock slice briefly through his own body. The story from the emergency team, two fire trucks and an ambulance that crowded the whole of their dead-end street, who insisted that Owen saved himself, vaulting with superhuman strength far enough away that he was able to regain his voice and scream for help.

Owen's story he kept to himself. He formed it during the never-dark nights of his three days of observation at Children's Hospital, his thoughts repeating in time to the beeping of his heart monitor. During morning rounds, he was quiet and cooperative while the doctors showed his mother's classmates the entry and exit wounds left by the electricity, a black charred spot on his chest opposite his heart and another on the palm of one hand. He pretended not to hear while they told one another in the hallway that another thirty seconds on that floor would have killed him. His father pulled him off just in time; this is the story the doctors had heard. *Lucky for the kid he could scream,* they said. Owen never corrected them, letting his father, who had so little to be happy about in those days, be the hero. He enjoyed his mother's guilt, exaggerating his need for the inhaler whenever she stopped by his hospital room. He told no one about that moment where he was lifted into the air, hurled from danger, tossed a little too forcefully into the cement wall. There was a distinct feeling of actual hands yanking him from the pull of electricity. He didn't tell them that it wasn't until after he was saved that he began to scream.

The first time Danny comes in front of him, Owen is supposed to be asleep. They are in Danny's bed, and Owen hears the shuddery breath before he feels the quickening of Danny's hand as it catches the comforter. Owen is still facing the wall, so he doesn't see the moment where Danny's face seizes in near-pain, doesn't witness, though he will later, the release, which he had always assumed would make a noise, and is disappointed to discover occurs in pure silence. He's not even sure what has happened until Danny is done, and, as if he knows or hopes Owen has been listening, he whispers: "Do you spurt yet?"

Owen shakes his head without turning around. "Uh-uh."

"Wanna see?"

Owen rolls over, and before he can look, Danny takes his hand and places it against the smooth, taut skin below his belly button, where there is a little pool. There is both more and less of it than Owen imagined. It clings like snot, and Owen would like to let go, but he can't get over the sight of his own hand on that skin, and the little throb in Danny's groin is just like the one in his own, and most of all, Danny seems to want him to stay like that, so he leaves his hand until the cum begins to cool, and he must wipe between his fingers with Danny's *Empire Strikes Back* sheets, gently, so as not to wake his friend.

When they next sleep over at Owen's, Owen's mother meets Danny for the first time. For once she is not on call on a Saturday, and she makes spaghetti and veal sauce. Lena refuses to join them, claiming a newly acquired moral objection to veal, and Owen's father, who has gone into the office for some emergency deadline, doesn't make it home, so Owen must suffer twenty minutes at the table in between his mother and his best friend. His mother asks Danny inane questions about school, his hobbies, his ethnic heritage. Owen is mortified; his mother—whom he had gotten used to during the years she rarely changed out of flannel pajamas, when she looked old, witchlike, her eyes shot through with bloody veins, dandruff gathered at her part—is suddenly beautiful. Her hair has bounce, she is bright-eyed, she appears to be wearing lipstick. This must be what she looks like at the hospital. Owen is jolted by the difference, and the realization that it happened a while ago, he just hasn't noticed until now. Danny answers all her questions, using full sentences instead of the grunts and nods he uses with his own mother. He nudges Owen under the table, and once opens his mouth to reveal masticated spaghetti and baby cow swimming in milk. Owen's mother listens to Danny's answers with her eyebrows raised. Danny is known for his charm around mothers, but she doesn't seem that impressed. Near the end of dinner, when Danny offers to load the dishwasher, Owen's mother smiles and cocks her head.

"Did you say you're in Owen's class?" she asks. Danny nods. "The fifth grade." She adds this like a test, the way she gives Owen one last chance to tell the truth before she calls him on a lie.

"Yes."

"You're not ten, though," she says. Danny grins with the same smile he reserves for their female teachers—Madame Cecile in French, Mrs. Wrinkle who leads the chorus.

"I'm almost twelve," he says. "They kept me back when my dad left and we moved here."

Owen's mother expresses her sympathy, and excuses them from doing the dishes. But later, when they're propped on their elbows watching *Nightmare on Elm Street* and she brings them bowls of chocolate M&M's ice cream, she glances back in a way that makes Owen feel as if he's been found out. Though his mouth waters for it, he lets his ice cream melt into soup. He spends the rest of the film guiltily imagining his mother slashed clean out of his life by a bad guy with knives for fingers.

In bed later, separated by the expanse of Owen's red shag rug, Danny says good night without hesitation, no hint that the darkness and ample covers might promise more. Within minutes he is breathing with the regular oblivion of sleep. Owen lies awake and furious, convinced that this return to innocence is somehow his mother's fault. He wants to live with his father, who leaves him alone, and not with a woman who suddenly, after three years of crying in her bedroom and two years of medical school, seems to think she has a right to be suspicious of his friends.

Tonight, as he often does, he lulls himself to sleep with prayer. He can't remember the words to official prayers, except for one, taught to him by his grandmother, that he interprets mainly as a plea to live through the night, and which once made him too terrified to sleep if he repeated it. Owen's prayers usually involve the repetition of a single phrase, an incantation. *Make them divorce, Make them divorce.* Occasionally, for good manners, he interjects a *please*, but generally he doesn't bother with formalities. It's not as though he's speaking to God.

Owen believes in angels now. He is sure that his brother—who was never declared dead, but whose search was abandoned anyway— is now a winged, half-naked creature guarding the leftovers of his family. He has no further evidence to support this theory, no visions of Hugh lit from behind by a divine bulb. He doesn't actually remember the feeling of hands pulling him from danger, only the ruminating he did about it later on. He believes in the idea that his brother saved his life so devoutly, his occasional bouts of labored breathing don't worry him. If the need should arise, his brother will save him again.

When Owen wants something, he prays directly to Hugh for it. When he feels shame, or the urge to confess things he suspects are some category of sin, he does not imagine kneeling in penance before a priest or God or a Jesus with an exposed, thorny heart. He imagines a painting that once hung in his father's office, an angel with six wings folded in toward his body like the petals of a flower. Wings that look strong enough, even in repose, to lift someone from mortal danger. In the middle of these wings Owen imagines the face of a ninth-grade boy, set against the photographer's background of blue sky. The creature hovers somewhere above his right shoulder, not judging or cajoling like parents or peers, but simply smiling, as if he has already seen it all, and nothing Owen decides to do will surprise him.

Not even his hands on another boy.

5. scissors

I can tell it's my mother by the knock—hard, official, trying to be brave. My father's knuckles are tentative, embarrassed, they barely make contact. He started using this knock when I was twelve, like he was afraid of catching me naked. Owen just kicks the base of the door with his sneaker when he's told to call me to dinner. Last year, I made a sign with a red Sharpie marker saying that no one is allowed in my room.

I turn the music down and go to the door, opening it a crack, feeling the scowl form around my mouth before it even has a reason to.

"What," I say to my mother, whose mouth is also set, expecting me to be rude.

"I'd like to talk to you," she says.

"I'm doing my homework." I slouch against the wall and hold the door barely open with my thigh.

My mother sighs. She still has her white hospital jacket on, a stethoscope around her neck, as if this will give her some sort of authority.

"I hear you're spending time in Harvard Square."

I look at her with perfect blankness.

"Jeremy Lispet saw you there," my mother prompts. I blink at her.

"So? I was waiting for Tracy by the T. I told you we were going to the movies."

"I thought you were going in Brookline. I don't want you in Harvard Square alone," she says. "It's easier than you think to fall into trouble."

I roll my eyes at this. *Since when do you care?* I want to say, but I have rules about what I will say to my mother. Nothing that might make her think of Hugh. This is harder to accomplish than you'd think. My mom's new life is not solid, it's a thin layer that could crumble at any minute, sending her back to bed. I go back and forth between trying to protect her and wanting to devastate her.

"Whatever, Mom. I'm not hanging out anywhere. Relax."

"What's that smell?" she says, peering over my shoulder.

I've been smoking cloves, wide, brown cigarettes with gold filters that leave the sticky taste of apple cider on my lips.

"Incense," I say. My mother looks me in the eye.

Once even a fib was so obvious on my face that my family could tell even before I opened my mouth. Hugh never trusted me with secrets; teachers relied on me as an informant. Lying is easy now. I just let my face go limp, stare straight into my parents' (or teachers' or friends') eyes and forget the truth. I even lie when I don't have to, just for the thrill of being believed. Lies have boundaries that are easy to focus on, not like the truth, which can stretch in any direction, out of control. It is the truth now that makes me feel self-conscious and terrified, like I'm about to be found out.

Most of the time my parents don't seem to notice my new talent. Only occasionally, when I am lying, will my father or mother look tired, defeated, like they know everything I've ever lied about, they just don't have the energy to call me on it.

Now my mother looks relieved, enough to try to smile before I shut the door in her face. I go back to my bed and flip through my binder, looking at old pictures of her. Hugh loved to take pictures of my mother. There are whole rolls of just her, her face thinner and tighter, her hair long and occasionally in pigtails, which strikes me as kind of immature. She is always laughing, even when she's trying to pose like a serious model. Her smiles used to be real.

I listen to the Beatles while I label the contact sheets I developed today, which are of the Furey family reunion at my father's childhood home. They are from the summer after second grade, when Owen was diagnosed with asthma, and my parents sent my cat Mitsy to live with my grandparents. That year, I won the seven-year-olds' race in their backyard and got to pick first from my grandmother's table of plastic and balsawood toys. There is a picture of this, my grandmother in a minidress with Marimekko flowers, her dark hair sprayed in a perfect bun. Even old, she's really pretty; everyone was always talking about her legs. She has a gin and tonic in one hand, a cigarette in the other. I'm standing next to her looking miserable, a balsa plane limp in my hand, my hair as short and ratty as a boy's and my knees scarred from picking scabs. My grandmother had just told me, after I barreled into the prize table fresh from my victory, that I was not very ladylike. I was trying not to cry. Not that I cared about being ladylike, but she had beamed and given Hugh a huge hug when he'd won the egg toss.

I spent the rest of the reunion in the garden shed killing spiders. Hugh came to find me eventually, cheering me up with a few shrugs and careless insults, as if it hardly mattered what anyone else thought of me, since he thought I was great. Then he helped me look for my cat, but we found no evidence that she'd ever been there. I never asked my parents about this. I was afraid of finding out the truth.

In the morning I organize my backpack as if I'm really going to school. Biology lab book, geometry notes, even my gym clothes. If my parents searched my bag, my props would be convincing. But they don't bother.

I only walk halfway, stopping in a small, diamond-shaped park by the old-age home. There are two old men at one end of the park, wearing large-brimmed dark hats, so similar they look like emaciated twins, feeding pigeons from a waxed Dunkin' Donuts bag. I sit on a bench facing away from them, take out my cigarettes and smoke for twenty minutes straight, until my throat is dry and stinging. I want to buy a hot chocolate, but I'm afraid the clerks will wonder why I'm not in school. It starts to drizzle, half-frozen drops that pelt the shoulders of my Levi's jean jacket. The old men make a big production of trying to hurry across the street and into the home, but their walkers block swift movements.

A guy in a white apron and Red Sox cap comes out and helps them over the lip of the sidewalk. Then he waves in my direction and starts across the street.

"Shit," I mutter. It's Jonah.

"Hello, Lena," he says when he gets close enough, and sits down next to me on the bench like he's welcome.

"Hey," I say back, trying to fit all my annoyance into one syllable. He takes out a pack of Marlboros, offers me one, and lights his own after I shake my head.

"I'm a volunteer," he says, as if I'd asked him, pointing back at the old-age home.

"Are you Catholic or something?" I say.

"No," he says, amused. "Do I have to be?"

"Catholic kids have to work here as part of their Confirmation. My . . . um . . . cousin did it." Actually, it was Hugh, but I wasn't going there.

"Mine's more like community service to avoid Juvenile Hall." He shrugs. "It's not so bad. They're all so grateful and interested, it's kind of nice. Different perspective, you know?"

Hugh had said something like that to my parents. Something about how easy it was to make people happy.

"Old people make me nervous," I say. "I always think they're going to have a stroke or a heart attack and I won't know what to do."

Jonah laughs. This is more than I've ever said to him in one sitting, and he looks surprised.

"Well, I'm not in charge of that part. I just turn the bingo wheel and hand out breakfast."

"Sounds depressing," I say.

"It's better than study hall," Jonah says. "I'm not allowed free blocks anymore." He grins, and I look away. He says it all so nonchalantly, not looking for sympathy or bragging like the other reformed delinquents in the Quad. I wonder what he did to get community service. I doubt they give it to you for trying to kill yourself.

Jonah finishes his cigarette, puts it out on the bench edge, and sticks the butt in his pocket rather than throwing it on the ground.

This makes me feel guilty for a second—I used to care about littering—then annoyed.

"See you in class," he says. I shrug. I won't be there, but I'm not about to tell Jonah that.

After he leaves I light another cigarette and smoke it, wishing that I hadn't given in and talked to him. I don't want him to think I like him.

When I know my father and brother must be long gone from the house, even if they are running late, I go back home and let myself in the back door. The house feels the same way it does when I stay home sick, as if it's trapped in a bubble, where even the air feels heavy and slow and protected from the real world. There won't be anyone home until at least three, but I keep thinking I hear the sound of the key in the lock, and every time a bolt of fear interrupts my breath.

I look in the kitchen cabinet for packets of Swiss Miss, but Owen drank the last one and left the empty box on the shelf. There is an inch of coffee left in the pot, the burner switched off but still warm. I fix a mug with cream and four spoons of sugar. It's like liquid coffee ice cream soothing my throat, and it leaves a pleasant prickle behind my eyes. Something like courage.

I take a quick shower to wet my hair, which has gathered into frozen slabs behind my barrettes. The only scissors I can find are the old yellow-handled ones from the kitchen junk drawer, so dull I wind up sawing away at my hair instead of cutting it. Halfway through, I have a moment of such horror at my reflection that I have to finish without the mirror, catching the top of my ear twice between the blunt blades. I flush what I cut off down the toilet; away from my head it doesn't even seem like hair, it's darker brown, coarse, like dirty straw. There is more of it than I thought there would be.

I get the box of hair dye from my room and read the directions quickly, before mixing the tube and squirting it all over my scalp. The stuff is impossibly runny, streaking purple down my temples and neck, racing along the whorls of my ears. I glance in the mirror and think of the time I was sent home by the school nurse after the annual lice inspection. My mother had to cut my already short hair close to my scalp, then lather it with shampoo so strong it made my eyes and nose run. My eyes are running now, and I have to breathe through my mouth to avoid gagging on the smell.

I get back in the shower stall to wash it off, bruise-black swirling into the drain like Halloween blood. Once out, I towel-dry and check the results. My hair is beyond black, so dark it makes me look paler than I actually am, highlighting the shadows that have formed under my eyes from too many late nights spent chain-smoking. The contrast makes my face look skeletal. I like the effect. I sink my fingers into Dippety-Do and slather it on, forming sharp peaks that stand straight up. I clip a few uneven strands, shellacking the whole thing with my hairspray. Before leaving the bathroom, I take a Maybelline eye pencil from my mother's cluttered makeup drawer. Except for the occasional lip gloss that tastes like candy, I don't wear makeup. But now I pull my bottom lid down, exposing red veins and a little pool of tears, and trace black along the inside of my lid, not the subtle shading my mother applies, but thick, the way the boys in the Quad do it. Dark, violent slashes under the eye that are the opposite of pretty.

By the time I get to Harvard Square the sleet has stopped, but the sky is still low and gray, not making any promises. There is hardly any-one in the Pit, just one skateboarder who looks about twelve and two bums yelling at a Jesus freak. It's only eleven A.M., and the black-boards outside still list breakfast specials.

I'm wearing combat boots I bought yesterday at the army-navy store in Kenmore Square. I got them three sizes too large and stuffed the toes with hiking socks. Since my ten-dollar-a-week allowance barely covers my cigarettes, I took the passbook from my desk drawer and started chipping away at my savings account from past birthdays and lost teeth. At the army-navy store I also got two pairs of fatigues, one black, one green, a thick leather bracelet with metal studs, and one pewter skull earring. From the glass case at the front I picked out a silver Zippo. The clerk who helped me was a boy from my school, who was smoking openly behind the counter, hand-rolled cigarettes he set aside when helping a customer, and picked up again if their decisions seemed to be taking too long. He asked me if I wanted the lighter engraved. I said no, remembering that Sebastian's had been blank. I wouldn't know what to engrave anyway. Not Lena, like the pencil cases and iron-on T-shirts that Hugh used to give me on birthdays. Even my initials would feel like I was giving too much away.

In Harvard Square I'm having trouble with the boots; I keep forgetting the length of my feet, tripping my way up stairs, miscalculating the amount of room I have in front of me. Even when I'm not stumbling, my walk is clunky, and I hope this resembles a tough boy's strut. I go to the newsstand to buy the last of my props: a red and white package of regular Marlboros. I light the first one, feeling the difference in my lungs. The filter is brown instead of white, and I have to remind myself to hold it between my thumb and forefinger, cupping the lit end in my palm as I drag.

I think my disguise is pretty convincing. I'm a tall enough girl to be an average-height boy, my hips are nonexistent, my shoulders wide and bony, my chest so small it disappears beneath the layers of an Ace bandage. While my features aren't exactly manly, I can pass for a boy who doesn't shave yet. Even my hands are big, the ends of my fingers stocky and thick with broad nails, which I clipped short after my last shower. I have my father's hands; Owen has my mother's.

I'm not so sure about my voice. I've been smoking more, clearing my throat and forcing hard coughs, anything that might bruise my vocal cords. I'm relying on what I know from having boys as friends in grammar school—I won't be expected to talk all the time. A few well-placed grunts and curses will get the same loyalty that a blabbing confession would from a group of girls.

I am so sure of myself as I walk across the street to Au Bon Pain, order a large coffee in a gruff mumble, sit with my legs splayed at a prominent outdoor table, that I am totally crushed when Sebastian shows up. He recognizes me instantly.

"Brookline Girl!" he says fondly, too loud, scraping a wrought-iron chair across the stone tiles to join me. He straddles it backward, and I note this for later, resisting the urge to cross my legs like a lady.

"Hey," I say, using my new, gruffer voice.

Sebastian raises his eyebrows. The skin on his forehead is pale and clammy, as if he is sick or scared. His expression, though, is amused. I brace myself.

"I give up," he says. "Who are you supposed to be?"

"No one," I say with my real voice.

"I know," Sebastian says. I sink lower in my chair. "You're starring in an after-school special about cross-gender identification."

"Leave me alone," I say, with more force this time, but still he pretends not to have heard me.

"You're having a sex-change operation," he says. "I've heard about this. You have to cross-dress for a year before they let you go under the knife—to make sure it's what you really want, right?" He reaches into the inside pocket of his jacket, then the outer pockets, looking for cigarettes.

"Jesus," he says, glancing under the table. "Your feet are *enormous*. Nice touch. You should do something about the jeans though." He gestures to my crotch. "A well-placed sock ought to do it. Don't want to be mistaken for a eunuch. Or maybe you do. I don't dare assume."

I sit forward, hunching over my lap. Sebastian chuckles across from me, looking delighted with himself. I take out my cigarettes, and Sebastian looks at them greedily, giving me an exaggerated smile and batting his eyelashes. I hand him one grudgingly.

I light my cigarette with the matches that came with the pack, not ready to use the Zippo in front of Sebastian. He's mercifully quiet for a moment, though his stare is uncomfortable. I realize he's waiting for me to say something, but I don't know where to begin. He isn't able to wait for long.

"I assume there's a reason you want to be mistaken for a boy," he says.

I nod my head, relieved.

"But you're not going to share it."

"Nope," I say.

"Suit yourself," Sebastian says. "Just tell me one thing." I wait, not committing. "What am I supposed to call you?"

"Lee," I say. I experimented with many names at home, but they all felt conspicuous. Lee is what Hugh sometimes called me; it will be easy to remember.

Once Sebastian is on my side, the rest of the day goes smoothly. In the next few hours I'm introduced to a dozen people, and they all take my being a boy for granted, because it comes from Sebastian. "This is Lee," he says. "He's an old friend." And instantly, I have a new identity, a bit of history. I speak up and, when no one questions my voice, I get almost chatty, for me. I even start talking to a girl. Normally I say all the wrong things to girls, but as a boy it's somehow easier. The girl, Katya, reads my palm. She tells me that my lifeline is alarmingly short, and the others peer enviously over my shoulder. When the manager of Au Bon Pain comes out to tell us we've loitered long enough without buying anything, some of the boys harass him, and though I would normally be mortified at such a thing, I join in the laughter. After the manager gives up and shuffles inside, I tell myself I did it to fit in.

Sebastian gives me a lesson on my new Zippo, and by the time I get home, before my parents so I can wash away the hair gel and smudged liner, my thigh already has an irritated red welt from the stone rubbing against my coarse army pants. I sit on my bed with only a T-shirt on, my wet hair as short and light as it was when I was little, the Dead Kennedys, who are starting to grow on me, playing on Hugh's turntable, tracing the redness with the cool silver of my new lighter. I think this is the first of many marks I'll want to keep.

6. Fur coat

The fifth-graders walk to the Muddy River Cemetery on a clear November morning, clustered into their natural division of boys and girls, bright parkas left open to the sun. They are like a funeral procession, Owen thinks, the undertakers played by Mr. Gabriel, Ms. Lieberman, and two parent volunteers, who flank all sides and wave the children forward to fill in lagging spaces. Traffic stops for the long stream of shuffling sneakers, which takes two whole cycles of the light to make it across.

Once inside the stone walls of the cemetery, the order explodes into the chaos of a gym class. The girls rush to claim the best stones, the boys scoff and pretend not to care, but secretly hope the girls have missed a few. Mr. Gabriel makes a general plea for forethought, reminding them that each student is allowed only one oversized sheet of rice paper. The class cheerfully ignores him, and within ten minutes, half a dozen children are whining about torn sheets and double images. They are loud enough to drive away the two couples, one elderly, one in their twenties, sitting on benches nearby. The Muddy River Cemetery, as well as being a tourist attraction, is considered a romantic spot. People propose to each other here.

Danny chooses a monument that looks like it will require two sheets to cover, and immediately four girls claim the graves on either side. Owen, who already decided which grave to do before the field trip was announced, wanders off alone, pretending not to care that Danny, after walking the whole way with him in one long tripping contest, doesn't ask where he's going.

The project seems to have grown in scale and importance since Hugh and Lena were in the fifth grade. In addition to the gravestone rubbing, they have been assigned a paper, which they have to research on their own time at the public library. Most of the people buried in this graveyard were from important families in the town. Not seeming to realize how creepy this sounds, Mr. Gabriel tells them that the occupants of their graves will be with them the entire year.

Owen is relieved his grave is far away from the volunteer parents: Mindy Turner's mother who is bossy and fiercely cheerful and chaperones almost every trip they take, and the small, overwhelmed, continuously nodding mother of the mortified Alan Ying. Owen's mother, who grew up the child of granite workers in Maine, was the expert volunteer for this field trip for both Hugh's and Lena's classes. Three weeks ago, when Owen brought home the permission slip, with a penciled note from Mr. Gabriel inviting her, his mother had asked if he wanted her to rearrange her classes and skip rounds to come along. Owen had shrugged as if it didn't matter (no one in the fifth grade, aside from Mindy Turner, wants their mother on a field trip), and ignored Mr. Gabriel's questioning glance when he handed in the slip, but now he is mad. His mother has never been on one of his field trips, not even in the first and second grades when the prospect of seeing her out of context was an exciting one. Before she was always at the hospital, she was always in bed. Owen suspects that when Hugh and Lena were his age, she was more like Mindy Turner's mom.

Owen releases the straps of his backpack and takes out his supplies, settling himself Indian style in the leaves that blanket his grave. He clears the top of the headstone of twigs and acorn caps and uses artist's tape to secure the veined silky paper over the rounded edges. He starts in the upper left-hand corner, rubbing the cigar-sized piece of charcoal with wide strokes. A swatch of gravelly, textured black spreads down for six inches before the grave's design begins to appear like a lithograph, the details in the empty spaces. Owen, lulled by the motion and his class settling down around him, shifts so he is resting his forehead against the paper as he rubs.

"Boo!" Danny says, jumping out from behind an ancient, gnarled tree. Owen's hand jerks, and his charcoal breaks, making a thick dark slash in the middle of a letter. He sits upright, retracing over the mistake with the broken piece. Danny plops down on the grave next to him, leaning his shoulders against the crooked slab. He lights a cigarette, glancing briefly around for Mr. Gabriel, who is trying to placate two girls whining about having to pee. He offers Owen a drag. He's wearing black wool gloves with the fingers cut off, and these, combined with the cigarette and the way he lets his hands hang limply from his upright knees, make him look at least sixteen years old. Owen shakes his head and continues to work, not wanting to give Danny the satisfaction of his full attention.

"Are you done with yours already?" Owen says, after a minute of Danny sucking so fiercely on his cigarette the filter is soggy from his lips.

"Katie's doing mine." Danny shrugs, grinning.

Katie Beck is Danny's girlfriend. They are the latest to fall under the class's new obsession with pairing up. Boys and girls have started "going out," a process that begins with an agreement over the phone and ends fairly quickly—two weeks is the current record—with a similar call in which the main couple is barely involved. During the time when they are a couple, the boy and girl rarely see each other alone, are lucky to steal a few minutes of hand-holding at recess or during a bold walk home from school. "Going out" doesn't actually involve going anywhere, since none of them are allowed out at night without adult supervision. There have been rumors of make-out sessions that get as far as second base. One already famous incident involved three couples, a latchkey kid, and an afternoon at his house that quickly turned into some sort of amateur orgy. This was according to the boys. Whatever happened, all of the couples broke up within twenty-four hours, and nothing like it has been attempted since. Danny is the most popular choice for a boyfriend; he has already had three ten-day relationships and seems to have at least a dozen girls waiting, impatiently, in the wings. Katie Beck is a timesuck; of every afternoon Owen spends at Danny's house, at least an hour is wasted on the phone with her friends.

"Better hope Gabriel doesn't find out," Owen says. Katie already does the majority of Danny's homework.

"She wanted to. I don't give a shit."

"Whatever," Owen says. He doesn't look up from his stone. He's almost to the end of the first name.

"Think Gabriel'd notice if we took off?" Danny says. "I hear Amanda's home sick today."

"He'd notice," Owen says quickly.

"Chrissy won't be there." Danny smiles. Owen hasn't been back since the pillow fight, but Danny has gone alone. While Amanda knows that Katie is his official girlfriend, Katie and her friends don't seem to know anything about Amanda. The social gulf between fifth and sixth grade runs too deep for them to find out. It's like something from *Dallas* or *Knot's Landing,* as if Danny is already a man gripped by midlife crisis, juggling a debutante wife and a slutty mistress he puts up in an apartment across town.

"So I get to sit by myself in the other room?" Owen says. "No, thanks. You're on your own. What do you *do* with her anyway?" he adds dismissively, as if his heart is not thumping wildly at the question. Danny shrugs.

"You know," he says, though surely he realizes Owen doesn't know at all. "Fuck around. I get to take her bra off. Sometimes she lets me stick a finger down there, but nothing else. Mostly I just try not to cream my pants."

This is both more and less than Owen imagined going on. He is relieved to hear that Amanda doesn't touch back. Somehow, that would seem more of a betrayal than Danny's frustrated fingerings.

Danny has masturbated in front of him five times now. Though Owen waits for it to the point of distraction, the idea seems to appear to Danny on a whim. It doesn't happen every time they are alone, and since the first time, he has not asked Owen to touch him. He has suggested that Owen join in on his own, and Owen has obliged, but only halfheartedly. He's too busy watching Danny to concentrate on touching himself. It's only after Danny falls asleep, or later when he is home in his own bed, that Owen will masturbate, moving to the memory of Danny's rhythm. For Owen there is still no big finish; he does it until his wrist grows tired, then gives up and falls asleep.

Something usually happens on the nights they play a police game. Danny is obsessed with cop shows—*T.J. Hooker, Chips, Miami Vice*— and likes to act them out. He chooses the best role and then gives Owen what is left over, either criminal or lowly partner. They pretend to have car chases, feign running through Florida streets, and always end up with Danny pointing his father's gun at Owen's head. Then Owen, in whatever character he has been assigned, must talk his way out of being shot. He doesn't like this part, though Danny shows him the gun is empty every time. It seems to Owen like the sort of bad judgment that neighbors would shake their heads over after reading about it in the paper. Owen is not sure why these games lead to Danny masturbating later on, except that they make him excited and overenergized. And so, even as he cringes at the cold metal of the gun pressed to his temple, Owen goes along because the anticipation of what will follow starts a stirring under the fly of his jeans.

Owen has spent a lot of time wondering if what they do can be considered "fucking around." Nothing has come close to the topic in Human Development, and his book only mentions it once, in passing, then refers the reader with questions to a section about homosexuality. Owen is afraid to read that section. He tells himself that it is not the same thing as what Danny does with Amanda, because they don't touch. Then he wonders what it means that he wants to.

"I don't think you should risk it," Owen says about Danny's plan to visit Amanda Peters. Danny laughs, an exaggerated guffaw meant to ridicule, and Owen realizes he didn't mean it. Danny has a tendency to dare Owen toward an idea he has no intention of carrying out. The first time he suggested Owen join him in beating off, Owen was sure it was some sort of trap.

When he is done laughing at him, Danny sighs. "This project is lame," he says.

"It's easy, though," Owen says. "Who'd you pick?"

"Some war hero," Danny says. "Probably a fag." He pauses for a moment, cocking his head, as if he is listening to the rasp of Owen's charcoal. "Hey," he says finally. "Is your brother in here?"

Owen looks up to see if this is one of Danny's jokes, but his friend is gnawing at a hangnail, his look too blank to be taunting.

"This is a *historical* cemetery," Owen says. "They haven't buried anyone here in a hundred years."

"I know," Danny says. "I was just kidding anyway." He stands up, brushing at the butt of his already filthy jeans. Owen feels sorry for him, and guilty for being so condescending. Most of the time, he does not think of himself as being smarter than other people. But Danny, even though he is better in math, often does not know simple facts that Owen has known for years. His geography is abominable, he never used a computer before transferring here, when he reads it is painfully slow, and he has the large, overly controlled handwriting of a first-grader. There seems to be a gap between what he sees and what he retains, and Owen has begun to wonder if it's because he is always stoned.

Danny leans so close that Owen feels a familiar thrill that is part arousal and part fear. He angles his head to read the grave rubbing Owen has almost finished.

Under the curved top is a worn-down outline of angel wings bordering a realistic skull. At the bottom, where Owen has pushed aside the overgrown grass, is an epitaph. *He is not here, he is risen.* The name appears on Owen's rice paper as white block letters in an abyss of black: BENJAMIN ASH 1775–1786.

"He was eleven," Danny says.

"Yeah," Owen murmurs, going over a dull letter with sweeps of his charcoal.

"What do you think happened to him?"

Though Owen has already imagined a short but highly melodramatic history for a dead eighteenth-century New England boy, to the point that he doesn't want to research him in the library because he prefers this made-up biography, he shrugs.

"I don't know," he says, as if, about this, as well as anything else they might discuss, he couldn't care less.

"Wanna play after school?" Danny says. His breath tickles the hair on the back of Owen's neck.

Owen makes an effort to breathe deeply, to keep his answer from tumbling out of him too soon—eager, transparent, and raw.

The fight that occurs after Lena cuts her hair is the worst Owen can remember in the history of his family. His parents rarely raise their voices in anger. His father, who ran group-therapy sessions when he was studying for the priesthood, is always trying to see someone else's side of things. Owen's mother grows silent when she's mad, her eyes bulging from the effort to hold it in. Why all of this restraint should suddenly fall apart just because of a bad haircut, Owen is unsure. Though he is sent to his room as soon as they glimpse the shining black remnants of his sister's hair, they are yelling so loudly Owen can make out every word. Lena's words are the most surprising—almost every other one is a curse. It's the abandon Lena takes in swearing at their parents that he finds the most frightening, though on some level it is also thrilling. All of the words he has recently learned to repeat nonchalantly with Danny, filling them in wherever they seem appropriate and sometimes when they don't,

Lena is screaming at their soft-spoken parents, people who, except for that one incident with the priest and an occasional slip due to bodily injury, do not use such language. Lena flings more swearwords in one performance than have been uttered in their house for a decade. Most of it goes something like this:

FATHER: We want to know who you've been hanging out with.

LENA: None of your fucking business.

MOTHER: Why have you done this to yourself? Is it a cry for help?

LENA: Fuck, that's deep. Been browsing the teen pamphlets at the hospital, Mom?

FATHER: What is this really about? Why can't you tell us?

LENA: Jesus Christ, you guys are clueless. You really are.

MOTHER: Fine. If you can't communicate like an adult, we'll treat you like a child. You're not to leave this house except for school and a trip to the hairdresser.

LENA: As if you could fucking stop me.

FATHER: Are you on drugs? Is that it?

LENA: Since when do you give a shit?

Owen thinks his sister has pushed things too far this time. He is sending mental messages to her to tone it down, but she continues to swear at them, hard, sharp curses, the silence afterward making them seem like slaps to his parents' cheeks.

Owen doesn't want to take sides. He would rather they all shut up. He would like to tell Lena to drop it and go to her room, his father to ignore her and escape to his reading chair in the living room. His mother to give that quick, impatient wave of her hand as she leaves the house, checking her pockets for the tools she will need at the hospital. Most of Owen's life, at least the part he can remember, has involved the members of his family sequestering themselves in their assigned chambers. He'd prefer it to remain that way.

Still, the fight is too tempting for Owen to stay in his room. He opens his door and creeps down the hall, stopping by the door to the living room. They are all yelling at once now, Lena spilling out foul insults, his mother sounding unhinged and hysterical with her battery of questions, his father trying to make an ultimatum above their chorus. Owen peeks in just at the moment that shocks them all. Lena rises from the sectional sofa, ready to storm off to her room in the way she has perfected, rattling the china cabinet from four walls away. Instead of their normal response to Lena's stomping, a roll of their eyes and exaggerated alarm at the damage she may cause, their father grabs hold of Lena's upper arm, tightly enough that Owen can see her fair skin bleeding white at the edges of his fingers.

"Sit down," he growls. Lena, momentarily stunned by this new tactic, allows herself to be pushed, a bit too firmly, back against over-stuffed maroon velour. The impact causes her to bounce a bit, and the sectional piece to misalign from its twin on the left. There is silence, all of them unsure how to react to this moment which seems more suited to TV than any scene from the Furey family. Lena looks down at her father's hand, still clamped on her arm, and back up again. Owen thinks he can see the corner of her mouth twitch with a smile at the opportunity.

"What are you going to do now, Dad?" she says. "Hit me?" There is a noise from Owen's mother, somewhere between a gasp and a remonstrative hiss. Owen's father lets go of Lena as if her skin has been burning his hand all along and he can't hold on for another second.

"That's enough, young lady," he says, not yelling now. Lena crosses her arms at her chest, mashing her lips together to indicate she's through. She rubs purposefully at the now-red stains her father has left on her arm.

"I don't care about your hair," he says simply, as though he hasn't been yelling about her disrespect for her body for forty minutes. "Leave it. You look ridiculous, but that's your business. You will not," he says, louder now, because Lena has looked up, squinting, as if preparing to let go with more, "disrupt this family just for the sake of doing so. I won't stand for this fabricated melodrama. I won't stand for it." When he repeats it, it is quieter, but just as cruel. It is not usual for their father to speak to them like this—his dealings with his children are sweet, if vague. Owen considers him the easy one. It is their mother who can clamp so naturally, almost happily, onto ultimatums. But their mother is silent, apparently shocked, by Lena or her husband Owen can't tell.

"Jeez," Lena says, with the same contempt, but not looking her father in the eye. "Excuse me for living." Their father can't seem to find a response to this, though Owen thinks he sees his jaw shaking on the edge of one.

After Lena is finally, mercifully, released back to her room, Owen's mother goes to the hospital and his father lies on the sofa with a book for about five minutes until he falls asleep. Owen pads down the hall in his socks and knocks quietly on Lena's door. With no answer he tries again, four knocks instead of two, using all his knuckles. He's beginning to wonder if she's even in there when he hears a low, runny-nosed response.

"Go *away,* Owen," she calls out, and he is so angry that he forgets completely his plan of comfort and allegiance—he was going to tell her that her haircut looks cool—and instead kicks the door and blurts out the first thing that comes to his mouth.

"Freak."

Owen and Danny go to the graveyard to drink. Danny provides the forty-ounce Budweiser bottles dressed in brown paper sleeves. In between barely lip-moistening sips, Owen pours the cold foam into the soil between his legs, feeding the bones. He doesn't like the way even a little beer makes him feel, heavy and drowsy and unguarded, images of himself pressing his mouth into Danny's appear frequently and without the usual alarm. He prefers the pot, which makes him hypervigilant. Rather than the smoke doing damage to his lungs, it seems to expand them, burning pockets of congestion the same way the red ember on a joint eats its way down toward his fingers. He likes passing it back and forth, the paper barely growing cold in the space between his and Danny's mouths.

Danny gets the beer by waiting around the corner from the liquor store, asking customers to buy for him. He takes Owen to show him how it's done. Sniffing out potential buyers is the tricky part. They must be old enough to have real IDs—college kids with fake IDs won't risk the double crime—but young enough that they don't have kids yet and haven't developed the moral superiority of a parent. Twenty-one to twenty-six seems to be the magic window. Men are more promising than women, though certain, slightly slutty women are guarantees if you flirt with them. Owen tests out his instruction on one twenty-something guy in jeans and a thin leather tie, and then on a punk girl holding a wad of money she has collected from her friends who are double-parked. He fails both times. Danny, annoyed and impatient, takes over and finds them a buyer in two minutes.

That night the first snow of the season has blanketed the graves, and a few days of melting sun and frigid temperatures has formed a frozen crust thick enough to hold them. Owen takes meager sips of the beer; a taste he will not be able to separate from what happens next for the rest of his life.

Either because he gets drunker this time or because, as Owen hopes, Danny, too, can no longer stand to wait anymore, in the middle of Owen's tirade against his sister, Danny puts a hand on the back of Owen's head and pulls him against his mouth. The kiss is much more gentle than Owen imagined it would be; somehow he thought if it happened it would be quick and hard and dirty, something they'd need to get out of the way before losing their nerve. But Danny kisses him as delicately as if he is a frightened girl, at times barely touching his lips in a way that flares every inch of Owen's half-frozen skin. He has to make a conscious effort to remain quiet, because the capture of Danny's mouth, the taste of the cloves and beer on his tongue, and the welcome fall as he is pushed back against the crust of ice, which breaks with a series of pops, all make Owen's chest tighten with the urge to release an unbidden, mournful sound. Like a cry of pain.

It's the kissing Owen likes, the kissing that, every time they go to the graveyard or into Danny's room, or the bathroom at Woolworth's or, once, in Owen's closet while his father is making tacos in the kitchen, he tells himself is all he really wants. Despite the feeling that always takes over, after a few minutes of teasing wet mouths, that he can't press himself hard enough, that his hands can't move fast enough, that kissing itself is such a pale imitation of what he really wants, the details of which are still unimaginable, but still give him the urge to bite Danny's lips in frustration.

Other than pressing him against hard surfaces, and the occasional caress of his father's gun, Danny won't touch him, so Owen makes up for this lack by touching anywhere and in any way his friend seems to want. This mostly involves the imitation of what he has watched Danny do to himself, often enough that he can reproduce the process with identical timing. Most of the time the whole process—the feeling of his spit-soaked palm rubbing dry, the sight of

Danny's pubic hair tangled with sweat—makes him nauseated and angry and flushed, as if someone has made a public fool of him. He has to close his eyes and press blindly on. But then there are the other times, when he forces himself to watch Danny's face and witnesses the moment of helplessness that passes across it, where he seems to be begging Owen both to stop and not to stop at the same time. As if there is something about the pleasure he simply cannot stand. This makes Owen almost proud, like he has finally pinned Danny down in a wrestling match and demanded uncle. He enjoys the look of anguish that mottles Danny's face the second before he comes and often imagines, though he knows better, that there is real pain involved. The first time he saw this he stopped, and Danny, who then hid his face in his *Star Wars* pillow, let out a cry and grabbed his hand back. Owen asked afterward what coming felt like, and Danny was lulled and grateful enough to tell him.

"There's a part where you know you're gonna explode and there's no way you can stop it and it's almost scary," he said. "You're scared you're going to and scared you're not all at the same time." Though he didn't say it, Owen could tell that when he was involved it added another fear. Danny was scared he was going to refuse.

No matter if he enjoys it or not, Owen, at the end of these encounters, whether Danny rolls away to sleep or turns his back to hastily zipper the stained crotch of his jeans, is always left with the wish that they could go backward, back to before they ever touched, when he wanted something but wasn't quite sure what it was.

Thanksgiving is followed by Danny's twelfth birthday. He has a roller-skating party at Spin Off, and in between skating laps hand in hand with Katie Beck, he sneaks off to the boy's room to receive a quick hand job from Owen, in a wooden stall crowded with graffiti about fags. December passes quickly into Christmas, a holiday his family has ruined either with overenthusiasm or apathy every year

Hugh has been gone. On New Year's Eve, Owen goes over to Danny's, and his mother, working as a waitress for the First Night party downtown, leaves them cream soda and Smartfood for their date with Dick Clark. They drink the soda mixed with vodka Danny acquired earlier in the afternoon, by lifting it from the cardboard box full of bottles next to a woman rearranging her purchases in the hatchback of her Saab. They play the Nintendo Danny's father sent him for Christmas and slurp from spiked soda cans until a half hour before the countdown, when they unplug the game to watch the crowd in Times Square. A reporter with a handheld camera is entering clubs and bars, giving them unsteady glimpses of the parties. In one club scantily dressed people are dancing to Prince's "1999," and a chuckling news commentator remarks that the song will be around every new year until the millennium. Owen makes the calculation in his head. In 1999 he will be twenty-four and Danny will be twenty-six. This sounds depressingly old.

At the countdown to midnight, the boys recite the seconds with exaggerated boredom, growing excited when the bright ball appears to stick for a moment in midair. At zero the television speakers blare with cheers and the atonal bleating of noisemakers. The camera sweeps across the crowd, settling on a spot for an instant before someone comes to their senses and jerks it away. In the pause before the mistake is realized, Owen and Danny have a clear image of two men, heads shaved, rings studding their ears, kissing deeply and with abandon, their lips parting just long enough for a glimpse of the muscular underside of a tongue.

Danny jumps to his feet, spilling the popcorn and his foaming soda can. "I'm gonna puke," he cries, laughing and holding his stomach all the way to the bathroom. Owen can hear him retching in there, spasms interspersed with self-conscious giggles. Though Owen waits for forty minutes, turning off the TV and cleaning the glop of soda-soaked popcorn from the rug, Danny doesn't come out, and finally Owen goes to bed alone, taking his place nearest the wall on Danny's futon. When he closes his eyes, the room whirls, and he wonders if Danny has finally managed to get him drunk.

He wakes to the sound of his own voice begging, calling *stop* over and over again, sweeping his free hand to dislodge the force that pulls at him in the darkness. There is something cold and heavy weighing his other hand to the mattress. His eyelids are gluey and it takes a few tries to pry and keep them open. There is a form crouched over him, perpendicular to his bottom half. Blinking, he makes out the shape of Danny's shoulders, the perfect shiny darkness of the back of his head. It takes Owen, confused by his own shuddering, the wrenching of his whole being toward one point at his center, a few seconds to realize that the soft wet abyss he is plunging into is his best friend's mouth.

"Stop," he says again, but Danny ignores him, moving faster. And then Owen realizes he doesn't want Danny to stop, he wants everything else to stop—the world, his brain—so that the feeling of falling into dangerous ecstasy never ever ends. He clenches his fist around cold hard metal and knows without looking that it is Danny's father's gun.

More than one thing happens that has never happened before. Owen seizes up and bends uncontrollably at his middle, half sitting as the unbearable arc explodes, and just as Danny pulls his mouth away Owen comes, emptying himself with a cry somewhere between relief and horror, the tears in his eyes blurring the figure in the doorway. It is Danny's mother, still in her coat, arms akimbo, lit from behind by the hallway's bare bulb, looking like a jaded, faux-fur winged angel there to tell them about the end of the world.

7. white dress

The first day I go to school after cutting my hair off is a disaster. Even though my mother's hairdresser softened the edges, and I wear a headband to girl it down, I still get stares in class. In the lunchroom, I pass by girls from my grammar school and one of them sings out: "Nice *haircut,*" sending the whole table into hysterics. By the time I leave the lunchroom, I have thought up a bunch of comebacks—nice nose, nice zit, nice excuse for a brain—but I never remember these when I need them. Girls insult me, and I blush and smile pathetically as if apologizing for myself. Long after they've forgotten all about it I'm still fuming, and it's hard to say who I hate more—me or them.

In Geometry, Tracy widens her eyes. "Interesting color choice," she says, as Mr. Herman hands out quiz papers.

"It was an accident," I say. She raises an eyebrow at this. "Did you study?" I whisper. Mr. Herman announces we'll get automatic zeros if we say another word, and Tracy waves me away.

I get a zero anyway. I don't understand any of the four problems, so I flip the quiz over and record the time, minute by minute, until the bell rings and we are set free.

The only person who compliments me is Jonah. In Photography, where I'm printing photos from another roll of Hugh's film. This one was taken at a concert, multiple shots of a band on a small stage, punk kids dancing in a frenzy, dark pockets revealed by the glare of Hugh's flash. A few photos of corners, one guy sitting on a dirty floor with his head in his hands, another homeless man wrapped like a mummy in an alley next to a marquee. Hugh liked to take pictures of sad, solitary people, which I find strange, since he was never one of them.

"Do you have a fake ID?" Jonah says. He startles me, and I drop my tongs and have to dip my fingers in chemicals to retrieve them.

"Just wondering how you got into the Rat," he says, pointing to the photo with the marquee. I vaguely recognize it as a club in Kenmore Square, rotting black clapboard and no windows.

"Are you stalking me?" I say. It's funny how I can always think of rude things to say to Jonah, but he never gets insulted by them.

"Your hair looks nice like that," he says. This is so obviously a lie, I laugh out loud. I'm looking right at him and it's like I can see my laugh sort of bouncing around in his eyes.

He seems very proud of this, even after I go back to scowling.

I get sent to the social worker after failing my geometry test. I've never been here before and the office is really cluttered—scratched-up leather couches, student art and photographs and dreamcatchers tacked up next to posters about drugs and date rape. There are two counselors—one for boys and one for girls. The girl one is a huge middle-aged woman with too much hair and jewelry and hippie clothes. She tells me to call her Patty, then asks if I want to talk about anything. I don't.

"High school can be hard," she says, flipping through a file on her messy desk. "Especially if you're having trouble at home."

"It's not that hard," I say. She must think I'm stupid.

"I didn't mean academically," she says, smiling in an annoying way, like she's so sincere.

"Did your family get any therapy?" she says then. "After losing Hugh?"

"No," I say, kind of mortified at the thought of this—my family stuck in an office like this one, expected to speak to one another. Patty nods like she knows everything.

"Mr. Allen says you're doing well in photography lab," she says. I shrug. "Try putting a little more effort into your other classes, okay? You got all As last year." I shrug again.

"You can come talk any time you feel overwhelmed," she says.

"Did my brother ever come here?" I say.

"A couple of times," she says. She closes the file. I know that tone. She's not going to tell me any more.

For the first two weeks I only go to Cambridge after school. I change quickly at home; transforming into a boy goes faster than trying to make myself look like a girl in the mornings. I find Sebastian in the Pit, often in casual, low-toned conversation with someone, exchanging money and tiny packages in the time it takes to blink. I look for Lionel, who has shown up in more of Hugh's photos, but he never appears while I'm there. His last visits, usually right after I leave or before I arrive, are spoken about like sightings of a rock star.

Sebastian takes me with him into Harvard Yard, where we are buzzed into dorms and climb metal stairways, knock on the doors of students who are never fully dressed. They answer in their underwear or maroon bathrobes, the closet-sized rooms behind them darkened by blankets tacked over the windows. They invite us in, give Sebastian cash, and take whatever interests them from his backpack. Inside it's like a salesman's briefcase, with pills, papers, powders, and leaves, all organized into tiny plastic jewelry bags or rolled into the larger Baggies meant for peanut butter sandwiches. Sometimes the college kid, especially if his friends are around, will invite us to do a line of coke or share the first joint. Sebastian almost always accepts, and after one dorm visit he is so high he has to take a break in the Pit, resting his head in the lap of one of the many girls who fawn over him. I haven't taken anything from Sebastian's backpack, which is pretty ironic. I've never done drugs and I'm practically a drug dealer.

I think about Hugh while we sell drugs. I wonder if this is what Hugh was doing with Lionel. If he smoked from bongs with the ease and confidence of someone not afraid to lose himself. If he was murdered because he was an informant, or owed so much money for drugs he ran away to avoid the mob. If he hadn't disappeared, would he be in one of these dorm rooms, and would he smile when he saw me, or scowl at the intrusion?

When we're not at Harvard, or in the Pit, when Sebastian gets too cold or wet or bored, he takes me to people's houses. In the streets behind Harvard Square, beyond brick sidewalks and ancient trees, are massive houses he strolls in and out of as if they are his own. There is rarely anyone home, but Sebastian always finds a back door open, a window cracked, a key hidden under a moss-covered pot. He punches numbers into alarm pads, resetting them when we leave. After a dozen, I stop asking him if the houses are his. They never are.

We raid refrigerators, linger with magazines in spotless bathrooms, turn stereo knobs up to ten. In family rooms—something I always wanted as a kid, a second living room where you keep the TV—we lounge on sectional couches and play Nintendo or watch *General Hospital* while Sebastian explains the plot lines to me. During *Donohue,* Sebastian usually falls asleep, and I wander around whatever house we're in, looking at their photographs. One child getting older in a straight line up the stairs, or badly focused vacation shots perched on pianos and mantelpieces. Some only have photos of holidays, everyone dressed up and an inch or two taller than the year before, boys and girls in birthday hats blowing out candles on brightly frosted cakes. Some people care about photos, you can tell by the print quality and mounting, and others, with no thought of the future, pierce them with tacks to corkboards in the kitchen. A few houses have no pictures displayed at all, and I have to go looking for them, in shoe boxes on bookshelves, in albums tucked under coffee tables. It's like their memories are something they take out only when they're ready, like they don't want to round a corner and come face-to-face with themselves, ten years younger and clueless. I flip through these albums and watch people change. Children grow bigger, get awkward, settle into their faces. Parents get old, until they barely resemble the way they looked in the washed-out, square photos from twenty years ago. I used to think once you turned eighteen, that's what you would look like for the rest of your life. The truth is, you just keep changing, just when you think you've gotten used to your face. Pictures show you what you've changed into, ruining the image in your head.

In one house we visit a few times, in the photos crowding every available surface in mismatched frames, one girl goes missing. She is there until the age of ten, thin and pale with gaps in her teeth, and then she is gone, and her younger brother and older sister keep growing without her. Christmases and beach houses and school plays continue to be recorded, she is simply not there. I think she died. If she'd disappeared, if they were still waiting for her, unwilling to let time go on until they knew for sure, they would have stopped taking pictures. Like my parents. They always let Hugh be the family photographer, but they never bothered to take on the job after he was gone. The only pictures we have for the last five years are the ones taken in school. The office always sends home samples, even if your parents refuse to order any prints.

I've stolen some of these other families' photos. Badly focused Polaroids half-buried on a bulletin board, doubles from a CVS envelope shoved in a desk drawer. The ones no one will miss. At first I compare them to Hugh's photos, looking for the kids he knew who might have lived here, who would now be in college or working full-time. No one is familiar, but I keep them anyway. I put them in the plastic pages of my binder: a family of four at Disneyland, a velvet-clad toddler screaming on Santa's lap, two children next to a massive sand castle, the older brother with his arm wrapped in mock threat around his sister's delicate neck.

Not all of the houses are empty, sometimes we visit kids my age or a little older who Sebastian knows. They hang out in their basement rec rooms, with wall-to-wall carpet and pool tables, built-in shelves that hold board games and videotapes, stereo systems with speakers the size of small children. These rooms are like playhouses the parents build so their kids will stay home and out of trouble. Instead, this is where they smoke pot, drink gin straight from the bottle, place little tabs of paper printed with moons and stars to dissolve on their tongues. Often parents call on the phone, and the kids have to get themselves up off the couch, putting their hallucinations on hold while they go preheat the oven or take chicken thighs out to defrost.

Though they're obviously rich, these kids all look like Sebastian, holes wearing through the elbows and knees of their clothes, hair unwashed, the soles of their combat boots peeling off their heels. The rich girls in my grammar school all had closets full of clothes, a rainbow of sock colors to match their sweaters. But these kids, mostly boys, wear the same thing day after day, even though they can clearly afford whatever they want. They give their money to Sebastian instead.

One day starts out warm but gets chilly in the afternoon. I have on only a T-shirt and Hugh's leather jacket, and as we're leaving a house at dusk it is starting to snow. Our host goes into the hall closet and takes out two dry-cleaning bags. They are ankle-length men's wool coats with Brooks Brothers labels, one gray, one black.

"Keep them," he says, as we rip through the plastic and remove the paper-lined hangers. "My dad will never notice."

When I start skipping school, it's not to go to Cambridge. In the beginning I miss my classes to hang out in the Quad, just a hallway or a stairwell away from my former life as a high school girl.

It's Sebastian's idea. He's been to my school already, selling joints and acid and Ecstasy. He asks me to meet him there one morning, and after everyone leaves my house, I walk to school as a boy, my spiked hair freezing solid in the wind. In the Quad, Sebastian introduces me to people I have been watching for more than a year. Boys who never glanced in my direction nod respectfully and offer me cigarettes, New School girls who would normally turn up their noses smile and flip their hair. One group of sophomore girls with tight braids sprouting from their half-shaved heads whisper and stare at me and call Sebastian over. When he comes back, he puts a brotherly arm around my shoulders.

"Apparently you're *gorgeous*," he says. I avoid them for the rest of the morning. Later I look at myself in the mirror in the girl's room, which I sneak into when the halls are deserted, to see if they're right. I see only what I've seen my whole life, my face. A face nobody huddled and whispered about when it belonged to a girl.

The Quad's rhythm follows the daily class schedule. In the ten minutes before every hour it is crowded with students passing through on their way to their next class, stopping to suck down a cigarette or two before the bell rings. At the end of these waves comes a tense limbo, when students decide whether to trudge off to class or hang back and miss it altogether. The people with free blocks put pressure on those with classes. Some kids torture themselves out loud. *I haven't been to physics in a week. Do you think he'll give me a do-over, 'cause if I take the test today I'll flunk.* They beg for excuses and their friends dole them out like cigarettes. The more experienced delinquents are nonchalant. Their friends head off to class and they wave at them absentmindedly, as if school is a hobby they've grown bored with. If asked what class they're skipping, half the time they don't even know. Sebastian is an easy convincer. After a visit from him most kids are too stoned and paranoid to make it to History or Oceanography.

For me, that first day is torture. At every bell I picture whatever class I'm supposed to be in, my chair glaringly empty, teachers asking what has happened to me. The urge to run at the sound of the bell is so great, Sebastian has to stop me a few times. At one point I worry out loud about missing my vocab quiz, and he laughs.

"Go if you want," he says, but he knows I can't. Who would I say I was?

As the day goes by, the sun moving across the stones of the Quad, I miss one class after another and nothing happens. No one comes out to look for me. By afternoon I half believe I am no longer expected anywhere. I have stepped outside of it all as cleanly as Sebastian.

Just before the last period, I watch Tracy march through the Quad. I am sitting on a low, wide stone step with three boys, all of whom are playing with fire, setting matches or lighters to the frayed edges of their clothing, pinching out the flames when they approach bare skin. She doesn't even glance at me—I am the sort of boy she naturally avoids—but I know she is walking through the Quad hoping to see me. She would go by the hall otherwise. One of the boys makes a whinnying noise and another snorts in encouragement. She is wearing one of her horse-barn T-shirts. I am glad she doesn't seem to hear them, and that she has no idea who I am when I grin in appreciation of their insult.

I spend the last period wishing I could show up just for Photography. That I had a spare girl outfit in my locker. Or that I could be invisible, that I could move through the darkroom developing Hugh's pictures without anyone asking me who the hell I think I am.

The next roll I develop is of Hugh's Confirmation and my First Communion, which happened on the same day. Hugh is in a suit jacket slightly short in the wrists, I'm in a white eyelet dress with a satin sash, my hair yanked into pearl barrettes. We're posed in front of the church, in our front yard by the lilac tree, with our parents, Owen, our grandparents, and a few of my father's colleagues from BC. Hugh looks happy—that's the day my grandparents gave him the Leica—

and I look furious. While arguing with my mother that morning about wearing the dress, Hugh had passed by the open door of my room and said: "It wouldn't kill you to look like a girl for once." He spent the whole day taking himself too seriously. My grandmother asked if he'd had the calling yet, and he put on a thoughtful expression, and said he wasn't sure. I wanted to tell them all he was full of it, that he had no more plans to be a priest than to be Miss America. But they wouldn't have listened to me.

Later, after the party guests had gone home, and I had changed back into my uniform of worn corduroys and Little League T-shirt, Hugh came by my room. I'd set up a fort with the dining room chairs and king-sized sheets. Inside I had a fan, a bowl of leftover Easter candy, and a pile of Roald Dahl books. Hugh had taught me how to make this fort, but he rarely joined me anymore. That day, he took photos of me eating a Cadbury cream egg and lounging on pillows.

"I'm supposed to be a man now," he said. "According to the church." I looked at him and squinted, trying to see a difference. He seemed to get taller every day, but no older—he was just stretching up. His nose looked a little bigger, maybe. But it wasn't like he had a mustache or anything. I remember wondering if what they meant about becoming a man had something to do with his soul instead.

"Are you one?" I said.

He shrugged. "I feel old," he said. He was thirteen. He would start high school that fall. "But not like a man."

At the time, I nodded, pretending I knew what he meant, though really I had no idea. I was just glad he was in my room.

On the Friday before we're let off for Christmas, with the promise of midterms I am unprepared for looming ahead in January, I'm sitting in an almost abandoned Quad when it starts to snow. Huge quiet flakes that build up fast, layering white on the wrinkled arms of Hugh's jacket. I'm waiting for Sebastian, who has gone off with a New School girl. I assumed it was a drug deal, but they've been gone so long I'm starting to wonder if they're hooking up. This possibility makes me blush harder than is really attractive for a boy. Luckily, the cold is a camouflage. The girl's friend is with me, waiting for them to get back. She has terrible posture; she hunches her shoulders and hides her face in her hair. She keeps glancing up expectantly at me. She's not as pretty as her friend but clearly has an even bigger crush on Sebastian. When he's around she doesn't talk but gazes at him from beneath her hair, eyes wide with the fear of rejection. He hasn't noticed her. It's because I know exactly what she's waiting for that I do what I do next. I huddle with her like we're the only two people in the world, dragging the flint of my lighter back and forth across her denim-covered notebook. I make us each a sparkly cigarette and we smoke them while watching each other, our eyelashes collecting the snow. I am both embarrassed and triumphant at how delighted she seems, at how she starts and giggles at every spark, and how she smiles up at me as if I've given her something worthy of worship. I had no idea how easy it was to impress a girl.

Two days into the Christmas break, a notice comes in the mail, generated automatically by the school's new computer system and accidentally addressed to me. It says that I have seriously exceeded my allowed absences for the semester. I tear it into shreds and burn it in my mother's ashtray, watching my name seize up, then disappear.

8. thermometer

On the first day, Owen fakes a stomachache and his father lets him stay home without interrogation. He is surprised how easy this is; his mother is always suspicious of vague ailments. She would have tested him by offering pancakes, held a hand against his forehead, and waved him off to school. But his mother has already left for the hospital by the time he starts malingering, and his father is so inexperienced he actually asks Owen's opinion on whether or not he should miss school. He brings Owen a bottle of ginger ale and a jelly glass, settles him on the sectional couch with a lap quilt before leaving for the office, promising to call in a couple of hours. After he is gone, Owen grazes in the pantry, eating small portions from various boxes so as not to leave evidence of his appetite. He watches seven straight hours of television—game shows then soap operas then talk shows, getting up only to relieve his bladder of ginger ale. By the time his sister and father come home he feels pasty-mouthed and light-headed, as though he has made himself genuinely sick by pretending to be.

When his mother comes home she visits his bedroom, where he is hiding from the tempting odor of Shake 'n Bake. She brings him chicken soup and saltines, which he eats tentatively, hunched over the faux wood tray on his lap. All he has to do is let his mind focus on what it has been flitting away from—the image of Danny's mother in the doorway—and he begins to gag. Halfway through he rushes to the bathroom and vomits. His mother stays in the bathroom with him, smoothing his hair as he retches and heaves over the brown-streaked bowl. After this is over he develops a genuine wheeze, heavy enough to guarantee him another day at home.

The same performance the next night gets him Wednesday, but Thursday requires new tactics. If he fakes an asthma attack it means the emergency room and his mother staying home to watch him. So when she puts the yellow glass thermometer in his mouth and leaves the room, he folds the silver tip inside the heating pad stashed beneath his covers. The gauge shoots up past 106 and he shakes it down to a respectable 100.2 degrees, high enough to back up his symptoms but not so spiked that he ends up at the doctor. He presses the warm flannel pad against his face for a few seconds when he hears his mother's clogs making their way back down the hall. She frowns in sympathy as she tilts the thermometer in front of her eyes.

"Poor buddy," she says, kissing his searing forehead. "Must be the flu." She brings him more ginger ale, and he lies in bed, ravenous, until they all go to sleep and he can raid the Tupperware containers of leftovers in the fridge.

On Thursday night he throws up a bland rice and butter dinner and displays a 101-degree temperature. His parents conference outside his bedroom door about a visit to the pediatrician. Since his father has an important meeting and his mother two exams, his checkup is postponed. He goes to sleep relieved and looking forward to a symptom-free Saturday. He plans on asking for a grilled cheese and keeping it down. There are moments when the concentration involved in such lying allows him to forget what he is avoiding in the first place. Instead he congratulates himself: he has missed an entire week of school.

Danny's mother didn't say a word. She shut the door, releasing them back into darkness. Owen struggled with his pajama bottoms, wiping away his virgin semen with the flannel. He shoved the gun under his pillow. Danny didn't lie back down but sat on the edge of the futon, head in hands, barely breathing. In five minutes the door opened again, and Mrs. Gray, her coat and skimpy outfit replaced by a limp terry-cloth robe, grabbed Danny by the arm and led him from the room. Owen spent the night alone, his crotch pulled as tight and raw as his lungs.

In the morning, he waited for someone to come and get him. The sun moved across the floor and by the time it hit the futon he could hear the sounds of breakfast from the kitchen. He dressed quickly in yesterday's underwear, jeans, and shirt, ignoring the whole new day folded inside his backpack. He opened Danny's door to the smell of coffee and burnt toast. In the breakfast nook he found Danny hunched over an untouched bowl of Cap'n Crunch, Mrs. Gray with her hair in rollers, smudges of last night's makeup hollowing her eyes. She sprinkled a packet of Sweet'n Low over half a pink grapefruit and didn't look up when she told Owen he wouldn't be allowed in her house again. Owen, who had spent the night imagining the expression on his father's face when he came to pick him up, was confused by this anticlimax and stood there for a minute, the kitchen linoleum sticky under his sneakers.

"Didn't you hear me, you little faggot?" Mrs. Gray spat, looking up. Her eyes were an ugly, red-rimmed blue. "Get the hell out of my house. If I see you here again I'll call the police before I call your parents."

Owen hurried, grabbing his bag and coat and taking the stairs two at a time to the street. It had snowed overnight, camouflaging the dirty plowed piles from the previous storm. In his teary scuffle for his belongings he'd forgotten his hat and mittens, but couldn't go back for them. By the time he walked all the way home, taking the shortcut through the graveyard, his ears had gone from burning red to numb and white at the tips. Confused by Mrs. Gray's last sentence, he expected to find his parents bereft in their own kitchen, phone not replaced on its hook, too ashamed to come pick him up. But when he let himself in with his key, no one was home. Half an hour later, his father returned from his daily run to find Owen taking the first unprompted bath of his life.

On Sunday afternoon he makes himself throw up again, then pretends to fall asleep on the couch. Later, his mother takes his temperature in the living room, which he spikes by holding the tip of the thermometer against a light bulb. It is agreed that Owen's father will take Monday morning off to bring him to the doctor.

The pediatrician's office is across the street from Children's Hospital, and the hallways of the building are narrow and dim and smell of disinfectant and plywood tongue depressors. Owen has to direct his father, who has never been here before, to the third floor and the correct office. Owen plays halfheartedly with the wooden train set he coveted as a small boy while his father reads *The New Yorker* and waits for their name to be called.

In the exam room Dr. Cloherty jokes with Owen's father about being a med student's spouse while Owen strips to his briefs and undershirt. The doctor pops a thermometer in Owen's mouth and Owen presses down hard with his tongue, willing the mercury to rise.

"Normal," the doctor announces, then proceeds to look in Owen's throat, nose, and ears. Mercifully, he seems to decide Owen is too old for the "Let's look for bunny rabbits in there" routine. He feels Owen's neck and announces that his glands are slightly swollen. Owen tries not to smile at this sudden good fortune. His lungs manage a convincing wheeze, but he passes the breath test. He lies down on the paper-lined table and claims sore spots as Dr. Cloherty prods his stomach.

"How's school?" the doctor asks, writing something on his clipboard. Owen shrugs, then speaks up when his father shoots him a don't-be-rude warning.

"It's okay."

"Playing baseball this spring?"

"I guess so," Owen says. He is not very good at baseball but continues to play it mostly because he likes the accessories: the T-shirts, the cleats, the leather mitts, and wooden bats. He looks forward to the team photo and seeing himself crisp and official, like every other boy on the team.

"Using your inhaler a lot?" the doctor asks.

Owen shrugs. "Sometimes," he says. Lately, he has only needed it after a night of smoking with Danny.

"No signs of puberty yet?" Dr. Cloherty says casually, and Owen blushes.

"I dunno," he mumbles.

"You'll know." Dr. Cloherty winks at Owen's father. "Maybe another year for you. I think your brother's voice started to change when he was thirteen." Owen's father looks taken aback, but Owen is impressed at how casually Dr. Cloherty mentions Hugh, as if he is out by the train set, waiting his turn. People rarely mention his brother, and when they do it is usually in a hushed, solemn voice.

"I'm going with your wife's diagnosis of flu," Dr. Cloherty says to Owen's father, indicating that Owen can put his clothes back on. "It's a hanger-on this year. Push the fluids and watch his lungs. Have his teachers send extra work home. That'll cure him fast." Dr. Cloherty winks at Owen and leaves, shaking his father's hand vigorously on his way out.

That night, to his delight, Owen wakes with a genuine fever of 103 degrees and diarrhea that keeps him in the bathroom staring at checkered tiles until four A.M. Real symptoms milked to their limit, a few fake ones, and the PTA's half-Friday buy him his second full week at home.

When his father suggests he call Danny about bringing his homework by, Owen's temperature retreats to normal. On Monday he dresses for school with the care of an invalid, willing down waves of genuine nausea. He walks to school the long way, avoiding his usual shortcuts. Along with the rhythm of his snow boots he chants a hopeful, desperate prayer to Hugh. *Let Danny be gone, Let*

Danny be gone. He doesn't bother to provide an idea of where Danny might be.

The first kids he comes across outside the school are Katie Beck and three of her friends. They giggle and look away and, though this is what they do for ninety-eight percent of their encounters with boys, he is convinced it means something. (Though Danny broke up with Katie more than a month ago, it was said to be "mutual," and his latest girlfriend, Meredith Gulch, still sits with Katie at lunch every day.) When Owen enters his classroom, Mr. Gabriel is standing in his usual place by the door and greets him with a raised eyebrow and a "Welcome back" that sends Owen's heart racing. It never occurred to him that his teacher would suspect. He takes his place at the foursome of desks he shares with two of Katie's friends and Danny, and waits, his face bright red and emanating enough heat to fool even his mother.

Danny enters alone but doesn't glance Owen's way. Instead, he grins at someone across the room and lopes over, sitting down at a block of desks with Brian Dowd and two girls who are known for being obsessed with horses instead of boys. Owen tries not to stare, leans his head down, and glances at the name tag of the desk diagonal to him. Instead of Danny Gray the name on the sticker is Tom Fisher. Just then Tom himself, a tall, bony boy who never stops reading and is generally considered a sissy, sits down and half smiles at Owen. Owen imagines pity in the tilt of his mouth and it is all he can do not to bolt from the room. Only a phone call from Mrs. Gray would have resulted in this change of seating. Mr. Gabriel is notorious for ignoring such requests from students.

Owen operates in a fog until recess, adrenaline and paranoia drowning out the morning's curriculum. On his way to lunch he passes by the nurse's office in the hope of refuge, only to find a note that says the nurse is out sick and all emergencies should be reported to the principal. Suspecting that Dr. Felsenfeld has already had a conversation with Danny's mother, Owen has no choice but to follow the tide of children toward the lunchroom. He has brown-bagged it to avoid walking across the cafeteria with a tray. He sits at a table in the corner near the eighth-graders, whom he knows consider themselves above the gossip of lesser grades. He can't locate Danny but still only manages to worry down one square of his quartered peanut butter sandwich. It is as heavy as an organ in his stomach. Tom Fisher sits down at the far end of his table but doesn't acknowledge him. He props his book so it stands open in front of his tray and reads while he eats. The seats between them are empty.

Owen spends the half hour of recess sitting on a toilet in the boy's room, trying to muffle the explosions of his bowels, reading graffiti about fags, which does nothing to settle his stomach.

He spends the afternoon reviewing a pile of missed work from Mr. Gabriel. He fills out three vocabulary sheets and spends a meditative fifteen minutes copying into his highest-level handwriting book. At a quarter to two, he takes the first deep breath of the day, knowing that it is almost over and that if he hurries out he can avoid confrontation. But Mr. Gabriel keeps him after. He schedules a time for Owen to make up two math quizzes and the history test. He reminds him that the graveyard paper is due next week and asks if he's had a chance to go to the library. By the time Owen is set free, every kid in the school is loitering on the playground, waiting for rides or forming into their groups for the Extended Day program. Owen considers hiding inside until the playground clears, but the teachers haven't left yet, and he doesn't want to be questioned. He pulls his coat on and throws himself to the crowd.

Danny and a group of fifth-grade boys and girls are sitting on the wooden benches by the baseball diamond, cupping cigarettes in their palms in case a teacher looks out the window. From a distance, Owen catches Danny's blank glance, and for the next thirty seconds, as he walks straight toward them—he can't get home without passing that spot—his heart unclenches and he believes it will be all right. Danny, like every other time, will simply pretend that it never happened, or that what happened is unrelated to their daytime roles as regular boys. He will punch Owen's arm, they will spend the afternoon shoplifting, and though they won't be able to face Mrs. Gray, there is still the promise of an unsupervised afternoon at Owen's house. He even feels his penis nudge the fly of his jeans with hope. He is smiling, about to raise his hand in a wave, when Danny leans over to say something to Brian Dowd. Brian laughs, exaggerated and knowing, a noise that turns Owen's spine to ice and makes every other member of the group look up at him. His hope grows cold and foolish, and he speeds toward them, looking down at the faded lines in the cement marking the fifty-yard dash. After he passes them, as he rounds the red-painted START line, he hears exaggerated snickers and catcalls, and one stiff, vicious word from the throat of his best friend.

"FAG."

On Tuesday morning he has a relapse. His mother, though witness to his violent vomiting, stays in the room while taking his temperature, straightening surfaces and collecting his laundry. When it comes out normal she remarks that his stomach must still be sensitive and she'll let him stay home.

"Only today, though," she says. "I'm afraid you're getting too used to the lazy life." She gives him a searching look, but Owen feigns exhaustion and turns his head to the pillow. His mother sighs.

"Your father's at a conference but call the hospital if you need anything, okay?" Owen nods and closes his eyes. He has become so used to faking a weakened, nauseated expression that it is now the natural resting position for his face.

When his mother has been gone long enough, Owen jumps out of bed and gets dressed. He takes twenty dollars in ones from the jar labeled SAVE on his bureau and his father's black peacoat because his own blue ski jacket seems conspicuous. The coat reaches almost to his ankles.

He walks to Coolidge Corner hunched against the frigid wind, waiting for walk signals at corners and bouncing on his toes to keep warm. At the pharmacy he buys two glass thermometers identical to the one in his parents' medicine cabinet and half a dozen Snickers bars to keep in his room for fuel. On his way by a small stationery and arts supply store, he ducks in on a whim. The door jingles, and a man with glasses, a receding hairline, and one earring looks briefly up from his place behind the counter. He seems disappointed to see Owen, as if he were expecting a more interesting customer. Owen slips down the Post-it aisle, out of the clerk's sight.

He calculates what's left in his pocket and picks out all the supplies he can afford. Two extra-long pieces of charcoal, five sheets of rice paper, a black hardbound sketchbook, and drawing pens of different thicknesses, which he tests out on a block of peel-away scrap paper. He brings his purchases up to the narrow counter.

"I thought the fifth grade already did their grave rubbings this year," the clerk says, and Owen looks up, blushing.

"I'm home-schooled," he says quickly. He is immediately worried that he will have to answer questions about this lie. He doesn't know anything about home-schooling, only that in the third grade Jason Bartlett was taken out of his class to be taught at home by his mother, and no one ever saw him again. But the question the clerk asks him next is fairly easy to make up an answer to.

"Don't you get lonely?" he says. He has unrolled the sheets of rubbing paper and is rerolling them all together to slip into a yellow cardboard tube. Owen concentrates on smoothing out his damp dollar bills. He tries to remember what Danny told him about earrings on men. He can't remember if it's the left or the right ear that means you're gay. The clerk has a small silver hoop in his left ear.

"No," Owen says, handing over his money. Though the clerk seems nice enough, Owen is contemptuous of his assumption. As if staying at home could be any lonelier than the fifth grade.

He goes to school only on the days after his parents ask if something is troubling him. Each time is a variation on the same. Danny surrounded by a group of smirking children, looking like a bored prophet, releasing one or two words that cause Owen's anus to clench in fear. One day he is cornered in the boy's room by Brian Dowd and Mark Flint, who take hold of his elbows and slam him back against the tiled wall until his head rings.

"Don't look at me, you faggot," Brian says, and Owen closes his eyes.

"He's thinking about sucking your dick," Mark says, and Brian punches Owen hard in the abdomen. Owen slides to the floor and, before he can stop himself, wheezes out, "Please."

Mark laughs. "He's begging now. Begging for his boyfriend."

Brian kicks Owen hard in the ribs. "Shut the fuck up," he says. "Save your begging. Danny's got something planned."

After this, Owen stays home for another straight week. His parents hang around while taking his temperature, but there is always a moment where a lapse in their attention allows him to replace the thermometer in his mouth with a preheated twin he hides in the elastic waistband of his pajama bottoms. On his next visit, Dr. Cloherty sends him over to Children's Hospital, where they take X-rays of his abdomen and five tubes of bright blood from the vein in the crook of his arm. Though it makes him woozy, Owen forces himself to watch his liquid insides rush to fill each tube, thinking of Anne Rice's vampires and the salty flavor of his best friend's neck.

He is sketching with his new pens, propped on the couch in his pajamas, stopping occasionally to shovel handfuls of popcorn into his mouth or sip ginger ale through a straw. He freezes when he hears the key in the front door, suddenly aware that the whole house smells of popcorn and oil. He barely has time to hide his bowl under the lap quilt when a teenage boy, a sweet-faced punk with spiky black hair, a leather jacket, and complicatedly laced, heavy boots strides into the room. It is only when another, almost identical but taller boy comes in that Owen realizes the first boy is his sister.

"If you tell them I was here I'll show them your thermometer collection," his sister threatens. She gestures for the twin to follow her to her room. They stay there, music thudding under the door, for long enough that Owen begins to blush at the thought of what they might be doing. When they emerge, the reek of marijuana teasing Owen's memory, Lena's friend winks at him on their way out. Only then does Owen realize that he has been holding himself in anticipation, waiting for another glance at these two, so much like the figures he has been drawing with thick black strokes in his sketchbook, tall and dark-haired and magnificent, the mere suggestion of wings folded in promise behind their backs.

9. bicycle

I develop a roll of negatives of someone with spiky black hair, and at first, though I haven't taken any pictures, I think it's Sebastian, or me. Then I realize it's Hugh. There's a girl in the other frames, first with long blond hair, then with hair cropped and dyed to match Hugh's. The haircuts are the same as mine, the smiles are from a different life.

Hugh started high school when I was in the fourth grade. I remember teachers asking about him, like he'd moved to another country. "Tell him to stop by some-time," they'd say. I didn't bother to explain that he had forgotten them. He was a *teenager* now, a word my parents said with mock dread, smiling at his closed door, his loud music, his grumpy morn-ing mood. I wasn't sure what any of this meant. If it was a stage or a permanent transformation. It didn't seem at all funny to me. As far as I could tell, being a teenager meant that he had no interest in any-one from his childhood. Including me.

I couldn't understand why Hugh and his new friends hung out in the park by the grammar school. (Now I know it was because, as ninth-graders, they were still babies at the high school, and they felt older in the park.) On the same benches where I waited my turn at bat in Little League, Hugh and his group of fidgety boys and squeal-ing girls with feathered hair and tight jean skirts spent hours doing absolutely nothing. They didn't play games, or act things out, they just moved around one another in little circles. Hugh, like the other boys, would sit on the bench, lie prone on the bench, roll off, lean against the fence, circle the group, then sit on the bench again. The girls stuck closer together, pulling at their miniskirts, crossing and recrossing their legs.

I was obsessed with the book *Harriet the Spy,* and I crouched in the bushes behind them, recording everything they said in a black composition notebook. I didn't come away with much. Most of their sentences were unfinished; they were always interrupting them-selves. Half of what they said made no sense at all, inside jokes they repeated over and over, until I wondered if even they knew what they meant. They bored me; I gave up on them after two spying ses-sions. The only exciting part was the five minutes where Hugh, who used to refuse phone calls from girls (he made me screen female voices), let a pretty girl with blond bangs frizzled by a curling iron sit on his lap. This seemed to mortify them both. They didn't speak to each other while it was happening, but to their friends on either side, and other than her butt on his thigh, there was no physical contact; Hugh's hands gripped the bench and the girl's were folded in her lap. After five minutes they popped apart without even looking at each other, and were swallowed back into the group. They acted like it had never happened.

For the four long months between Christmas and spring, this girl, Emily Twickler, was Hugh's girlfriend. She called him every night, and Hugh stretched the phone as far as it would go, so that the base was in the middle of the hallway and the white spiral cord was pulled out of shape under the edge of his bedroom door. On the afternoons that my mother was out doing errands with Owen, Hugh and Emily would disappear into his bedroom, shut the door, and play music so loud that I couldn't hear a thing even when I went outside and listened by his window. I didn't understand why my brother wanted to spend so much time with a girl. Emily Twickler wasn't smart, I could tell by the way Hugh dumbed himself down when talking to her. I knew about sex, but couldn't believe it was that great, or that it took up three whole hours behind a closed bedroom door.

It was Emily who dyed my brother's hair, along with her own. They locked themselves in the bathroom one afternoon, where I imagined them taking a bath together in the same tub where I once bathed with Hugh. I had to leave the house and do laps around the block on my bike to calm down. At dinner, my parents joked about Hugh's head, so black it was almost purple, the dye left in so long his scalp was only a few shades lighter than his hair.

"I hope you didn't use the good towels," my mother said, spooning pasta onto Owen's plate. Hugh was preoccupied with himself, running his hands through his hair every few seconds, though it fell immediately back into his eyes. My father announced that he'd once had hair to his shoulders, and Hugh looked unimpressed.

"You look like a bug," Owen said, and this made our mother jump up to get more water from the kitchen.

The thing is, I was the only one who was angry. I was the only one with an urge to punish Hugh, scream and hit and shake him back to himself, because I was already having trouble remembering his real hair, what he looked like and who he was my whole life up until that afternoon.

Since I dyed my hair my parents gang up to talk to me. Probably because I lost it last time, screamed and swore at them, which I'd never done before. They're scared of me now, which is just fine. Once I said that stuff out loud, I wanted to say it over and over again. They're better off ignoring me.

They knock on my door together, standing side by side like police officers there to deliver bad news.

"What," I say, hiding my smoke-filled room by holding the door open just enough to stick out my head.

"Come out and talk to us, please," my father says, pretending to be a normal, reasonable parent. He forgets I know better.

I go only as far as the kitchen table, still within bolting distance of my room.

"We got a progress report from your teacher," my father says. I forgot to check the mail today. I sigh and roll my eyes like I'm bored by this news.

"So?" I say. My mother takes over.

"You're failing Geometry," she says.

"Not really," I say. "I just have to make up a test." They look skeptical.

"Where do you go every afternoon?" my father says.

"To the photo lab," I say.

"With who?" my mother pipes up.

"By myself," I say, slowly, as though they may have trouble understanding me.

"Not with a . . . boyfriend?" my father says. I laugh. I have never had a boyfriend, but I guess my father doesn't know this. Why would he?

"Have you been skipping school?" my mother says.

"Just a couple of classes," I say. "Everybody does it. It's no big deal."

"If I call the school, is that what they'll tell me?" she says. I shrug. I doubt she'll call the school. She's far too busy. Still, my insides clench at the thought of it. I've burned progressively serious notes from the office, including one that requested my parents come in for a conference.

"We want you to start coming home right after school," my father says.

"Am I grounded?"

"Put it that way if you want. We want to know where you are and your brother could use the company."

I can't help it, I let out a snort at that.

"What's that supposed to mean?" my mother says. She looks upset. Her eyes are starting to glaze over in that way they used to before she stopped looking at all of us and focused only on school.

"Nothing," I mutter. They have no idea that Owen is taking them for a ride. He's missed something like three weeks of school already. I hate that they're so gullible, but I'm not going to be the one to say so.

"We want you home every day by two-thirty," my father says.

"What about the drama club?" I say, thinking of something I heard in the Quad. "Play rehearsals are every day."

"Since when are you in the drama club?" my mother says.

"I take the pictures. It's part of my assignment for Photography."

My parents look at each other, deciding whether or not to believe me. I sit still and look bored and innocent. My mother finally shrugs, looking so exhausted I know they're about to give in.

"Fine," my father says. "Come home right after that."

"Sure," I say. "Can I go now?"

"There's one more thing," my father says. He looks to my mother for support, but she's rubbing her eyes, no longer paying attention.

"Yes?"

"We were thinking you might like to talk to someone."

"Like who?"

"A therapist," my father says. He's blushing. My mother snaps back to attention. She fakes a smile, trying to pretend, I guess, that this is a reasonable thing for my father to be suggesting.

"You're joking, right?" I say quietly. My head is pounding.

"No," my father says.

"No way," I say. I don't look at them. If I do I will swear or spit or scream, and I'd rather get every minute I can away from this house even if it means not telling them they're the stupidest parents alive. *Too little, too late,* I almost say.

"Think about it," my mother adds.

I go back to my room and turn my music up loud, drowning out their voices and all the things in my head that I might say if they were the kind of parents you could tell the truth to.

Sometimes I wonder if Hugh figured this out. If they were like this before and I just didn't notice until after he was gone and I grew up.

In the morning I make a point of loading a fresh roll of film into Hugh's camera and strapping it around my shoulders. My father smiles and says good morning when I pass through the kitchen, as though yesterday were some sort of bonding experience. I leave with my hair still wet, just as my father asks Owen how he's feeling. Owen looks genuinely sick at being stuck there. Instead of books I stuff my backpack with a change of clothes, eye liner, and hair gel, and change in the Dunkin' Donuts unisex bathroom. I take the T to Cambridge, hunching down in my seat when we pass the Longwood stop, the one near the hospitals, where men and women in scrubs and white jackets climb on and off the train, plastic IDs clipped to pockets or worn on chains around their necks. Something about their uniforms and badges makes them look like they have a purpose, like they are members of an exclusive world, where everyone speaks the same language. This is why my mother became one of them, I guess. When she has her ID on, even just around the house, she moves faster, like she has somewhere important to go.

It's after noon by the time Sebastian shows up at the Pit, hungover and smelling like he slept in his clothes again. I'm still not sure where he sleeps, though I assume he crashes in the houses of the kids we've met. He seems to know a number of girls who act like they'd love to have him sleep over, but I try not to picture that.

Today he is moody, and I'm a little pissed from waiting so long. He doesn't have any cigarettes and smokes half of mine and makes me buy him a coffee. He asks if I'm coming with him to campus. He's never given me any money for helping him deal, not that I'd take it, but somehow I end up paying for stuff for him half the time. I don't know what he does with all the money people give him. I have a headache from the cold and it's making me testy and this is how we end up in our first fight.

"When are you going to introduce me to Lionel?" I say. I've never even glimpsed Lionel, or the other kids in Hugh's photos who congregate around him. I've pretty much figured out that Lionel supplies what Sebastian sells, but he never talks about him.

"I've introduced you to lots of people," Sebastian says. "What's your hard-on for Lionel?"

I try not to flinch at that expression. Sebastian talks to me sometimes like I'm a guy, even when no one else is around.

"I just want to meet him," I say. "I told you that in the beginning."

"So come out at night. He rarely shows his face in the day anymore."

"I'm grounded at night."

Sebastian looks delighted. "How *sweet*," he says.

"Can't you just bring me to his house?" I say. "We've been to everyone else's."

"Stop nagging," Sebastian says. "You sound like somebody's mother."

After that he wanders away to talk to some of the other kids at Au Bon Pain while I fume over the fact that I have no money left for hot chocolate and seriously consider going home and crawling under the covers and never coming here again.

He comes back in twenty minutes and pretends nothing is wrong. When I tell him I'm going back to Brookline to develop photos, he offers to come with me and I let him, mostly because the thought of not being with him for the rest of the day leaves me anxious, as though I'll miss something I can't afford not to have.

We stop by my house so I can change again. Owen is on the couch eating popcorn and he stares at us with his mouth open, yellow husks in his teeth. I forgot he'd be here and don't like that he's seen me, but he's easy enough to threaten.

"What's wrong with your brother?" Sebastian says, after we've closed ourselves in my room. He's lying on my bed smoking, and I'm half inside my closet, my back turned to him as I pull my arms into my shirt and unwrap the Ace bandage around my chest.

"Nothing," I say. "He's faking to stay home from school."

"Why?" Sebastian says. While tented under my huge shirt, I slip my arms through my bra, noticing how pilly the white cotton is under the arms. I fumble with the back clasp and feel the cool air where my shirt rides up with the movement of my elbows.

"I don't know," I say. I hear the creak of springs as Sebastian gets off the bed, feel goose bumps rise on my back as he approaches. I let go of the bra and try to pull my shirt back down. But his hands are already blocking it.

He reaches up and, very gently, without pulling tight or fumbling, fastens the two metal hooks on my bra. I barely feel his fingers brush against my back. I hope he doesn't mistake my goose bumps for pimples. Then he walks back to my bed, sits down, and lights a joint. I pull my shirt down and add another layer, a gray sweater large enough to fit a whole other me inside it.

By four o'clock it's almost dark out and the Unified Arts Building is deserted. I use Mr. Allen's key to let us in the photo lab. I collect the last photos I printed from the drying rack, while Sebastian opens every cabinet and sniffs hopefully at chemical bottles. He's not putting anything back where he found it and I can't decide what to do about this. I don't want to leave the place a mess and show we were here, but I know what his reaction will be if I suggest he pick up after himself. I end up putting everything away myself while Sebastian locks himself in the negative closet to see how long he can last in the dark.

I show Sebastian the latest photos to see if he recognizes anyone.

He barely looks at them, just keeps shaking his head. Finally he points to a kid holding Lionel in a headlock, a handsome boy with long curly brown hair escaping from his ponytail.

"That's Max," he says. "He's from Cambridge. He still parties with Lionel sometimes. He looks different now, though."

"If I could get out at night, would you take me to one of Lionel's parties?" I say. Sebastian shrugs.

"They're not usually planned," he says. "We'll see." I have an urge to shake him until he promises.

"Wait here," I say. "And stop touching stuff." I close myself in the negative closet to break open two more rolls of finished film I have taken from Hugh's box. It's been two weeks since I showed up for Photography. I need some new pictures. Even if I don't know who they are or what they mean, I can't stand leaving them locked in plastic.

When I'm halfway through the second roll, I hear voices outside the door. Someone is talking to Sebastian. In my hurry to finish I fumble and have to restart the roll. When I open the door, a canister in each hand, I have to blink my eyes to adjust to the fluorescent lights.

"Hi, Lena," a voice says. It's Jonah, standing in a tough-boy pose I've never seen him use, legs apart and arms across his chest. He looks taller because he's standing straight instead of hunching beneath his greasy hair. Sebastian is leaning against the Formica counter, casually rolling a joint. I wonder what they were talking about. They are quiet in that way people get after someone has said something unforgivable.

"What are you doing here?" I say to Jonah, moving over to the sinks to start adding chemicals.

"Looking for you," Jonah says. Sebastian giggles at this, and we both glare at him.

"You've missed a lot of class," Jonah says. "Mr. Allen's pretty pissed." I turn my back to him and start pouring chemicals into the canisters, swishing them in circles.

"I've been sick," I say. Sebastian giggles again. Jonah is blushing fiercely but still standing his ground.

"What's wrong with you?" he says. Sebastian finishes rolling the joint and lights it with his Zippo. He inhales deeply and blows the ash away from the glowing tip, causing black specks to rain to the floor.

"Brain tumor," I say. Sebastian laughs again while inhaling and starts to cough. Jonah glares at him, but his eyes linger for a second on the joint.

"You must have a brain tumor to be hanging out with this loser," he says.

"Now, Jonah," Sebastian says, loping over to him. Jonah stiffens when Sebastian puts a hand on his shoulder. "You used to be more fun than this." He takes a deep hit off the joint and turns it, ember in toward his palm, offering it to Jonah. Jonah frowns and takes a step away. Sebastian, mute from holding the smoke in until his eyes bulge, shrugs at me as if to say he told me so.

Suddenly I'm furious, though it's not really clear who is making me feel this way. I look at Jonah.

"You don't know anything about me," I say to Jonah. There is an uncomfortable pause.

"That's obvious," Jonah says. "See you around."

He leaves us alone. Sebastian finishes the joint with small, sharp sucks of his lips.

"You know him?" I say, when I'm sure Jonah is gone for good. Sebastian shrugs.

"Sure. He used to be a customer. I hear he went nuts, though."

"He tried to kill himself," I say.

"Loser," Sebastian says, shaking his head. This makes me uncomfortable, even though I've thought the same thing myself. I would never say it out loud. I turn away from him.

I stand over the sink with a canister in each hand, turning them upside down and right side up again, making sure that they don't stand still, not even for an instant. Photos can be ruined by the same solution that develops them.

I hang the negatives to dry just before it's time for me to head home. I pull the first roll straight and try to guess at the images by holding them against the light. They are of Christmas, multiple shots of the tree, Owen surrounded by wads of wrapping paper, my parents with bed heads, laughing in their bathrobes. One of me, still in my pajamas, posing on my new red BMX bike. I had asked for the boy's version, with a crossbar. Then more pictures of Emily Twickler, her black hair showing up white, her smile a dark slash across her face. I drop the end, letting the negative spring back into a spiral. I have no desire to see Emily again.

Sebastian has fallen asleep on the couch in Mr. Allen's office. I'm not sure how to wake him, so for a second I just watch him breathing. He doesn't look very peaceful, his forehead screwed up from some dream dilemma. Finally, I lean forward and put a hand on his shoulder, shaking gently. To do this I have to lean pretty close, and our faces are only inches apart when he snaps open his eyes, as if he's only been pretending to sleep all along.

"Hey, handsome," he says. He smells like tobacco and wet leather and someone in desperate need of a change of clothing. I can't remember when this turned into such a good smell.

During April vacation that year, Hugh went away with Emily Twickler's family. It was the longest I had ever been away from him. It rained the whole week, and I spent it sneaking into Hugh's room to read on his bed, which felt oily and smelled of dirty socks. I was avoiding Owen, who wanted to play Candy Land until I was brain-dead.

The first sunny day was Saturday, and I went out with my new BMX bike. I met up with three older boys from the Catholic school who dared me to do stunts with them. I traded bikes with the leader, a boy with a red crewcut, because he accused me of being a snob when I hesitated. After that, it was like being kidnapped. I had to stay with them and they made me do dangerous things on the bike, like dart across the trolley tracks just as the train was picking up speed. They refused to give me my bike back at sundown and told me to meet them in the morning. I went home and hid the Crewcut's bike behind Hugh's ten-speed. I couldn't tell my parents, they wouldn't have understood. They'd be mad I'd given my bike to a strange kid. I waited for Hugh, who was due to be dropped off by Emily's parents in time for dinner.

When he got home he stormed straight to his room, turned his stereo up to full volume, and refused to open his door, even when my parents shouted threats at the peeling panels. Dinner was just the four of us again, one of my parents rising every few minutes to knock on Hugh's door and offer to make a plate for him. After dinner, my mother called Emily's mom and had a quick conversation, then hung up without saying good-bye.

"They broke up," she said to my father. I was beaming from my spying place behind the door. I gave Owen the thumbs-up. He'd missed Hugh, too. Hugh lasted at Candy Land longer than the rest of us.

"I'll try ice cream," my father said. He was let inside Hugh's room with the entire quart of Brigham's, and I got stuck giving Owen a bath. My father came out after Owen was already in bed. He smiled wearily at me and gave my mother the look I knew meant they'd postpone discussion until after my bedtime. Hugh still didn't appear, and I started to worry. If he spent the rest of the weekend in there, I'd never get my bike back.

After I'd lain awake for hours, listening to Owen's slight, wheezy snore, and my parents finally switched off all the lights and went to bed, I snuck down the hall and rapped lightly on my brother's door.

"What?" Hugh called out, somewhere between annoyed and whiny. I opened the door slowly, careful of the squeak that grew higher in pitch the faster I pushed against it.

The room smelled like cigarette smoke and damp spring air. Hugh was on his double bed, still dressed, clean sweat socks looking like bandages around his enormous feet, leaning against the headboard that was painted the same glossy black as his new hair. The Brigham's carton was on the floor, filled to the rim with balled-up tissues. I wondered briefly if he had a cold and then realized, horrified, that he'd been crying. His eyes were puffed up and raw, his voice, when he finally spoke, clogged and halting, as if it might break on the wrong word.

"Leave me alone," he said, not looking up, raising a cigarette he'd been holding out of sight to his lips and inhaling. Though the cigarette, or at least the casual way he smoked it, surprised me, the phrase did not. We had been saying this to each other all our lives. Naturally I ignored it.

"Hugh," I whispered, wanting to tell him every detail of my awful day, to admit how terrified and thrilled I'd been, to tell him I wanted those boys to feel as small and threatened as I had felt on that old rusty bike, performing tricks like a circus monkey. But all I got out was his name.

"I said leave me alone!" he yelled, picking something up off his bed and whipping it at me. I ducked and it hit Hugh's framed chess championship certificate, then clattered to the floor. I looked down, stunned, at the weapon. It was a spoon.

I wanted to laugh at first. A spoon was less serious than some of the things I'd thrown. But Hugh wasn't supposed to be the one with the temper. He had never tried to hurt me before; the closest he'd come were headlocks to hold me still when I was in a rage. Between the black hair, his swollen eyes, and the fury that made him whip utensils at me, I was beginning to wonder what had happened to my real brother. I backed out and closed the door. Once I was gone, I was too embarrassed to go back in.

In the morning I waited as long as I could, lingering over the pancakes my father made to lure Hugh from his room. It got too late, and I left for the park with a heavy, roiling stomach, pumping the Crewcut's pedals with weak knees.

The boys led me to a construction site and dared me to ride on steel girders set across a ditch. I wasn't afraid anymore, so mad at Hugh I didn't care about anything else. I fell, with the bike, down into the ditch and landed on my arm. I felt strange, like I didn't care enough to get up. The boys ran away when they saw I was actually hurt, leaving my bike behind. When I finally got tired of lying there, I got up and pushed it home with my good arm.

My mother took me to the emergency room where I got an X-ray, a cast, a sling, and a Jawa figure from the gift shop. I got a lot of attention at school and at home for my broken bone. I told no one how it had really happened, not even Hugh, who felt guilty for being mean to me and drew on my cast—an entire comic strip of imaginary BMX adventures starring the two of us.

I didn't ride my bike much that summer. I told my parents my arm was bothering me, but really I couldn't stand to look at it, with its bright red crossbar. It just made me too mad.

10. envelope

There are days when his father barely fights him, is too busy to check his temperature, says nothing when Owen stays in his pajamas long after the time he should be dressed and ready. Even his mother sometimes forgets to ask, when she returns home after a thirty-six-hour shift at the hospital, whether or not he made it to school. Owen keeps up appearances just in case, complains of stomach upset and head pain, keeps spiked thermometers ready at all times, either refuses to eat or loudly vomits up his dinner. He waits for a knowing look to pass between them, some evidence that they are on to his charade. But they are rarely in the same room, and when they are they move around each other in a complicated swirl of chores. They unpack groceries, do dishes, fold laundry, and collect new loads for the machine, swerving or bending to give each other room, passing baskets and dishes and wrapped stacks of cold cuts, moving at the last second out of the other's vision, their faces never lingering on the same plane.

After the battery of tests comes back with negative results, Dr. Cloherty decides that Owen has a stubborn, mysterious virus which can only be battled with rest and time. After this announcement, he asks Owen to wait outside while he confers in hushed tones with his father. Owen's father comes out looking sad but preoccupied, and says nothing. Owen is sure he has been revealed, that his father is simply waiting for his mother so they can confront him together, but nothing ever comes of it. Whether they believe him or not, they all seem to have decided to let him stay home.

His parents always call at the same times—his father at eleven after morning meetings, his mother at three when the hospital shifts change—so Owen has a safety zone of four hours. On clear days, he packs up his supplies and walks to the graveyard. The weak winter sun makes his eyes hurt, and he is grateful when clouds move over his work area. He has chosen a group of lichen-spotted stones around his original boy. He rubs his charcoal methodically, pleased by the slow revelation of eye sockets and wings, letters spelling out the names one by one. Gabriel and Sarah Ash. Their children, Gabriel, Michael, Seraphina, and Grace, their ages recorded in years, months, and days, none of whom made it to eighteen. Epitaphs in old-fashioned spelling promise their eternal happiness in heaven. The same skull with feathered wings decorates the top of each headstone except for Grace, who was only two, whose headstone is carved from white granite and is a third the size of the others. A sleeping lamb curls above her name. At home, when his parents and sister are asleep or gone, he tacks the rubbings on the wall next to his bed, in the order they are arranged in the graveyard, shoved edge to edge, the three-letter last name repeated until it looks like a word of instruction. The remains of an entire family.

At the end of January there is a nor'easter. Even though the radio announces that school is canceled, Owen spiked his fever the night before, so sick-day rules apply. The T is still running, and both of his parents go in to work. Lena goes back to bed after hearing the forecast and appears to intend to sleep all day. Owen is trapped inside.

After three bowls of Frosted Flakes (his parents will think it was Lena) and *The Price Is Right,* Owen is bored. He sneaks past Lena's doorway and, hearing no evidence of life, opens the back door and goes down two flights of narrow, curved stairs. The basement is split in two by the cement hallway. On the left is a dank storage space and the dreaded laundry room, on the right his father's office. No one comes down here anymore; his father reads in the living room with news programs droning in the background, his mother studies in her bedroom or at the kitchen table. Junk has started to accumulate in the office entrance, thrown hastily in as though space has run out across the hall: large plastic bins holding their summer clothes, Owen's bike and skateboard, twenty-four packs of toilet tissue and paper towels. When Owen tries the light switch, the ceiling bulb illuminates briefly then extinguishes with a pop. Snow has drifted over the small windows near the ceiling, blocking the daylight.

Owen makes his way across the room, weaving around dark shapes, banging his shin on a low table, reaching for the lamp he knows is on his father's desk. The lamp is bright yellow, with a bendable metal arm and a long fluorescent bulb. When Owen holds the button down, the bulb flickers, hums, and comes to life. His father once let him play with this lamp, which, with its dimming feature, seemed so modern, but now seems old and slow to respond compared to the sleek black model Owen has upstairs. Owen sits back in his father's oak desk chair, surveying the room.

It is so hushed he can hear his own breathing. Dust is everywhere, tickling his throat and eyes and threatening an attack of allergies. A long bulletin board covers one wall, Hugh's Missing posters tacked across it like repetitive, desperate wallpaper. A toll-free number is listed under his photo. At one point there was a hotline, Owen remembers, a room full of volunteers at the local TV station manning the same phones you saw during fund-raising shows. When Owen went there, he was left in the care of a young female caller, who let him drink from her soda, slipped him bull's-eyes, and held his hand so tightly while walking him to the bathroom he cried and demanded she let go. She apologized and gripped him even tighter.

Owen gets up from behind his father's desk and walks over to the wall. Stacked beneath it are the boxes from Copy Cop, and to the right of these, shoved in the corner, a tower of banker's boxes his family uses for storage. Owen opens the first one. More paper, bundles of it wrapped in rubber bands. He removes the top stack. *Every Visible Thing: A History of Angels in Religious Thought,* by Dr. Henry Furey. His father's book. The manuscript is battered at the edges, with red margin notes throughout in his father's miniscule writing. Underneath are notebooks, each one labeled with raised lettering on bright green plastic strips. ANGELS IN JUDAISM, one says. ISLAM, ORTHODOXY, ZOROASTRIANISM, SERAPHIM, ARCHANGELS, MICHAEL AND GABRIEL.

There is a folded poster that Owen opens to reveal a chart of concentric rings, each one labeled, the title at the bottom THE CELESTIAL HIERARCHY. Owen closes the box, sets it aside. Behind the sofa, the arms of which were shredded by a cat Owen can't remember, he finds half a dozen framed prints and a cardboard art tube. He remembers some of the prints that used to hang on the walls, and can re-create their positioning by the picture hangers still in the plaster, and the squares of slightly whiter white that have not yet faded into the surrounding wall. Owen pulls them out, one by one, into the light. In the largest one, an angel with long curly hair stands on top of a writhing serpent, pressing a sword to the serpent's neck. In another, two bright yellow angels climb up a ladder while a bearded man sleeps, smiling, beneath them. The print Owen is looking for is the last in the collection, the size of a notebook, set in a delicate, gold-leaf frame. Owen sits back against the couch with it cradled in his lap. An angel with a grave, manly face, dark curls, and six powerful wings—two wings at his shoulders, two rising like a crown above his head, and two folded like a cloak in front of him, with only his feet peeking out at the bottom. Tucked in the bronze and amber feathers of each wing are dozens of black eyes. They cluster in some spots and are missing in others, like hives. Owen doesn't remember this detail, and wonders if this is the wrong painting. Surely he'd remember a rash of creepy eyes? The label along the mat reads: SERAPH, BYZANTINE MOSAIC, 13TH CENTURY.

Owen leans over the couch again and picks up the artist's tube. Looking for more angels, he is surprised when he pulls out two sheets of rice paper. He unrolls them, revealing the familiar skull and wings on one, and what looks like a weeping willow on the other. His sister's and brother's names and fifth-grade class sections are written along the bottom in charcoal.

Owen rerolls the rubbings, stacks the print, one Copy Cop box, and the tube on top of the banker's box, and hefts the pile with difficulty. He has to stop and rest every few stairs, setting the box above him so it is pressing into his chest. The seraph stares at him. He looks bored and contemptuous, as if his thoughts are far too serious and world-altering to interrupt for the bother of a child. It is the way his father's divinity students once looked at him, mostly the men, when Owen sat coloring in the university office on the rare days his mother and sister were not around to attend to him.

In his room, Owen tacks up the new rubbings next to his own. Lena's gravestone belonged to a girl barely ten. Hugh went the traditional route, choosing an elderly man. He had no reason to dwell upon the death of children.

The crank calls begin on Friday. Lena answers the first one on the extension in her room.

"Owen!" she barks, mouth at the crack in her door. "It's for you!" Owen, stomach already gripped with fear, goes to the kitchen wall phone that hangs beside the corkboard. He lifts the receiver slowly, listening for the click of Lena hanging up before he dares to begin.

"Hello?" he says weakly.

"Suck any dicks today, faggot?" a boy's voice says in high-pitched disguise. Even so, he can tell it's not Danny. He thinks he can hear Danny's laugh leading the chorus in the background. He hangs up quickly, imagining their laughter seeping through his brain and out his other ear, trumpeting through the house.

The phone rings again three minutes later. Lena, clearly fed up, calls his name, and his father looks up from his newspaper and raises his eyebrows. Luckily, his mother, who would ask what was going on, is at the hospital. Owen returns to the kitchen, picks up the receiver, and instinctively closes his eyes.

"Pussy," a voice hisses. "You should get a sex change operation. Then you can be a hooker and get paid for what you do best, which is suck—" Owen hangs up again.

When it rings the third time Lena bellows for him to get it himself, and Owen walks toward the ringing phone as if it is a bomb. He thinks he hears the click of Lena picking up as well, and hangs up the instant the voice starts with the word *faggot*. Owen stands in the kitchen for three more calls, hanging up soon after answering, but still able to distinguish that each call has a different voice. There is a party somewhere, and Owen is the entertainment.

"Owen?" his father says, standing in the kitchen doorway, paper folded in his hand. "Everything all right?"

"It's just Danny," Owen says. "We keep getting disconnected." His father looks skeptical, but nods and wanders away.

The next time it rings, Owen raises his hand, rubbing a few escaped tears on the arm of his pajamas, but before he can get it, a hand reaches over his shoulder and grabs the receiver.

"I've called the cops," Lena barks into the phone, not waiting for them to speak first. "They've traced your number and are driving over to cut your little dicks off."

She hangs up, turns around, and, in a gesture so rare Owen almost starts in response, puts a hand on the crown of his head as she passes by.

"Boys," she says with scorn. She disappears back into her room, slamming the door.

He is having the dreams now, the ones he was warned about by his father and Mr. Gabriel and the sex book, but they are not what he expected. Owen's wet dreams are nightmares. He is usually in a crowd, either in the classroom or on the playground or at a birthday party, when Danny begins to touch him. Because Owen resists, Danny is rough, pushing the gun to his neck, tearing at the zipper of his jeans, forcing him down to the ground. As he works Owen with his hand or, in and out of his mouth, Owen is paralyzed by mortifying pleasure, unable to push him away. At some point he realizes, from the comments and stares of the crowd who stand by and watch, that Danny is invisible. All they can see is Owen writhing, his pants around his ankles, his exposed erection. The boys from school laugh, the girls shriek with disgust. Mr. Gabriel makes notes in his attendance book, Dr. Cloherty on his clipboard. The worst dreams are when his parents are there; his father tries to pick him up and pull his pants back on, confused at the invisible force keeping them down, and his mother pops a thermometer in his mouth. No matter what anyone does, his ascent to climax can't be stopped, and eventually, jerking like a puppet, he explodes and Danny disappears. He wakes still convulsing, the crotch of his pajamas full and warm. He has to change and hide the soiled bottoms in his laundry bin, and washes them himself while his parents are at work.

He takes out *Changing Bodies, Changing Lives* again, hoping to find some comfort or explanation. He reads the section he'd been afraid of: "Exploring Sex with Someone of Your Own Sex (Homosexuality)." It goes on and on about a horizontal line, a spectrum with gay at one end and straight at the other and how most people are somewhere in between. A few stories about boys who fooled around with other boys and grew up normal, and others who did nothing but ended up gay. He finds out what anal sex is. All in all, it is not very helpful or enlightening. It doesn't tell you what to do if your best friend gives you a blow job and the whole school finds out.

———

Owen finds his father's manuscript frustrating and hard to understand. The parts he does understand disturb him. In the introduction his father states clearly, and with such repetition Owen can barely read on, that angels are not human. They are a separate race of beings created by God, spiritual in nature, without bodies or the finite lives of their inferior human friends. Though popular culture holds that people can become angels when they die, there is little of this tradition in most major religions. Dead people can be, and often are, returning ghosts, but they are never angels.

Owen stops after this. He feels as he does when he tries to speak to his father while he is reading or on the phone, and he is waved away with impatience. Rejected, but also righteous in his anger. His father was supposed to be one of the brightest professors at the divinity school; Owen has heard this phrase whispered, emphasis on the past tense, at PTA meetings and family reunions. He was a leading authority on angels. And yet he knew nothing. Even Owen, eleven years old and a mediocre student, knows he is wrong.

He prefers reading his father's notebooks, full of collected facts and illustrations, particularly the ones about modern angel experiences. For years, his father interviewed people and pasted the typewritten transcripts into the pages of the book. Most angels were not seen, only heard as a voice of comfort or warning, or their presence felt in times of great danger. A number of people told of invisible hands lifting them up, moving them just out of reach of a speeding car or collapsing bridge. Sometimes an interview is followed by a skeptical comment in his father's handwriting. "Inconsistent details," or "Seems flaky." Owen flares with anger at these add-ons. The people interviewed all seem very sure, some slightly amused at his father's questions. "What makes you think it was an angel," his father asks over and over. "What else could it have been?" is one woman's reply.

When Owen is supposed to be asleep and his parents are still up roaming the halls and liable to peek in on him, he bides the time by daydreaming about life-threatening situations. An overturned bus teetering above a ravine. An airplane hijacked by terrorists. Alone in a sailboat on a stormy sea. In each fantasy, Hugh arrives at the last moment, unscathed and handsome as a superhero, massive wings aiding the rescue. Sometimes he is invisible and Owen merely feels him, his man-sized hands gripping under his arms and lifting him as easily and familiarly as his parents once did, when he was still young enough to be carried.

Mr. Gabriel rings the doorbell. Owen sees him coming up the porch steps and crawls across the rug to turn the TV volume down. He crouches beneath the front window, trying not to breathe as Mr. Gabriel rings the bell again and then knocks on the glass-paned inner door, calling Owen's name with the same impatience he uses in class. He stands there for a long time while Owen sweats and his legs cramp from squatting, and he starts to get the feeling that Mr. Gabriel can see through the wall. Can see his crumpled, orange-juice-stained pajamas, his greasy, dandruff-flecked hair, even smell that sort of musty, cheesy smell that takes over when he spends too many days inside. He is about to give himself up when Mr. Gabriel shuffles some papers, sighs, and leaves. Owen peeks out at him walking down the front steps and across the street. He looks strange and out of place, not like his teacher at all, in a black wool overcoat and a ridiculous hat with ear flaps.

Owen checks the foyer and finds a thick manila envelope with his name written on it in Mr. Gabriel's neat cursive. Inside are assignments for him to do at home, including a fractions test he has to take under a parent's supervision. There is also his graveyard paper, which his father brought to school for him last week. Owen had not been able to find anything about the Ash family at the library, so he'd created an imaginary life for them, with children who died as often and as easily as hamsters and parents who had no time to grieve, just replaced them with new babies and moved on. Mr. Gabriel has given him an Incomplete.

On his wall, bordering the grave rubbings, Owen hangs a series of drawings he has done in the sketchbook and removed by running a craft razor along the spine. They are reproductions of the seraph mosaic, three pairs of wings fanning out from the center, the feathers varying shades of gray and black, or red and fiery orange, sometimes blue-green like a peacock, as they are described in his father's notebooks. Eyes like clusters of pox run up and down the layers. Instead of drawing a seraph's face, he makes a collage by cutting up the pages in the Copy Cop box. He pastes Hugh's ninth-grade photo, blue sky cut away, at the center point of all the wings, so that the drawings look like a series of otherworldly paper dolls. Hugh doesn't look bored or preoccupied like the seraphim and cherubs, or fierce like his mother, or absent like his father, or bright and feverishly determined like Lena. Hugh is the only member of Owen's family who actually looks at him.

11. igloo

Sebastian talks a lot about sex. Though it makes
me feel kind of sick and trapped, I can't get him to
stop bringing it up. He's kind of obsessed with sex,
in my opinion. And I'm a little curious, underneath
feeling sick to my stomach.

Once, in the Store 24, he asked me to lend him
five dollars, and along with a pack of Marlboros he
bought a small square box of condoms. I was mortified. First of all, the guy behind the counter looked

at me instead of him. Then, when we got outside, Sebastian opened the package right on the street and offered me one. I backed away and shook my head, and a homeless guy laughed at me. Hugh's wrinkled condom package was still hidden in the pocket of my leather jacket. The condoms Sebastian bought were a different brand; one side of the package was clear and you could see the rolled, flesh-colored latex underneath. You might as well have been looking at a penis.

"I don't actually *need* one, remember?" I said. Sometimes, I suspected that Sebastian was beginning to forget that I was a girl.

"I know more girls who carry them than guys," Sebastian said.

"Yeah, well, I'm not one of those girls," I mumbled.

"Are you a virgin?" Sebastian said, smiling as though this had just occurred to him, though he'd asked me before. I'd just avoided answering so far.

"Pretty much," I said. This was an exaggeration. Except for one incident in the eighth grade I choose not to count, I have never even been kissed. Sebastian smiled at me as though he found this information adorable.

"You're not, I guess," I made the mistake of asking. I flinched when he laughed.

"No," he said. "Not since I was twelve."

"You did it when you were *twelve*?" I shrieked. "With who?"

"My brother's girlfriend." Sebastian shrugged, as if this were a traditional family activity. "It was my birthday present."

"That's disgusting," I said before I could stop myself. Sebastian didn't seem offended; he laughed.

"What about all those girls," I said quietly. "The ones you go off with?" Sebastian had a lot of girls who liked him, and he was always finding new ones at my high school or in Harvard Square. He often left me alone for an hour or two while he disappeared with one of them, and returned cheerful and generous with his cigarettes.

"Yeeees?" Sebastian joked.

"Do you have sex with them?"

"Most of them."

"The first time?"

"What did you think we were doing? Playing Monopoly?"

What I imagined was endless kissing. I don't know how to imagine anything else.

"I just thought you were fooling around."

"Like in grammar school?" Sebastian laughed. Then he stopped and squinted at me in a way that made me squirm.

"You're sort of innocent," he said. "It's sweet." I couldn't decide between my two urges. One was to punch him, the other to bury my face in his neck. I did neither, just shrugged and walked toward some people we knew so he'd have to change the subject.

What I don't understand are the girls he does it with. The girls I know, or overhear talking at the high school, are saving sex. Not for marriage, which is considered old-fashioned, but for true love or senior year or at least for the man they think they might marry someday. Sex is something boys want and girls try to put off until the right moment. I thought only sluts actually slept around. I never realized there are so many girls willing to do it, and so casually, as if it were a kiss in a game of spin the bottle instead of the farthest you can go with no coming back. I wonder if they even think of it as far, or if once you do it, it's no longer a big deal. I hope this isn't true. I like the idea of it being important. I would never tell Sebastian this. Clearly, it is exactly this kind of thing that makes me innocent.

One afternoon in the Pit it starts to sleet and everyone disappears. Sebastian brings me to a house we've never been to before, with a red-tiled roof and a tall stone wall enclosing the yard. He punches a code into the back-door alarm pad, letting us into a huge kitchen with a butcher-block island in the middle and copper pots hanging from the ceiling. The refrigerator, the fancy kind with side-by-side doors and ice and water dispensers, has next to no food in it. We find Frosted Mini-Wheats but no milk, so we eat the rectangles straight from the box. Behind the kitchen table is a wooden desk with bills and papers organized into piles by size. A picture of two boys, a blond one about seven, the other a brown-haired toddler, posing on the low branch of a tree, is on the windowsill behind the desk. I figure these kids are grown by now. This house doesn't feel like it has a family living in it.

"C'mon," Sebastian says, and I follow him up narrow back stairs to the second floor. Upstairs there are two long hallways separated by an open, skylighted foyer that looks down over the main staircase, which turns twice and is carpeted with oriental rugs. The doors to all the rooms are closed, but Sebastian walks purposefully to one at the end of the hall and turns the knob. It's a boy's room. I can tell by the cheesy sock smell before I even see the race-car and punk posters. There is an expensive-looking stereo system in a built-in cabinet along one wall, and a television. The green carpet is almost completely hidden by volcanoes of dirty clothes and towels.

Sebastian kicks off his boots, adding a new level to the unbearable stench, and roots around in a bureau for socks. I've never seen him take clothing from people before, but I don't say anything, just find a semiclean spot on the bed and try not to watch him change. He grabs a flannel shirt from the closet, layering two T-shirts, one long-sleeved and one short, underneath it. There is a distinct gray circle where his neck meets his shoulders. He occasionally borrows showers, but I guess it's not his priority today. At first I thought it was gross how he went day after day unwashed and in the same clothes, but now I understand it more. I've stopped showering every day. It's like being a little kid again. There's a smell that develops that's not bad, just strong, and kind of comforting. Because it's your own, I guess.

I look away while Sebastian changes his dirty blue jeans for black Levi's. I didn't mind seeing his ropy shoulders, but the backs of his thighs, with curly brown hair sprouting from potato-white skin, make me feel like I'm hurtling too fast at something I don't want to be anywhere near. While he's buttoning his fly, I hear the sound of a car pulling in, then a door slam.

"Shit," he mumbles, peering between the slats of navy blue blinds.

"What?" I say. I've dreaded this all along, people returning while we are in their house.

"Be cool," Sebastian says. High heels march purposefully up the back stairs and pause by the door to the room. It's as if someone is deciding whether to knock.

"Sebastian," the woman says when she finally pushes open the door. She's dressed in work clothes, a suit jacket and skirt, heavy nylons shimmering at her knees. A gold chain snakes against her protruding collarbone and diamonds sparkle at her ears. The only thing about her that isn't perfect is her hair, which is trying to escape her bun in angry, springy curls.

"Hi, Mom," Sebastian says, ignoring my stare. "We were just leaving."

"I don't think so," his mother says, looking at me with a quick, dismissive flick of her eyes. "We haven't seen you in weeks. Dr. Ackerman says you've missed three appointments. You can't treat this as your home only when it's convenient for you."

"You kicked *me* out, remember?" Sebastian says.

"No one kicked you out, Sebastian. You were given an ultimatum you refused to agree to. You are the only one to blame for where you are."

"That's rich," Sebastian says. His hands are fisted in anger.

"Maybe I should go," I say in the tight silence that follows.

"No," Sebastian says at the same time his mother says: "Please do." I rise from the bed then freeze, not sure which one I should listen to.

"At least wait downstairs." His mother sighs, and I hurry out, relieved at not having abandoned him completely.

I creep down the big staircase without touching the mahogany banister. The house is freezing, the big living and dining rooms drafty and spotless, like no one is ever in them long enough to leave a trace. There are cold, clean fireplaces in every room. On the mantels are pictures of Sebastian—I recognize him now in the eyes and chin—with a little boy's nose and soft, mousy-brown hair in a bowl cut. His older brother poses next to him, smiling knowingly or hamming it up, stealing the camera's attention. In one later photo, his brother is our age, and his hair has been bleached white and spiked with gel, looking like their mother around his forehead. His smirk is aimed at someone off camera, his face turned away from whoever is trying to take his photo.

A man walks into the living room while I am studying this picture. He is sorting through a pile of mail, a briefcase still tucked under one arm. He is not surprised to see me, and doesn't ask what I'm doing there. He just looks, then wanders off to the kitchen. I follow him.

"They're upstairs," I offer, though he hasn't asked. I forget to disguise my voice, but he doesn't seem to find this weird. He nods, but makes no move toward the stairs. Instead he fills a red kettle with water from the tap and puts it on the huge black stove, turning the gas on with a violent pop. With the sounds of argument tumbling down the back stairs, the man makes us tea, adding honey and milk without asking if I want it, placing the fat pottery mug on a coaster on the island and gesturing to an empty stool. He doesn't say anything as I sit down and start to drink it, just flips through the mail, glancing at return addresses but not opening anything. When he gets to *The New Yorker,* he turns the pages and reads the cartoons first, just like my father and Hugh used to. The tea is delicious. I wrap my hands around the mug and let the steam rise up to my face.

After what feels like hours but is probably about twenty minutes, Sebastian comes thundering down the back stairs, a Carhartt sweatshirt added to his layers of leather and wool coats. I step away from my stool, not wanting him to see how I've been sucked in by the enemy. And that all it took was tea.

"Hi, *Dad,*" Sebastian says, in an exaggerated imitation of a cheery young boy. Sebastian's father says nothing, doesn't look up, just continues to page through the magazine, no longer pausing to read the captions. Sebastian might as well be invisible. Which is weird, since I was sure his dad was waiting, with the tea and the mail, desperate for a glimpse of him. Sebastian's mother stands behind him, red-faced, as though she's trying to think of one last thing she can say that will change everything. But Sebastian is looking at me now.

"Let's go," he says, and we leave the way we came in. As I turn to close the glass door behind us, both of his parents are looking, and it's up to me to give a small, weary smile, as if I'm apologizing for a lifetime of disappointing them.

Outside I have to jog to catch up to Sebastian's angry stride. Things are quiet for a while, until Sebastian finally senses that he's not the only one fuming.

"What's *your* problem?" he barks. I take a breath, trying to steady my real voice.

"Why didn't you tell me Lionel was your brother?"

He was in the family pictures. The same blond spiky hair and mischievous grin as in Hugh's photos. I'd always assumed Sebastian's brother was off at college like everyone else's. He'd only mentioned him that once. I never suspected he was the drug dealer I am sure knows something about the night Hugh disappeared.

Sebastian ignores me for the rest of our trudge through dirty snow to Harvard Square. Back in the Pit, he turns his charm on full blast, flirting with every girl there. I'm left sitting in a corner, my killer looks ignored. When Sebastian disappears with a tiny punk girl, without a word to me about when he'll be back, I decide to leave. My father is probably home by now, and the drama club excuse is running thin. But I can't make myself go. Even when it starts hailing I sit huddled in the T station stairs, waiting for Sebastian to come back. He is my only friend, he knows the only person left who might remember something different about my brother. He comes back after seven, with a Tootsie Pop to offer in apology.

"I'm just moody. I hate running into the 'rents," he says.

"Why won't your father talk to you?" I say. I've been thinking about his parents a lot, the way his mother looked sad but acted angry and his father looked as if he had no choice but to be so mean.

"He's given up on me. Wish my mother would, too. She's a child psychologist. It would look really bad if she fucked up both her kids."

"Do your parents talk to Lionel?" I ask.

"No," Sebastian says. "They don't even say his name. They say: 'Do you want to end up like your brother?' Like he's dead or something."

I'm quiet after this. No one has ever said this in my house, though they think it, I'm sure, all the time.

"Can you get out tomorrow night?" Sebastian says.

"Yes," I say. I know how to sneak out. I've just been waiting for the invitation to do it.

"I'll meet you here and bring you to Lionel's party," Sebastian says. He lights his Zippo and extinguishes it again, repeating the movements on the thigh of his jeans.

"Thank you," I say. He shrugs and avoids my eyes. I can't stop thinking about his parents in that big, beautiful house. How they let them go, both of their children, one after the other out the door, just like that.

All I've been developing lately are pictures of Emily Twickler. There are endless rolls of them, all basically the same. During his freshman and sophomore years, Hugh and Emily broke up and got back together eight times. Every breakup was like the end of the world, with the phone ringing in the middle of the night and Hugh mopey and bleary-eyed, chain-smoking and refusing food. Their reunions were quieter; sometimes Emily would show up at our house like nothing was wrong when we thought they weren't speaking. My parents had fake, worried smiles around her, and they stopped taking Hugh's side, because he always held it against them when she returned.

Hugh's schoolwork suffered for the first time in his life. When a report came from the school that he had too many unexcused absences, my parents confronted him. I listened from the hallway.

"Where were you on the days you missed school?"

"Emily needed me. Some things are more important than school."

"Nothing's more important than school," my parents said in unison.

"Spare me the 'first in your families to go to college' speech," Hugh said. "Everybody cuts sometimes. Don't worry about it."

"Your chemistry teacher says you're failing."

"I just have some homework to make up."

"This relationship with Emily is starting to worry us."

"What's that supposed to mean?"

"She's not a stable girl."

"Fuck you. You know nothing about her. Or me."

I had never heard my brother swear at our parents before. Everyone was silent for a minute, not sure what this meant. My father wouldn't even say *God* or *Jesus Christ,* but instead said *Jiminy Crickets,* which never failed to make us laugh.

My parents reminded Hugh that Emily had broken his heart half a dozen times. That she had cheated on him with other boys and then told him about it just to make him mad. That she called screaming in the middle of the night. That she might be involved with drugs and had been hospitalized for depression. I was impressed by this list. Emily was a lot more interesting than I'd thought. Hugh just got angrier the longer they went on. He repeated over and over that they didn't understand. Not Emily, or him, or anything about real life.

"If you try to break us up," Hugh said, "you'll regret it. I'll make sure of that."

"Who *are* you?" my mother asked, but Hugh refused to answer that. Like he didn't even know himself.

All of this ended when Emily was sent away. Her parents sent her to a boarding school for delinquents in western Mass when she failed out of Brookline High and was caught doing drugs. At first, Hugh claimed they kidnapped her to keep them apart. (Emily's parents were as tired of Hugh as mine were of Emily. They had telephone conferences together, all trying to decide what to do with their love-blind teenagers.) She was taken away one night with no warning, and they wouldn't tell Hugh where she was. He found out the name of the school from her younger sister, but when he called there, a week before Christmas, he was transferred and cut off so many times it was almost an hour before someone leveled with him. Emily was not allowed to receive phone calls.

"Is she in a school or a prison?" Hugh yelled before slamming the phone down. He barked at his parents' attempts to comfort him and locked himself in his room for days. He came out for half an hour on Christmas morning, only after Owen made a special request. He went back to bed while our mother was still stuffing wrapping paper into a garbage bag.

Hugh asked my father to drive him to see Emily and screamed and threatened to run away when he was told no. Then Emily sent him a letter. It was eight pages long. She told him she thought their relationship was unhealthy and asked Hugh not to contact her anymore. She mentioned a new boyfriend and a writing class and seeing inside herself. The letter, on peach-colored stationery, was dotted with perfectly formed tear splashes and tiny sketches of her pouting face. I read it when Hugh, who carried it around for days, accidentally left it by the sink in the bathroom.

Hugh stayed in his room for the rest of Christmas break, but the morning school started again he was up early, his backpack and camera on his shoulder, ready to face the world. He didn't mention Emily again, and the rest of us, relieved, didn't bring her up. One morning after he left I overheard my parents whispering.

"Maybe now we'll get our son back," my mother said.

And my father said, "I hope so."

On the night of the party I get ready in my room, avoiding the bathroom, which is sandwiched between my parents' and Owen's doors. All I have for a mirror is the little beauty station my grandmother gave me for Christmas in the seventh grade, a plug-in three-way mirror framed in light bulbs that can be switched to mimic different situations: daytime, nighttime, or fluorescent. I've never liked the way the mirrors reflect on one another, showing my profile. The first time I saw it, it made me feel lonely, because I didn't look anything like I pictured myself. Tonight I have a cluster of pimples on my chin that I wish I could put tinted Clearasil on, but boys don't wear it.

My mother is on call tonight and my father can sleep through our fire alarm, so I'm not too worried, but I sneak through the kitchen in my socks and put my boots on in the back stairwell. I can see my breath in the moonlight shining through the window at the bottom of the stairs. I tie triple knots in my boots. The house doesn't protest as I leave it, just vanishes behind me like it's seen this a million times before.

Sebastian is waiting for me in Harvard Square, which is much more awake than Brookline. He tells me his brother is house-sitting for a Harvard professor spending a semester in England. Normally, Lionel lives in an apartment in Somerville. We trudge away from the sounds of buskers and into suburban streets.

In all the movies I've seen about teenage parties, there are hundreds of kids crammed like sardines, kegs on lawns, noise pollution, and permanent damage done to the house. Lionel's party is nothing like this. The only difference from other houses on the street is that more lights are on, including the one on the back deck. Here there are four guys sitting around a wicker table, the sun umbrella still open and slick with ice. They are passing a bong around and, though they nod at Sebastian, they are all in various stages of holding or expelling breath, so no one says anything. Sebastian opens a sliding glass door that leads into a kitchen. This looks more like I'd imagined; it's trashed. The counters are a mess, piled with bottles, dishes, and takeout containers of food that were clearly opened days ago. Every utensil in the house looks like it's been used and left to gather mold. There is another group around the kitchen table playing cards. At a sign from one of them, they all hold a card to their foreheads, facing out. The one girl in the group is giggling so hard the boys are annoyed and clearly want her to shut up. But her giggling also wobbles her chubby breasts, so the boys sneak peeks in between rolling their eyes. There is a couple by the refrigerator, the girl sitting on the counter, the boy standing in between her long legs. He is telling some story and every few words she leans in and interrupts him with a kiss. I wonder what that feels like, permission to kiss someone whenever you want. Instead of waiting for something that never comes.

The girl looks up and squeals with delight. "Sebastian!" She waves, leaning so far off the counter the boy has to hold tight to keep her from falling off. He doesn't look pleased.

"You guys seen my brother?" Sebastian says.

"I think he's upstairs," the girl says, smiling and leaning back in a sexy pose. She bangs the back of her head on the cabinet behind her, and the guy with her laughs and squeezes her thigh.

"Shut up," I hear her say, then the sound of smothered mouths as we move to the next room. Every room has between five and ten kids in it, some stoned, their legs draped across furniture, others bouncing on the balls of their feet, waiting for something to happen. In one room there's a pool table, and there's a game of tackle football going on in the snow in the backyard. In the hallway, two boys are playing hockey with intense concentration, not holding back shots even when people walk through. Someone hands us plastic cups of yellow beer from a keg. I take a sip without thinking and spit it back into the cup. I hate the taste of beer.

Sebastian shakes his head and takes my cup away, abandoning it in the soil of a ficus plant.

"Why is it all high school kids?" I say. It's louder near the back of the house, a stereo blaring Pink Floyd's "The Wall" while a group of small-pupiled kids sitting on the floor sing along and point out details of the blue-flowered wallpaper to one another. "I thought your brother was twenty-one." Sebastian shrugs.

"He never grew up," he says. "He hates the Harvard kids he deals to. And most of his friends from high school are gone now."

Sebastian asks a few more people where Lionel is, and is told that he's off in a bedroom with a girl.

"Might as well have fun while we wait," Sebastian says. He hands a few tabs of what I know is Ecstasy to a group that comes asking, and downs one himself with what's left of his beer.

"I know what you need," he says, grabbing my hand and leading me back to the kitchen. On one counter is a cutting board strewn with triangles of lime and lemon. He cuts the puckered edges from two slices of lime, pours two shot glasses full of brown liquid from a squat, thick glass bottle, and tells me to give him my hand. He licks the spot on my hand between my thumb and first finger. His tongue is slightly rough and my palm immediately starts to sweat. I try to pull my hand away, but he holds tight, raining salt from a plastic picnic shaker onto the damp spot. He repeats this on his own hand. He hands me a wedge of lime and the overflowing shot glass.

"What is this?" I say.

"Like so," he says, grinning. He licks the salt, downs the shot, then shoves the lime in and sucks, screwing his face up. He waits for me.

I barely taste the alcohol, just feel it burn my throat and warm my stomach. Suddenly, I feel great, more alert than I have in months. I lick the remaining salt from my lips and smile at Sebastian.

"I think she likes it," Sebastian says. I do my own salt this time, and we swallow two more shots. He stops me from pouring a fourth.

"Tequila's a great high, but it's the worst sick," he says. "Take it easy."

At first I think the shots haven't affected me, but when we leave the kitchen I know I'm drunk. It's not the kind of drunk I've been before, which made me feel alone and foolish and even less like everyone else. This drunk is magic. It's making everyone smile at me, making me not wish I was somewhere else, but perfectly happy to be right here, right now. I'm not even anxious about Lionel anymore.

Sebastian starts flirting with two girls from Arlington and calls me over. He lights a joint and passes it around. I take it without thinking. I know as I inhale that I have some big reason for boycotting it so far, but I can't really remember it. My conviction to remain drug-free seems childish and very far away. The pot sears my lungs as if I'm inhaling the ember as well as the smoke. I hold it in and pass it along. When the joint comes to me again I take an even deeper hit. One of the girls, the one wearing a red plaid miniskirt with combat boots, settles herself into my lap. It doesn't occur to me to argue. I don't even know what we're saying, just that I'm laughing like we're the funniest people in the world. The sharp happiness of the tequila has turned into a hazy film between me and everything potentially serious. I feel like I'd be calm in the face of a nuclear war. Like I know better than anyone that none of it matters. I wonder if Sebastian feels like this all of the time.

The girls take our hands and lead us upstairs, and Sebastian shushes me when I try to confess. We end up in a kid's room, a blond bunk bed broken into two singles across the room from each other, one with an *Empire Strikes Back* comforter, the other with scenes from *E.T.* The girls leave for a minute, escaping into an adjoining bathroom that barely muffles their excited voices. I pull Sebastian over to the window. I'm feeling suddenly sober, and sick.

"This isn't funny," I say. "Tell them I'm a girl and let's get out of here."

"Relax." Sebastian laughs. His pupils are the size of pinpricks. "Think of it as educational."

"What am I supposed to do?" I hiss. The toilet flushes once, then again.

"Whatever you'd want done to you," Sebastian whispers. As he says this he puts two fingers just at the edge of my army fatigues, lifting my shirt an inch and grazing the bare skin of my stomach. It's like being punched. I can't speak or move, and when the girls come tumbling back into the room, I let one of them take my hand and lead me to the *E.T.* bed, while the other pulls Sebastian away. I don't have to make the first move, since she kisses me pretty fast. For the first few minutes I keep my eyes open, watching across the room, as Sebastian holds himself above his girl with his arms taut, and how this makes her squirm and pull on his hip bones to get him closer. Then my girl asks why I have my eyes open. So I close them and imitate what I've just seen, hovering and kissing her into the mattress until I hear a little gasp in her throat, holding myself away until my arms are shaking and she pulls me down and our identical hips press together in a way that promises to never be enough. At some point the ringing in my head focuses to a single realization: I could make this girl crazy. Just like Sebastian does, with a mouth that smiles while holding back a kiss. The thing is, I'm not sure I want to.

She passes out before I have to do much. I fall asleep for a couple of hours, then get up to use the bathroom. I walk in on someone, a guy standing and peeing into the bowl in the darkness.

"Hey," he says sleepily, nodding in my direction. I try not to look as he shakes himself dry. He turns to wash his hands in the sink. The moonlight reflecting in the mirror from the window illuminates spiked blond hair and a gaunt face barely recognizable as the one that once smirked for my brother.

"All yours," Lionel mumbles and leaves by the other door, the one that leads to the hallway, scratching one white buttock as he goes.

I sit on the toilet until I can see details of the bathroom—a sea horse shower curtain stained by mildew, the sink top cluttered with razor blades, prescription bottles, and a curling iron—and I know dawn isn't far off. I go back into the bedroom. Sebastian's backpack is propped against the wall. I take two joints, sliding them into the empty space in my cigarette pack. I leave Sebastian sleeping with a girl he doesn't know, go home, and sneak in the back door. I smoke a whole joint alone in my room, looking at photos of when I was still a little girl and Hugh was the delinquent teenager.

One of the last rolls Hugh took was of me and Owen when we had the chicken pox. Owen is usually the one who gets the sickest, but that time I had it worse, with sores in my throat that kept me from eating anything but soup and ice cream. After ten days, my pox transformed into greasy, dark red scabs that I peeled away whole from my skin, leaving craters my mother warned would be with me for life. So I limited myself to picking at the ones on my scalp, where my mother wouldn't see the damage, which was less satisfying, because I couldn't see it, either.

I fell into a routine of sleeping late and napping in front of daytime television, which meant I was often up in the middle of the night scrounging for snacks. This was how I caught Hugh, his combat boots and a heavy wool overcoat making him look like a storybook giant. He had his hand on the back doorknob when I came into the kitchen, wearing a pair of Spider-Man pajamas that used to be his. It was after midnight.

"Shit," Hugh said, when I asked where he was going. He sat down with me at the kitchen table, talking in the secret-pal whisper I had been missing. He had been using it only on Emily and his friends. I knew he was trying to keep me from telling, but I liked the attention, so I let him go on for a while, growing warm and drowsy inside the magic winter light of our kitchen. Outside the window snow was falling quietly, the kind of snow that promised to go on for hours.

"I'm just meeting the guys," Hugh said. "We're going to see this band. I'll be back before Mom and Dad get up."

I wondered what sort of band played in the middle of the night, but thought he would laugh at me if I asked. Maybe it happened all the time and I was too young and naïve to know about it.

"You'll get caught and they'll ground you," I said.

"They'd never ground me," Hugh said. "Anyway, I won't get caught unless you tell on me."

"Can I come?" I said, suddenly excited. I'd been in the house for two weeks, and the idea of roaming the white streets of our neighborhood, the reflection of snow lighting the sky, Hugh beside me while the rest of the world was asleep, suddenly seemed like the best idea in the world.

"Not this time," Hugh said. I scowled at him.

"Tell you what," he said. "If tomorrow's a snow day, I'll build a fort with you."

Until he was twelve, Hugh built elaborate forts in the snow in our backyard, with tunnels leading to different rooms, shelves carved into the walls for treasure. He let me help with the digging and gave me my own royal igloo. I had been begging him to do it again for three winters; every time I tried it by myself the walls collapsed on me.

"Promise."

"I promise. Just don't tell."

"Deal," I said. Hugh smiled like the old days, when we were a team. He had the chicken pox before I was born and still had an oblong white crater above his eyebrow that winked when he smiled.

"Go back to bed before they wake up and catch us both," he said. He loped toward the back door. I waited, then as he closed the door I thought of something. I ran over and turned the knob.

"Hugh!" I called down in a loud whisper.

"What?" he said, annoyed. The stairwell was dark, and I could barely see the shadow of his spiky black hair against the lighter wall.

"Don't get in any black vans," I said. A rumor was going around my school that a black van with tinted windows was cruising Brookline neighborhoods, picking up children stupid enough to give directions to strangers. It was said to be driven by a clown, who kidnapped kids, molested and killed them, and buried them in the outer suburbs.

"I'll see what I can do," Hugh said.

"I'm not kidding. You'll never come back." I knew he was barely listening. I used to think Hugh took me more seriously. But lately, especially when I was annoyed at Owen, I wondered if Hugh had been pretending. If I was an irritating little sister he had placated all along.

"All right, fine. Go to bed now, Lee," he said.

And then he was gone, giving me a glimpse of the sparkling white world before he closed the door. The stairwell filled with a cold, biting swirl of air. I shivered and thought—what if I never see him again? But it was the anxious, melodramatic kind of thing I thought too much when I was ten, and my parents and teachers were always telling me to stop. So I did.

When the police asked me if I knew anything about Hugh's disappearance, almost twenty-four hours later, I had already denied it so many times to my parents that to change to the truth seemed more dangerous than sticking to my story. I wanted to be on his side. By the time it was obvious, even to me, that something had gone very wrong, after there were Missing posters lining the walk to school, and the kids who usually teased me pretended instead that I was their friend, after my mother fell to pieces and my father turned his whole life over to the search, I couldn't bring myself to admit the truth. That I was the one who had let him go.

12. toothbrush

Owen stops going to the graveyard in February.
He is out of rice paper and can't bring himself to
return to the art supply store. Coolidge Corner
seems a world away to him now, and the thought
of weaving in and out of mothers with carriages
and men on their lunch hour makes him paranoid.
It is only a matter of time before he bumps into
someone he knows.

 He has gotten to the point where he'd rather

not leave the house at all. If his father orders a pizza, usually on the nights his mother is on call, he brings Owen along to run in and pay. The pizza place is the one that the fifth-graders sometimes hang out at after school, and though by nighttime it is mostly families and older teenagers, just walking across the linoleum and stating the name Furey to the man behind the high counter causes odd physical reactions Owen can't explain. His throat closes up, leaving barely enough room for his saliva, so he has to swallow repeatedly to keep himself from drooling. He needs to shade his eyes from the fluorescent lighting, as harsh as a lamp switched on in the middle of the night. People's faces are ugly and disturbing; he has trouble looking them in the eye. He focuses instead on some faulty detail—the razor burn on the pizza guy's neck, the ripe pimple on the nostril of the boy who rings him up. By the time he returns to his father double-parked outside, the pizza box seeming as large and unwieldy as a wooden door, he is gasping with fear. This makes no sense to him, feeling terror over nothing. At first he thinks it is some sort of precognition, that he is sensing the danger that Hugh will ultimately save him from. But nothing happens. It seems all it takes are strangers' faces, bright lights, and the air outside his house to liquefy his bowels and leave him weak, shaking, and reluctant to venture out from the safety of his bathroom. Now, just the mention of school is enough to squeeze his lungs and drain the color from his face, so that one close look at him and his parents abandon the suggestion.

Mr. Gabriel doesn't come back to Owen's house. Instead, he recruits Tom Fisher to bring Owen his homework. Tom comes by on Monday afternoons to drop off assignment sheets and collect Owen's work from the preceding week. Tom seems even more awkward than Owen remembers, he won't meet Owen's eyes, is careful not to brush against any part of him while folders exchange hands. The packets come with instructive, impersonal notes from Mr. Gabriel. Occasionally Tom must give him verbal instructions as well and he does this in a monotone, looking somewhere above Owen's right shoulder, as if he is practicing an oral report. He has a prominent Adam's apple, like a Super Ball bouncing in his neck. His fingers are long and tapered and starkly pale. He has been teased for having girly hands, but to Owen they look otherworldly. He tries to memorize them for sketching later, but never gets them right. Tom's eyes behind clear plastic-framed glasses are blue on sunny days and green when it's cloudy.

On a rare day off, his mother is home when Tom rings the bell. To Owen's horror, she invites him in, offers chocolate milk, asks him where he is from (Atlanta), and what his hobbies are (he's in the school musical), all of which he answers with polite, unenthusiastic sentences. When her beeper goes off, she uses the living room phone to call the hospital, leaving Owen and Tom alone in the kitchen with a plate of cookies. She spent the morning making them as a treat, but got caught up studying while they were in the oven and burned the bottoms. Owen picks at his, crumbling the cakey bits and eating only the chocolate chips. Tom has put the napkin Owen's mother offered in his lap and uses it to wipe prissily at his lips. *Like a fag,* Owen imagines Danny saying.

"I have to go," Tom says, after he has dutifully polished off two cookies.

"I'm not *contagious,*" Owen mutters. He winds his ankles around the chair legs, as if expecting to be knocked off.

"I didn't say you were," Tom says, looking at him for once.

"What is everyone else saying?" Owen asks, before he can look away. "At school. About why I'm not there."

Tom shrugs, taking a sip of chocolate milk. Owen's mother has given them swirly straws, as if they are in the first grade. Owen waits while the plastic tubing clouds with brown milk, then empties in reverse circles when Tom releases his lips.

"Some people think you're dying," Tom says. "Of AIDS. Like Ryan White. And that they won't let you come to school."

"You're kidding," Owen says, almost smiling. He had begun to think everyone knew he was lying, twenty-four hours a day, with every exaggerated swallow and hand to his abdomen, so this rumor of terminal illness is almost a relief. For about ten seconds. Until he remembers what people get AIDS from.

"What do you think?" Owen says.

Tom shrugs. "I don't really care," he says coldly.

Owen blushes. He remembers now, as if Tom had inserted it behind his eyes, a moment last September, Danny hissing *He sucks cock!* when Tom passed by them in the lunchroom. Owen had laughed out loud. He had done it automatically, without much thought to who Tom was. It doesn't seem that the boy he laughed at and this boy are the same at all, and he wants to explain this to Tom—that he hadn't meant it, he didn't know him, it could have been anyone, the giggle was merely to impress Danny.

But there is no reason for Tom to believe him.

For the first time that Owen can remember, except for Thanksgiving and Christmas, which include other people so they don't count, his family sits down for dinner together. It is his mother's idea, and she insists they all participate. Owen clears the dining room table of months' worth of newspapers and utility bills, setting four places with the plates they call the wedding china. The outer edges are rimmed with gold leaf that he remembers trying to scrape off and taste when he was little. The silverware in the velvet-lined box is crusted with green, so his mother tells him to use the stainless from the kitchen. Lena is given the job of chopping vegetables, which she does so slowly and inadequately she is dismissed with exasperation. Owen's father stands in the narrow kitchen galley, reading *Time* magazine and handing his wife utensils and spices as she asks for them.

When dinner is ready, they sit in cross formation at the table, their parents at the head and foot, red candles left over from Christmas sputtering in the middle. Owen has been told to change out of his pajamas for the occasion. Lena's hair is freshly washed and lies flat against her scalp without its normal glopping of gel. The heavy black eyeliner she usually wears has been washed off, making her look younger, vulnerable, as if she has just woken up from a night's sleep. The whites of her eyes are bright, flawless, and bleached by Visine.

Dinner is roast beef baked with crispy potatoes and onions. Owen's father carves while his mother doles out peas and salad. She is exuberant, talkative, seeming either not to notice or choosing to ignore the lethargic responses of the rest of them.

"I met my first AIDS case this week," she says. "A twenty-year-old boy. He's in isolation, no one can go in without gowns and mask and gloves, including visitors. Not that he has many. Lena," she says, distracted. "Is that all you're eating?"

Lena's plate is mostly white space, dotted with a few peas and potatoes, roast beef rejected altogether. She seems fascinated by the process of moving her food around with her fork. She graces her mother with a blank smile.

"I'm saving room for dessert," she says dreamily. Owen wonders if his parents are really this blind or just pretending to be. Can't they see that she's stoned?

"It's sad, really," his mother goes on. "No one visits him. I stopped by and talked to him this afternoon, just because he seemed so lonely. It's such a shame, the stigma that's developed around this disease. Even some of the doctors seem less than compassionate. The men, naturally. I don't even know if he's gay."

"Is he going to die?" Owen says. He speaks because it looks like no one else is going to. Lena is totally out of it, watching the reflection of the candle flame in her knife, and his father is eating with concentration. No one else is listening.

"I think so, sweetie," his mother says. She's looking at his father. She knows he's not listening, and she's getting angry.

"Will he go to heaven?" Owen adds, trying to get her to look at him instead.

"Of course he will." His mother blinks and turns to him.

This is when his father lets out a sound, somewhere between an angry huff and a guffaw.

"Nice of you to join us," his mother says. "Just in time to insert your expertise."

"Is that what they're teaching you in med school these days?" his father says. "How to reassure AIDS patients they're going to heaven?"

"Henry," his mother says. "Knock it off."

"Why wouldn't he go to heaven?" Owen says. His parents are staring at each other, gripping the arms of their chairs in a mirror reflection of each other, their knuckles white as bones.

"Because there isn't one," Owen's father says. He doesn't take his eyes from his wife.

"That's it," Owen's mother says, standing so quickly she knocks her chair over.

"That's what?" his father taunts.

"I've had enough. I try to do something nice, as a family, and all you can do is ruin it. You weren't even listening to me. I'm trying to live, Henry. Live my life. I won't be punished for it."

Despite the fact that no one is finished, his mother begins tossing the plates together roughly, gathering them in a lumpy pile to bring to the kitchen.

"Maybe you should be spending your time by your own child's bedside," his father mutters.

"I don't think," his mother says calmly, "that you really want to get into a neglectful parenting contest with me, Henry."

She hefts the plates onto one forearm, leans across Lena to pick up the Corning Ware bowl of peas with the other. Lena looks up and catches her eye.

"Why did you even bother?" Lena says softly. Owen wonders what she means. Having dinner, talking about work, fighting with their father?

"I have no idea," her mother says.

Tom's rumor embeds in his mind like a seed pushed into soil by a thumb. Then it sprouts. After his parents say good night, he sweats and struggles with deep breaths and thinks about his unexplained virus. He forgets at first that his diagnosis was based on fake symptoms. Even when he remembers, he cannot explain away his real symptoms—the ones that recur whenever he is forced to leave the house and sometimes now even when he's not. He tries to remember what Mr. Gabriel told them about AIDS, but the lesson in his memory is full of holes; he was barely listening. In his sex book, published in 1981, the term does not exist. He steals an article he sees his mother reading, but it is highly technical and says little about transmission. All he knows for sure is that gay men get it, that they get it from sex, and that Danny did something to him that his book called oral sex. Once his illness is revealed even his family will know what he has done. He wonders how long it will take for him to die.

He considers asking his mother. Though he is almost always angry at her lately, the scene at the dinner table, with a vulnerable, storytelling version of his mother, made him want to protect her, and she has been easier on him ever since. She hasn't taken his temperature in days, though Owen has gotten into the habit of taking it himself. It is always a degree below normal, and he is sure this means something.

Instead, he asks her about her patient. Every few days, when she is in his room putting laundry away, or fixing him a bland meal at dinnertime, he gets an update on the young man's condition. The pneumonia is receding, but he's developed a strange infection in his brain they cannot diagnose. He has sores lining his mouth and throat that make eating next to impossible. He plays Scrabble like a pro, knows all the obscure two-letter words, the uses of Q in the absence of a U. His name is David.

It doesn't occur to Owen to be jealous of the time his mother spends with this boy. He wants her to spend time with him. He wants to know everything about how he feels and what the doctors think is going on. He is collecting symptoms, ones he will recognize if he develops them later on. He checks his glands all the time. Swollen glands, according to his mother, are the first sign of doom.

"What does he look like?" Owen asks his mother one night, after a long explanation of Pneumocystis and Kaposi's sarcoma.

"Oh," his mother says, squinting as she thinks about it. "Well, they had to shave his head for the drainage. He has blue eyes. He's very thin. Looks more like fourteen than twenty."

"Does he look like Hugh?" The question escapes before he can think about it. His mother stiffens, the ease and friendly demeanor of their recent conversations is gone in an instant. She stands up from where she's been sitting on his bed, looking around for something, some chore that she can do. But the room is already straightened. She backs against the nearest wall.

"Why would you say that?" she says. He wants to get out of bed and hug her in apology, but she is looking at him with too much disgust. "Of course he doesn't look like . . . why would you say such a thing?"

"I don't know," Owen mumbles. "Sorry." But he is angry again, as instantly as she is cold. *Hugh!* he wants to yell. *Hugh Hugh Hugh Hugh! Why should I pretend I never think that name?*

As punishment, she takes his temperature, sitting on his bed so he cannot replace the thermometer, her eyes flitting around so they rest everywhere but on his own.

That Sunday, his mother is on call at the hospital, and Owen and his father can't find anything to eat for breakfast. No one has been to the grocery store, the milk carton is empty, the cereal boxes, when shaken, reveal nothing. There are no eggs, no butter, even the peanut butter jar is scraped clean, and the bread box reveals only one moldy English muffin. Owen's father leans on the open refrigerator door, looking exhausted, staring for an interminable few minutes during which Owen begins to wonder if he is waiting for a miracle. Finally, he closes the door with a plastic kiss.

"Let's go out for brunch," he says. He wakes Lena and threatens to ground her if she doesn't join them. She climbs into the backseat of the station wagon, her hair in her eyes, wearing a green army jacket and boots, grumbling about free countries and child abuse.

"Pancakes are not child abuse," her father says with false cheer.

They go to IHOP, a blue cement building with a brown shingled roof in the same lot as the Stop & Shop. A sign on the door boasts that it is the only business in Brookline open twenty-four hours a day. The hostess seats them in a booth and leaves them with menus the size of their torsos. At the inner edge of the booth are six syrup dispensers, the flavors in raised print stickers from a label gun. There are families who have clearly come from church, the children in dress clothes, printed bulletins folded and sticking out of fathers' coat pockets. One of these families, Owen realizes with a lurch of nausea, belongs to Brian Dowd. He is three booths down, in a light blue suit jacket and clip-on tie, grinning at Owen as if he's just made his day. Owen hunches down, propping up his menu and hiding behind it. When the waitress, who has a chipped front tooth and red-black welt like a leech under one eye, comes over for their order, Owen tries to delay her taking the menu away by being indecisive, but his father nudges him under the table. He orders blueberry pancakes and gives up his shield. Brian Dowd appears to have a family made up entirely of beefy men and boys with crew cuts. When he catches Owen looking, he winks at him.

"Dad, I don't feel so good," Owen says quietly. Lena rolls her eyes.

"What's the matter?" his father says. He has brought the Sunday paper and looks like he'd prefer to be left alone with it.

"It's my stomach," Owen says. This is not a lie. His innards have become as slippery as the vinyl bench.

"Do you want me to take you to the bathroom?" his father says.

"I want to go home."

"Owen." His father sighs. "We just ordered."

Owen starts to wheeze. He knows it is a single bathroom and doesn't want his father following him in while he has diarrhea. But if he goes alone, Brian Dowd will surely take the opportunity to follow. He tries to hold himself still, willing his intestines to be calm, but when the waitress thumps an oversized stack of pancakes topped with a wedge of melting butter in front of him, he can't wait any longer. He slides out and half runs, half waddles toward the back.

He stays on the toilet for a long time, reading the notice about employees washing their hands over and over until it repeats in his head like a commandment. He thinks he remembers his mother saying something about AIDS patients getting a lot of intestinal infections. It's possible his diarrhea isn't nerves at all. He wills Brian's family to leave and his father not to come looking for him. There is an innocuous knock on the door, followed by a more insistent one a minute later. Owen flushes, washes his shaking hands, and opens the heavy door. The bathroom entrances are set in a small alcove, so when Brian Dowd pulls him out and slams him against the dark wood wall, shoving a meaty forearm under his neck, they can't be seen by anyone in the restaurant.

"Hey, faggot," Brian hisses at him. His chin looks sticky, his breath reeks of strawberry syrup. "Long time no see." Owen tries to struggle away and is punched in the stomach for it.

"I hear you're dying of fag cancer, that true?" Brian says.

Owen shakes his head no.

"Good. Because Danny wants to kill you himself."

That's when a hand grabs onto Brian's ear and pulls, hard.

"Ow!" Brian whimpers, backing up to relieve the pressure and revealing Lena holding on to him, her hand in a fingerless glove.

"This is no way to treat people in a pancake house," his sister says in a low voice, twisting harder. "Let's hear an apology."

"I'm sorry," Brian whines. He looks furious. Owen is angry, too. Was his sister never eleven? Doesn't she know she's making things worse?

"Stay away from him," Lena growls. "I know people who will set you on fire with a Zippo if I ask. Got it?"

"Yeah, dude, let go." It takes Owen a second to register this. Brian thinks his sister is a boy.

"Nice suit," she says sarcastically.

She lets go, and Brian trips away, not looking back. Owen is impressed, despite himself. Before this moment, he never would have used the word *tough* to describe any member of his family.

His sister looks him up and down, shoving a hand through her hair in a perfect imitation of a delinquent boy.

"Your pancakes are getting cold," she says. Then she struts into the ladies' room.

Though it is pretty much assumed he won't be going to school, Owen wakes every morning to tell his father he isn't feeling up to it. But now he goes back to bed as soon as the door closes behind the rest of them. He sleeps until afternoon, when the better television shows are on. He has almost filled his sketchbook with drawings of angels, their different anatomies gleaned from the pictures he finds in his father's research. He goes down to his father's office every week for more material. He finds a collection of blank notebooks, longer and thinner than the ones Owen uses for school, with hard covers and pages sewn into the seam. He uses one to keep track of signs from Hugh. He read in a book stolen from his father's bookshelf that guardian angels are mischievous about signs, that they have a sense of humor about the doubt over their existence, and so they are constantly leaving clues in everyday life. Owen keeps track of every time an angel is mentioned on a television sitcom, in pop songs on the radio, on the clues and answers in his father's daily crossword puzzles that he keeps in a basket in the bathroom. He notes any time he feels as if he is being followed from behind, any objects out of place in his room he knows his parents wouldn't bother to touch. He often finds his toothbrush in the wrong hole of the porcelain wall rack, the hole that has been empty as long as he can remember and always assumed was Hugh's. Sometimes a heaviness bleeds into his shoulder, just as if someone has pressed their palm there. There is a crow who, four times in two weeks, wakes Owen in the morning by pecking at his window. Owen lists these clues using a multicolored Bic pen that has four different nibs he releases by thumbing the tiny lever of corresponding color. He color-codes each sign, according to how strong he believes they are. Red clues are irrefutable, black are questionable and possibly explained away by human influence, blue and green lie somewhere in between.

He also keeps a list of suspicious symptoms that may be from AIDS. The fluttery feeling he gets in his stomach and chest, like there are birds trapped in there, and the heaviness of his lungs at night, that could be asthma or Pneumocystis. The small bruises that he can't remember getting, which could be cancerous lesions. Night sweats. Glands that are sore, and that he prods all day to see if they've changed. A small, angry red spot on the head of his penis.

He is not sure how Hugh will manage to save him from AIDS. Maybe he will reveal a cure to their mother. Or, Owen thinks sometimes, Hugh won't save him at all. Maybe Owen will die and join Hugh and all the other angels. This doesn't seem so bad to him, the dying part. It's the getting sick, going back to the hospital, having his brain drained, and his parents and Lena having to wear masks all the time that he is worried about.

He lives during the night now. His parents are both in bed by eleven P.M., and it is during the hours between then and dawn that Owen prefers to write his lists and draw, to hang his grave rubbings and sketches of Hugh on his wall and lie underneath them. He prefers the stillness of the world at night, likes the idea that he is awake while his entire neighborhood is comatose. The physical fear that plagues him during the day is absent in the hours before dawn, when it is neither morning nor night, but a stretch of time absent of definition. During the day he can't help but think, along with key moments he notices on the clock, of Danny doing math time tests, buying his lunch, being let out to smoke on the playground. About his mother on grand rounds, or taking a break to play Scrabble in her gloves and mask and paper gown. His father hunched in his cubicle. His sister disguised as someone else. At night, he has no one to keep track of. Until the night he catches his sister sneaking in.

He doesn't hear her leave as her room is at the other end of the house, off the kitchen. But at four A.M., an hour before his mother's alarm goes off and his freedom ends, Owen goes to the kitchen for a snack. He is unwrapping cheese slices and folding them into his mouth when he hears the telltale creak of the back door. He steps into the hall in time to see his sister, fully dressed, latching the chain. She turns around and sighs at him, glaring at the cellophane wrappers clutched in his fist. Her cheeks and the tips of her ears are bright red from the cold. She stomps her feet gently, knocking the snow from her huge boots. She sits down on the storage bench by the door, which holds all their snow boots, ice skates, hats, and gloves in a jumble of mismatched pairs. She begins to unlace her boots, picking at the frozen laces with the raw, bitten remains of her fingernails.

"Are you going to tell?" she says. With one boot off, she massages her toes through thin socks.

"Are you?" Owen retorts.

"I haven't yet, have I?"

"Where were you?" Owen asks. He checks her eyes. She looks tired, but sober.

"Why does your best friend want to kill you?" she snaps back. Owen looks away, shrugging.

"I thought so," Lena says. "Let's have hot chocolate."

"Okay," Owen says.

Lena makes a paste of unsweetened cocoa, sugar, and water on the bottom of a saucepan, then pours milk in and heats the whole thing over the stove.

"Why don't you just use the Swiss Miss?" Owen asks.

"Don't you like it better this way?" she says, pouring the steaming cocoa into pottery mugs with animals glazed onto the sides. Lena's is a porcupine, Owen's a giraffe.

"I don't know," Owen says. She looks at him strangely.

"This is the way Mom makes it," she says.

"Not for me," Owen says.

"She used to," Lena says. "When you were little."

They take the cocoa, marshmallow fluff blanketing the top, into Lena's room. Owen is stunned by the mess. There is hardly any bare floor space, the carpet piled with rejected clothing, dishes, notebooks, tapes, and records. Lena turns the overhead light on just long enough to find and light half a dozen candles, then flicks it off again. By candlelight, the grunge fades into the background. There is nowhere to sit but her bed. Gone are the rainbow quilt and throw pillows she had when they shared a room. Now she has a double bed with no frame, low to the ground and pushed into a corner, her desk turned the long way and pushed up against the other side, so the bed is almost completely hidden from the doorway. The mattress is covered with ratty paisley throws, her red flannel sheets wrinkled and stained in places with what looks like coffee. She has about a dozen pillows, and Owen props himself against two by the foot. It is more like an animal's den than a girl's bed.

Lena settles herself at the head, removing a carved wooden box from the top drawer of her desk. She takes out an orange packet of rolling papers and a large bud of marijuana, which she begins to separate into leaf and seed. She glances up to see if Owen is going to object.

"Can I have some?" Owen asks, when the joint is ready.

Lena laughs. "No way," she says.

"I've had it before," Owen whines.

"Jeez, you're starting early. I didn't even know what pot was when I was ten."

"I'm eleven," Owen reminds her.

"Well, in that case." She smiles, blowing ash off the lit end of the joint. She hands it to him.

After a few drags and a superhuman effort to hold them in without coughing, Owen sinks into the cave of her bed and sighs. It seems to him that he has been hasty hiding at home. Everything at school has surely already been forgotten. When he looks up, Lena is smiling at him.

"Don't let Mom and Dad see you so happy," she says. "They'll send you back to the fifth grade." Owen shrugs.

"Is that punk guy your boyfriend?" he says. "The one you brought home that day?"

"No," Lena says quickly. She presses the joint against the sides of the ashtray and extinguishes it with licked fingertips. "Sort of," she says. "It's complicated. I don't really want to talk about that."

"Are you in disguise or something?" Owen asks.

"I guess you could say that."

"Aren't you worried Mom and Dad are going to see you?"

"No. They don't notice anything they don't want to."

"Were they always like this?" Owen asks. It is something he has written in his notebooks, a question in varying phrases, leaving space afterward sufficient for detail, as if someday he might open it to find the answer penned in a different hue.

"No," Lena says. "Not always."

"What were they like?"

"You know," Lena says. But Owen shakes his head. "They were around more. They looked at each other. They laughed. Hugh made them laugh a lot. Especially Mom."

"I can't remember," Owen says.

"You're lucky," Lena says.

"What was Hugh like?" Owen whispers. "Was he Mom's favorite?"

Lena stares at him, then lights up a Marlboro the same way Danny does, cradling the flame within her hand.

"He was everyone's favorite," she says finally. "Even yours."

13. casserole

Kissing girls gets easier. Now I do it at every party, in the bathrooms or closets of houses in Cambridge, against the cold stone buildings in the shadows of Harvard Square. I've made my own rules. No more bedrooms with Sebastian; I can't risk going so far. I always kiss them standing up. I never try to get in their clothing or let them in mine. I kiss them till their knees are weak and then I stop. Some girls seem to take this as a challenge, and I have to be quick to knock away their diving hands. But I think a lot of girls like the idea of just being kissed, without wondering what they'll have to deal with next. I know this feeling. I never kiss a girl more than once, because the first time is the one everyone remembers. Second times lead to bases I don't want to go to. I've already developed a reputation. Sebastian says they call me the Kissing Bandit. I think he's a little jealous. I'm the one all the girls talk about now, when it used to be him. One day, a girl he's been flirting with drags me off instead.

"Don't blame me," I say later, when he scowls as I slide Chapstick over my swollen mouth. "It was your idea."

"No one told you to make a career out of it," he mutters.

"I'll stop if you want," I say, holding my breath.

"Free country," he says, shrugging.

Only part of me wants to stop. The truth is, when I'm kissing girls I don't feel awkward or ugly or dressed up like someone I'm not. It's also the only time that my crazy questioning head gets to stop for a rest. Smoking pot isn't as reliable as I thought it'd be. Sometimes it soothes me to the point of flat water, but other times, without warning, I end up with more in my head than I started with. Sebastian gives me Valium then, but that just makes me sleepy and not in a good way. So exhausted I don't even want to crawl into bed because it seems like I'll never be able to get up again.

I've been to three of Lionel's parties. They're actually the same party, which goes on all day and night, with people rotating in shifts. I've seen Lionel only once more; on the third night in the kitchen he was playing poker at the table. He interrupted the betting to stand up and slap Sebastian's hand.

"Hey, baby brother," he said, a cigarette stuck in the corner of his mouth, bouncing up and down like a conductor's wand.

"This is Lee," Sebastian said reluctantly. Lionel nodded, but he wasn't looking anymore. He'd gone back to his cards.

"Lee Furey," I said loudly. I thought I could startle or scare him into giving up a clue. But he threw a stack of chips into the center of the table, grabbed his cigarette with his thumb and forefinger, and took a deep drag before removing it from his mouth.

"Congratulations," he said. "I'm not sure Sebastian knows his whole name." The guys at the table chuckled automatically. "Why don't you get your little friend a drink, Sebastian," he said. And that was all, we'd been dismissed. He didn't even flinch when I said Hugh's last name.

Sebastian tried to cheer me up with tequila and a freshman who wanted to make out, but I declined both, going home early. How could I get the truth out of someone I couldn't even manage to startle?

Sunday's party feels different as soon as I get there. I was here last night and expected it to be a continuation. But I notice someone has tried to straighten up, and hung those three-dimensional tissue-paper hearts from the light fixtures, the kind you can fold back up again for next year. There are dishes of candy hearts with sayings branded into them and red hots, a big set of lips stuck to the refrigerator door. Lionel must have a girlfriend.

"Happy Valentine's Day," Sebastian says when he sees me. He leaves something in my hand when we slap palms. It's a baby-aspirin-colored heart, YOU'RE HANDSOME set off center. I drop it in a smoldering ashtray on our way to the basement.

I get as stoned as I can down there, and Sebastian cuts me off when I can no longer sit up straight. I'm lounging on huge pillows that were once white but are now too stained to be any color at all. Some girl I've kissed before keeps trying to get me to kiss her again. She's like gum on a sneaker, every time I scrape her away she springs back. Finally Sebastian insults her so she'll leave me alone. He lies down next to me and we both watch him flick his Zippo on and off his jeans as if it's the most fascinating thing in the world. He keeps lighting the pillow tassels on fire and stomping them out until someone asks about the smell. It takes me a few seconds to realize that my name is being called. Partly because it's the wrong name.

"Lena." The voice is annoyed at having to repeat itself. I look beyond my knees to the guy leaning over, peering as though he's trying to figure out exactly where I've hurt myself.

"Don't call me that," I say, before I recognize him.

"Look," Sebastian says with delight. "Your boyfriend's here."

"Hi, Jonah," I say. Then, to Sebastian, "Shut up." He's giggling like crazy. He rolls off the pillows and jumps up.

"God, I'm starving. Aren't you guys hungry? Save my spot," he says to Jonah, slapping him on the back. Jonah wobbles like he can't even be bothered to brace himself. "We all know it's the spot you want," Sebastian adds, and he lopes not so steadily away.

Jonah stands there looking stupid while trying to look superior. It's hard to focus on him; like everything else, he seems very far away.

"Sit down if you must," I say. I just want the space around him to stand still. I scoot up against the wall and manage to get out and light a cigarette without anything escaping from my insubstantial hands. I don't offer him one, even though I know he smokes the same brand I do.

"How'd you know it was me?" I say finally.

"Give me a break," he says.

"I've fooled people," I say.

"Not anyone who was really looking," he says.

He has his camera strapped around his jean jacket and he takes a few snaps of some people across the room. He does this automatically, without thinking, the way I inhale a cigarette or bite my nails. I left Hugh's camera at home tonight.

"Don't," I say, when he aims it my way. He shrugs, lowering it to his lap.

"Do you have any idea how much trouble you're in?" he says. I'd like to press my cigarette out on his lens. Instead I lean my head back and take a deep drag.

"My friend works in the office," Jonah says. "They're sending your parents a letter that says any more absences and they'll hold you back a year."

"I didn't think you had any friends," I say. "And why are you asking about me in the office?"

"This is serious," he says.

"I don't care," I say. I've been neglecting the mail lately. Sometimes my parents forget to check it anyway, and the box gets so crowded the postman has to pile things by the door.

"You don't want to be kept back," Jonah says.

"Like you, you mean."

"Yeah. I'm a seventeen-year-old sophomore. You think that's fun?"

"Like I said, I don't care."

"The thing is, I think you do."

"Well, you're wrong. Not to mention annoying."

"Fine," Jonah says. His jaw is tight.

"Why do you give a shit, anyway?" I say.

"I'm just trying to look out for you."

"Just because you ruined your life doesn't make you the expert on mine. You're like a fucking guidance counselor or something. Why can't you just leave me alone?"

"You're charming on drugs," Jonah says. But he's getting up to go.

"This isn't drugs," I say. "This is me. You don't know me."

Jonah brushes something from his corduroys. His legs from this angle look really thin and wobbly, like a calf's. "I guess I thought you were somebody else," he says.

He walks away just as Sebastian comes back with two overflowing plastic cups of Valentine punch. My throat is really dry so I gulp it at first, but it burns and I end up coughing.

"What's in this?" I say, trying to pretend I'm not watching Jonah thread his way up the exposed staircase.

"Everything," Sebastian says. He gestures and I obey, drinking deep.

When Hugh first disappeared, nothing stopped moving. My parents didn't sleep for days, calling the police every hour, taking turns driving our station wagon up and down the same empty streets. The neighbors brought food in covered glass rectangles, peering at the clutter of dishes and ashtrays in the living room. I would spoon out three or four sticky squares of different casseroles onto Owen's plate, trying to make it look like a balanced meal, which it wasn't because most of the casseroles were made with the same elbow macaroni. When a search party was formed, the headquarters started at our house, and my father's students showed up in groups and asked me where to check in. When it got too big to fit in my father's office, the local PBS station donated their calling room. After that my father was never home. And my mother went to bed.

At first it seemed temporary, like she had the flu. She would get up long enough to fix us breakfast, clearing the fliers with Hugh's face off our plastic place mats. But by the time I walked Owen home, she was in bed again, with the same pajamas and cowlicks she'd had in the morning. She nailed blankets over her windows, because the marker lines of light at the edges of the shades were too much for her to handle. She unplugged the living room phone and brought it in with her, nestling it on the opposite pillow. When her friends called she told them quickly that she needed to leave the line open for my dad. Sometimes, she said Hugh instead of Henry. Which everyone knew was what she meant in the first place.

She didn't sleep. She pretended to, and when I opened the door I found her with her eyes closed, too tight to be convincing. Sometimes I tested her by standing next to the bed and staring. She rolled away like someone in a dream. She kept magazines and the daily papers piled in the valley between her side and my dad's, but she didn't read them. It was too dark in there to see anything. My father thought she was sleeping too much and had a conference on the phone with their doctor about depression. He was too busy to see what I knew. My mother was not depressed, she was terrified. So terrified she could barely move, could only crouch, waiting for what she feared most. Like a game of hide-and-seek. Half of her wanting to disappear, the other half waiting, almost wishing, to be captured. I could feel my mother waiting, her whole room was coiled and ready to spring. When my father was home, he slept on the couch in his office.

Someone had to be in charge of Owen. I fed him, did his laundry, got us to school on time and him to bed. When he asked me questions about our mother (he never asked about Hugh), I gave him vague, cheerful answers, the kind people give to little kids, even though I never believed those answers when I was five. I gave him his asthma pills and listened at night for any sign of a wheeze. I learned to doze without really sleeping, the clip-on lamp on my headboard glowing for so many hours it warmed a circle onto my pillow. Any change in Owen's breathing, my mother getting up to go to the bathroom, my father coming in at four A.M., snapped me instantly to attention. I lived on catnaps of fifteen minutes, marking every quarter hour on the Snoopy clock next to my bed.

Mr. Gabriel sent a note home that said it seemed like I wasn't getting enough sleep, that I was having trouble memorizing vocabulary words, and didn't finish in the top spots on the math time tests anymore. I denied it, but still my father took the note into my mom for a conference. Two days later, my grandmother moved in with us.

At midnight, Sebastian makes me a strange proposition. I'm stoned and drunk and there are a bunch of voices flinging unhappy ideas around my head, the newest voice being Jonah's. All of this makes me not really hear him the first time he asks if he can kiss me. I assume he's joking.

"Come outside," he says.

We stand on the back porch, the light from the kitchen brightening him but leaving me in the shadows. There is a lot of snow on the bushes still, weighing down leftover strands of Christmas lights.

"I think I should kiss you," Sebastian says. He gives me that slow, calculating, gorgeous smile I've been watching melt girls for months. The thing is, now I know it doesn't mean much. It still works, though. My mouth has gone dry.

"Why?" I say. I'm just stalling, and he knows it.

"Call it an experiment," he says, reaching out and tucking a stiff piece of hair behind my ear.

"Are you going to dissect me?" I laugh. My lips are shivering already, though I can blame that on the cold.

"I'm collecting data for future conquests," he says. He's as close now as he can get without pressing against me. "Or maybe I just want to know what all the girls are bragging about." He still has his hand cupping my ear, but I can barely feel it. He is waiting for me to tell him yes, which is the same thing as saying I want to kiss him, which I don't really want to admit.

"Whatever turns you on," I say. He laughs at this.

"Let me lead," he says, and he plunges into my mouth just as I open it to answer back.

It's a good kiss. Slow and warm and building, sweeter than I thought he was capable of. I thought he'd go for sexy and demanding, but he's lingering on my mouth like he cares about every move. He's an expert, really. This is exactly what I try to do with my kisses. Make a girl feel like there is nothing on my mind but the worship of her mouth. Even like I love her a little.

Now I wonder if they all feel as lonely as I do.

When we go back to the party, there's some sort of commotion. There's always at least one melodrama a night. Last time a friend of Lionel's OD'ed and there was this big argument about whether to call an ambulance or find someone sober enough to bring him to the hospital. Tonight's drama is centered around the upstairs bathroom, with people hanging around the upstairs hall whispering rumors and trying to peek, like passing an accident on the highway.

"Sebastian!" someone yells. It's Lionel, at the top of the stairs. He thunders down, the crowd leaning away to give him room, and grabs Sebastian's arm, pulling him away to a corner. He says something, angry, and points upstairs. Sebastian shrugs and shakes his head. Lionel looks fed up and pulls him toward the kitchen.

I climb the stairs, piecing together clues from the murmuring. *It's not like she was his girlfriend,* a girl says. *She probably did it for attention,* says someone else. *She's always been kind of a freak.*

The bathroom door is open and I slide past a few people to get a peek inside. The first thing I see is blood on a white towel, which is being held to the arm of a girl Sebastian hooked up with last week whose name I can't remember. She's sitting on the floor and there is a boy sitting on the edge of the tub, holding her arm up, pressing the towel to it. The boy is Jonah. He looks up and sees me.

"Where's your friend?" he says. When I don't answer, he lifts the towel to check the blood, which is coming from long cuts on the outside of the girl's forearm. I leave the bathroom, I've seen enough. It's none of my business anyway. But someone should tell her that to kill yourself, you need to cut the other side.

At the end of the hallway is Lionel's room. I check to make sure no one's watching, then open the door slowly, in case there are people in the bed. There is no one. I slip in and close the door behind me. The bedside lamp has a black bulb in it, so the room is like a darkroom, tinged blue instead of red. The floor is covered with dirty clothes and shoes, crusty plates and empty beer cans. I have to weave my way over to the bed. It's a low platform with a futon mattress and embarrassing-looking stains on the sheets. On the bedside table are a tape player and an ashtray and a pile of unlabeled homemade tapes. I open the little drawer. Inside are different condoms thrown in together, looking like a selection of candy. Also a Swiss army knife, a marble pipe, a lighter, and rolling papers. I go over to the bureau and look through those drawers. In with the boxer shorts I find a bankbook, an official-looking paper telling Lionel to appear in court, and a strip of photos like the ones you sit in a booth and pay a dollar for. They are all of the same girl, older than me and sexy looking, posing like it is a porn movie. I've never seen her before. In the bottom drawer I find a Brookline High School yearbook. It is from the year Hugh was supposed to graduate. I've seen this already, in the library. Most of the pictures are of seniors. Hugh isn't in it.

I close the drawers and go back over to the bed. I sit down against the wall, putting my boots up on the filthy sheets. My hands look weird, like they belong to someone else. I've been biting my nails too much. I feel like I'm in one of those dreams where I have lost all my clothes, or I'm driving a car even though I don't know how, or I have to take a final exam and the last thing I remember it was the first day of school. I no longer know what it is I'm looking for. I can't remember if I ever did.

So I wait there, smoking, for Lionel to come in and find me.

When my grandmother showed up with a big blue suitcase, I watched to see which room she would take. My mother had picked up, vacuumed, and changed the sheets in Hugh's room soon after he disappeared. It was still waiting for him and was the logical place for my grandmother to sleep. But instead she put her suitcase in the corner of the living room, her fat makeup bag on the edge of the bathroom sink, and pulled the couch-bed out, making it up with old Marimekko sheets, an electric blanket, and hospital corners. Every morning she folded it away before Owen and I got out of bed. She made us gloppy oatmeal on the stove instead of letting us have the instant packages of cinnamon and sugar. At night she roasted slabs of fatty meat and had endless recipes for potatoes, which she bought in a twenty-pound bag. She vacuumed every day, so that the swirls on the carpet never had a chance to fade. She followed behind me and Owen with damp paper towels, like we were leaking. She laid out girly turtlenecks and corduroys for me to wear to school. She ironed all day, shirts, napkins, sheets, even Owen's little dungarees. She made me do my homework at the kitchen table while she ironed. She talked so much I couldn't concentrate.

She said, "Women take over in a tragedy."

Or, "Your father only has so much strength for this. You're a good girl for helping him."

And, "Your mother's never really done her part. She had a hard life, they say. But she'll have to get out of bed if this family is going to survive."

I didn't answer any of this. My grandmother was not the kind of person you talked back to. She just nodded to herself and sprayed water onto shirts, pressing the iron down with a sizzle.

She was always going into my mother's room. She brought trays of soup and crackers, soft, bland foods as if my mother had a cold. She pushed her way in with the vacuum, dusted the sills and the bureau with an old T-shirt. She suggested my mother take showers and, when she did, changed the sheets on the bed and made it up with decorative pillows. My mother tossed these to the floor when she crawled back in with her hair still wet.

My grandmother sometimes brought me in there with her, to clear dishes or flap the tacked blankets free of dust, letting a few seconds of gray light inside. When we were cleaning, though my mother never even opened her eyes, my grandmother talked. She talked the same way she did to me, in a monologue, not expecting an answer. Like she was allowed to say whatever came into her head.

I tried to sneak my mother sympathetic looks during these speeches, but she wouldn't look at me. I wasn't sure she even knew I was there.

In the end, my grandmother went too far. I was dusting the long bureau, the carved mahogany one with two tall mirrors that was my mother's. My father's was made of the same wood, but was a wardrobe with doors that opened out. This had always fascinated me as a kid, that the difference between boys and girls went as far as what bureau you got when you were married.

My grandmother picked up a picture frame and ran her cloth over it. The picture was one that I'd never liked, of my mother as a little girl. She was in a limp flannel nightgown with dirt smudged on her face and a teddy bear held strangled under her arm. She was scowling in a way that seemed more than the temporary annoyance of being photographed. She kept it, she once told me, to remind herself to make her children smile. I never knew what that meant. Hadn't she ever smiled as a kid? My grandmother, who had already dusted this photo half a dozen times, finally looked at it and set it down with the *thock* of wood against wood.

"I know what your life was like," she said toward the lump in the bed. "I know how you had to take care of things too young. We have that in common. But I won't sit by and watch you do the same to the children you have left. When was the last time you looked at them?" She grabbed my arm and turned me toward the bed. "Look at your daughter, Elizabeth." I dared to glance up, but my mother hadn't moved. My grandmother let me go with a noise of disgust. She turned back to wipe violently at the mirrored tray that collected odd earrings and extra change.

"You act as if you're the only one who mourns him," she said.

The crash happened so fast it was like the mirror had cracked just from my grandmother's words. It took me a minute to connect my mother kneeling upright in bed, her hair wild with electricity, with the tea mug that lay chipped and leaking on the carpet in front of the bureau.

"Get out of my house," my mother said. My grandmother, her face changing from confusion to fear to anger, opened her mouth to say something else. But I spoke up first.

"Leave her alone," I said loudly, causing both of them to stare at me. And though I'd never seen my grandmother take a suggestion let alone an order from anyone, she nodded stiffly and left the room. "Just leave her alone," I added, after she'd gone. When I turned to look at her, my mother had already reburied herself under the covers.

My grandmother moved out the next day, taking her makeup bag and suitcase, her mouth still tight from the talk she'd had with my father in his office. I figured her leaving would cause some big melodramatic change, that my family would band together. This is what would have happened in a book. But nothing changed, except our house got dirty again, my mother stayed in bed, my father in his office or at search headquarters, and I went back to listening to Owen breathe.

The next September, no one sent the check in for school pictures, so Owen and I were only allowed to pose with our classes. I didn't like the idea of missing a year. I took Owen to Woolworth's, paid with quarters, and drew the curtain across the booth. We got one strip of the two of us together. You always saw kids goofing off in those photo booth pictures, but Owen and I just sat still and forgot to smile.

Lionel is really pissed to find me in his room. He actually grabs me by my jacket and pulls me off the bed, slamming me against the wall. My neck snaps back and I hit my head hard. The look on his face makes me wonder why I never noticed in all those pictures that he was crazy. That sparkle I thought was mischievousness is now a flash of something else. He looks like he is enjoying how angry he is.

Sebastian stops him. "C'mon, Lionel, lay off," he says. This isn't his normal voice, but the whiny, powerless voice of a little brother getting picked on. "She's just a girl," he adds.

Lionel blinks, then lets go of me like I'm burning his hands. I don't realize he's holding me up until my feet land on the floor.

"A girl?" he says doubtfully, looking at my chest. "What are you, a dyke?"

I shake my head.

"Well, whatever you are, it still doesn't explain why you're in my room. Looking for something?"

It suddenly occurs to me that Lionel thinks I'm stealing drugs. I might laugh, if my head didn't feel like it might explode with the effort.

"My brother," I say softly.

"What the fuck is she talking about?" Lionel asks Sebastian. Sebastian looks confused, like he's missed something because he's so stoned.

"Beats me, her brother's like ten years old."

"My other brother," I say, louder now. "Hugh Furey."

Lionel runs his hands through his hair, rearranging the stiff spikes. I've looked at this face so much, it's odd to see it close up and moving. Recognition passes over it. I wait for anger or panic or guilt or fear, but he just shakes his head, baffled.

"Wasn't he that kid who disappeared?" he says.

"Yes," I say. Sebastian looks from me to Lionel, waiting for someone to explain.

"That was like five years ago. The police interviewed everyone about it. What, you think I've had him in the closet all this time?"

"No," I say stupidly. I am confused. He said the police interviewed him, but I thought they'd never seen the pictures. I was sure only I knew about Lionel.

"Didn't you," I start. I'm blushing now. "Weren't you his friend?"

"I sold his girlfriend weed. We weren't exactly buddies. He was pretty straight and narrow."

"But he took pictures of you," I say. Lionel is bored with me. He turns around, takes his T-shirt all the way off with one pull at the back collar. His back is smooth, with sharp clean bones rising like wings behind his shoulders. He is much taller than Sebastian, almost as tall as Hugh. I think he is the best-looking guy I've ever seen in person. He sits on the bed and lights a cigarette with his Zippo, swiping it across the thigh of his jeans like Sebastian.

"He took pictures of everyone," Lionel says. "I can't help it if I'm photogenic." He bats his eyelashes at me and tells me to get out of his room.

I can't move. After the party winds down, and people either leave or find a corner to sleep off their hangovers, after I explain myself to Sebastian, and he grows tired halfway through and falls asleep with his head in my lap, I still don't get up. I don't know what's wrong with me, but for some reason I want to wait. I wait for dawn to arrive and the T to start running and my parents to wake up. I wait until I know that it's too late, until I'm sure I've done the worst thing of my life. Then I fall asleep.

14. hammer

Owen's father always wakes him gently. He raises the shades first, then sits on the bed and pulls the covers slowly away from where Owen burrows his head. He repeats his name in a soft, coaxing voice. If he has found this more difficult lately, since Owen started going to bed an hour and a half before he's due to get up, he has yet to lose his patience and change the routine.

His mother's technique is more direct. She

throws open the door, letting the knob knock against the perpendicular wall. She flicks the overhead switch and calls his name the first time as though she has already been calling him for an hour. He doesn't mind that she is rarely around to do this anymore.

They never wake him together. This is how he knows, immediately, that something is wrong. The room is dark, and he opens one eye to his father's soft but anxious voice, then both eyes with his mother's bark. His first thought is that he has told the truth in his sleep. He snakes a hand down to check and see if his pajamas are wet.

"Owen," his mother says urgently, so he looks up. They are back-lit by the hallway, which means it's too early for the sun to be up.

"Where's your sister?" she says.

He wonders why are they looking for Lena in his room when she moved out of it years ago. Then his mind gels and he remembers.

"She must be late," Owen says.

"Owen!" his mother grabs his shoulders, shaking him. "Are you awake? What do you mean, late?"

"Nothing," Owen says, rubbing his shoulder. He feigns confusion though he is now fully awake. "I mean, did you look in her room?"

His mother, frustrated, turns around and marches away. Owen looks at his father.

"Your sister isn't in her bed," he says. Then, ridiculously: "Go back to sleep."

Owen swings his feet out of bed and toes into his slippers, following his father out of the room.

The hall clock reads 5:30. Owen must have fallen asleep earlier than usual; he has no memory after two A.M. He assumes Lena left the house when his parents went to bed, but he was sketching in his room and doesn't really know.

His mother is on the kitchen phone, responding to someone's questions with clipped, angry answers.

"Fifteen," she says, then pauses. "Yes. No. I don't think so. Nine o'clock. Yes, last night. No. No. Not that I know of. Of course not."

"Listen to me," she says after a pause, quiet and fierce. "I will not wait twenty-four hours. I won't wait twenty-four minutes. Send someone now."

Owen's father steps forward and takes the phone from her hand. She gives it up more easily than Owen expects her to, but doesn't move away, so they are standing closer together than they normally do. If one of them curled an arm out, they'd be hugging.

"This is Henry Furey. I want to speak to Chief Brody," Owen's father says. "That's fine. I'll wait while you call him at home."

Owen's mother stares directly ahead at her husband's chest, as if she is contemplating resting her forehead there. Owen peeks out into the hall, at the unlatched back door. When Lena walks in, there will be quite a scene.

Three hours later the kitchen is bright, and a tall, lanky man his father's age, wearing a suit with a gun strapped underneath, stands on their linoleum and writes short answers in a little spiral flip book. This is Brookline's chief of police, whom his father seems to know well enough to call "John." He has gray hair cropped to his head in a buzz cut, and a tiny piece of toilet paper bull's-eyed with blood on the edge of his jaw. He smiles and says hello to Owen, calling him by name though no one has introduced them. His parents haven't looked at Owen in hours; he sits at the inner corner of the breakfast table, hoping not to be sent away. The chief turns down his mother's offer of coffee.

"Please sit down, Elizabeth," he says. She doesn't. "Take a breath. Tell me what's going on."

"What's going on is the same thing all over again. She's gone from her bed. She was there last night and this morning she was gone."

"All right," the chief says, noting something in his book. "Has she been acting out lately? Fighting with you, talking back?"

"She's a teenager," Owen's father says. "Of course she has."

"Any reason she would run away?"

"Only if she were the cruelest child in the world," Owen's mother says.

"Elizabeth." The chief sighs. "My men have gone over the house. There is no sign of forced entry. I think it's safe to assume she left on her own."

"Your assumptions have been wrong before," she snaps back.

"You said yourself you chained the back door," the chief says softly. "The chain isn't broken. It was unlatched from the inside."

Owen's mother plunks down then, hanging her face in her hands. "Why would she do that?"

Chief Brody looks as if he has a suggestion, but seems to decide against it. "We'll find her," he says instead. "I'll put the whole department on it. We'll need a picture."

Owen's mother lets out a noise then, a horrible noise that sounds as if something small has just died in her throat. Chief Brody reaches into his inner suit pocket, pulling out a handkerchief, though his mother is not technically crying. A flash of silver catches Owen's eye. He squints. On the policeman's lapel is a tiny angel, pinned so tightly through the cloth it almost disappears, its wings slicing a cave into the fabric.

In the space of one sentence Owen goes from invisible to the object of the room's attention.

"She sneaks out," he says. His parents whip their heads around to look at him. "She sneaks out," he repeats to the police chief, who is looking at him strangely. "And she dresses like a boy."

It doesn't occur to him until later, after he has given them every detail, that he has betrayed Lena. The angel is the reason he told. It was a sign. This is what Hugh wants him to do. He doesn't think, despite the things she has said, that his sister would run away. Owen can't believe that Lena would insert that noise into her mother's throat, or the shake into his father's voice. Not willingly. Not when she has heard them before.

Owen forgets that it's Monday until he answers the door to Tom Fisher standing in the outer foyer, blue backpack hiked childishly on both shoulders. His mother hurries up behind him and looks annoyed when she sees who it is.

"Why don't you take Owen outside to play?" she says to him. Tom looks alarmed.

"Mom," Owen says. "It's like ten degrees out."

"Put a hat on," she says, waving them away. She goes back to the kitchen where she is making coffee for a policewoman and Jeremy Lispet's mother, passing the time as she waits for the phone to ring.

Owen asks Tom to wait. He dresses quickly, grabbing his folder of finished homework, and leads the way out into the frigid air.

"You don't have to stay," he says. Tom shrugs as if it doesn't matter. They stand on the porch for a minute while King, the dog across the street, barks furiously from his perch on the stairs.

"C'mon," Owen says. "Shut up, King!" Owen hates that dog. He never barks when you need him to.

He leads Tom down the driveway, under his own bedroom windows, then Lena's, and around to the back of the house. In between the house and the small, overgrown backyard is an old garage his father keeps asking the landlord to tear down. Owen is not allowed inside because the roof is missing in places and the whole thing is threatening to collapse in on itself. There is an old orange Saab inside, its engine long gone, abandoned by a previous tenant. When he was little, Owen and his sister played "Dukes of Hazzard" in this car. He hasn't thought of that in years.

"You drive," he says to Tom. He creaks the passenger door open and gets inside, the leather seats like ice against the backside of his jeans. Tom gets in the driver's side and, automatically, as any child too young to drive would, he jiggles the wheel, flicks the levers on either side, changes gears, and makes the small, happy noise of a sports car accelerating. He glances at Owen, embarrassed, and leans back in his seat.

"So how come the police are at your house?" he says after an uncomfortable silence.

"My sister is missing," Owen says.

"Wow. Didn't that happen to your brother, too?" Owen nods. "Interesting," Tom says with his characteristic tone, far too old for an eleven-year-old. This voice is why the majority of the fifth grade makes fun of him. "Maybe your family's cursed. Are you worried it will happen to you?"

"I wasn't really," Owen says. "Until you mentioned it."

"Sorry," Tom says. "Where do you think she is?"

"I think she snuck out and something's keeping her from coming home," Owen says. Tom nods at this, as if they are police detectives trading reasonable assumptions in their squad car.

"Are you ever coming back to school?" Tom says after a pause.

"Nope," Owen says. "Danny Gray wants to kill me." He's not sure why he's talking about this so freely. This morning's confession to the police has left him reckless.

"Why?" Tom says. He's not a good liar; it's clear he already knows the answer. One word and you can hear his heart beating with the fear of being found out.

"Don't you know?" Owen says, glaring at him. Tom blushes.

"Danny told everyone you tried to give him a blow job while he was sleeping," he admits.

"Yeah, well." Owen fiddles with the button on the emergency brake. "That's not what happened, but no one's going to believe me."

"What did happen?" Tom asks quietly. Owen looks up suspiciously. Tom seems too guileless to be trapping him. And he hardly cares anymore. He just wants to tell someone.

"We were fooling around. It wasn't even my idea. Not originally. His mom caught us."

Tom nods. "That happened to me," he says. "At my old school. My best friend told everyone I tried to kiss him."

Owen nods. He's not sure he wants to have this in common with Tom Fisher. They sit for a moment, both looking out the windshield, as if they are checking for traffic on an imaginary road.

"Did you like it, though?" Tom says finally, gripping the wheel, ready to swerve if he has to.

"It scared me," Owen says softly. "But yeah." His thighs are shaking.

"Me, too," Tom says. Then, without looking over, he reaches out and puts his hand on Owen's, still fidgeting with the emergency brake. Owen looks at it for a moment and considers pulling away. Instead he turns his own hand up so their palms meet, curling his fingers in with Tom's.

"I won't tell anyone," Tom says.

They sit there, holding hands, until his mother calls Owen's name from the back door.

His father spends the whole day patrolling Brookline and Boston in his station wagon, his mother answers phone calls and fends off sympathetic neighbors. His sister's picture appears on the local six o'clock news, along with a sketch done by a police artist based on Owen's description of Lena in disguise. Anyone who sees her is instructed to call the police station. That night there is another visit from the chief, but Owen is sent to his room for the update. His parents' voices through the closed door are shrill, panicked. The chief goes home around ten, but leaves an officer by the curb in a squad car to watch them for the night. Owen listens to his parents refusing calls that might tie up the phone, boiling the kettle, pacing the floors, rummaging in his sister's room, not going to bed. At midnight, he wanders out in new pajamas and finds them sitting on the sofa, the television on with the volume knob turned down, staring straight ahead at the phone that has been pulled to the coffee table. There is a haze of smoke as thick as storm clouds over the upper half of the living room. His father, who has been trying to cut down, lights a new cigarette from the remains of the filter in his hand.

"Can I stay up?" Owen asks. He can't stand the thought of being in his room, not with everyone else out here waiting. He moves toward the couch, aiming for the empty cushion between them.

"Go to bed," his mother says harshly.

His father looks at her. "Elizabeth?" he says.

"You're going to school tomorrow," she explains. Owen feels himself growing hot.

"I can't," he says. His voice is small and not very convincing. *I have AIDS,* he thinks. He says: "I'm sick."

"You'll be fine," she says. "It's time you went back." She's looking at his father.

"I have a fever," Owen whines. "Dad?" His father looks at his mother for a second, receiving some silent signal.

"Go to bed, Owen," he says. "I'll get you up in the morning. You can try one day and see how it goes."

Owen turns and heads back to his room, nausea welling up as strong as though it has been summoned. Just before he closes the door, he hears his mother say something, though he cannot make out what comes before or after.

"I don't want him around," is all he hears.

His father drives him. He double-parks by the front entrance, which Owen never uses because the side door by the kindergarten is closer when he cuts through the park. Seeing his school from this angle— the swarm of dropped-off students shuffling in through double doors—makes it seem more ominous. He spent the morning making vomiting noises in the bathroom, while sitting on the toilet with real but silent diarrhea. He spiked his temperature to 103 degrees—emergency measures—but his mother shook it down and claimed it was normal. He considered fainting, but couldn't muster the courage to let himself fall to the hardwood floor.

"Have a good day," his father says. He is wearing the same flannel shirt and jeans he had on yesterday, his eyes are webbed with red, and he smells like he slept in an ashtray. Under normal circumstances, Owen would make things easier on him. But he's desperate. He has already used every symptom in his arsenal, so he resorts to begging.

"I can't go in there," he whispers.

His father sighs. "Owen, we'll have a talk later, okay? When you get home. But right now I need you to go to school. We're busy looking for your sister and it would be better—"

"If I wasn't around," Owen mocks. "I heard her. Mom doesn't want me around."

"She's just trying to protect you."

"She hates me," Owen says simply.

"Don't be ridiculous. Your mother loves you."

"What*ever,*" Owen says, in a perfect imitation of his sister's scorn. This is not, apparently, the best tactic to get his father back on his side.

"Get out of the car, Owen," his father says quietly. "You're going to be late."

Owen opens the door, scrambles out, and slams it with all his might. He storms between manicured hedges toward the doors, anger quickly giving way to nausea as familiar faces turn to stare at him. He is sure he hears the word *Danny* whispered as he passes by, then *virus*. Almost to the door, he hears his name called but ignores it. He hears it again, closer now, and he turns at the hand that grabs his arm, cringing in expectation of an insult or a punch. But it is Tom Fisher.

"Didn't you hear me?" Tom laughs. He's out of breath. Owen shakes his head.

"C'mon, then," Tom says, and though once he would have avoided this at all costs, Owen feels strangely safe walking next to Tom, and even forgets to feel sick as they enter the foyer, their shoulders brushing to fit through the door.

The feeling doesn't last long. As soon as they get to their classroom, despite Mr. Gabriel's attempt to diffuse the whispered gawking by announcing a pop fractions quiz, Owen is the center of attention. Everyone takes turns looking at him, some with confusion, others with disgust, or worse, with small smiles that suggest they know something he does not. The only one who doesn't look at him is Danny. Danny pushes his chair back, balancing on the back legs, chuckling occasionally at something Brian Dowd says. His flicks his bangs out of his eyes in a gesture so familiar it makes Owen's throat hurt. He is surprised at how disappointed he is. He's afraid of Danny killing him, why should he care if he won't look at him?

During the fifteen-minute quiz, five notes are passed to Owen's block of desks. Tom handles them all, slipping them in his back pocket instead of forwarding them to Owen. There are whispers and snickers despite warnings from Mr. Gabriel's furious red face. When the quiz is over—Owen leaves half of his fractions undone—Mark Flint and Brian Dowd walk out of their way to pass by him. They make slurping noises and waggle their tongues. Owen wonders how long he can wait before his need for the bathroom becomes an emergency.

"Just ignore them," Tom whispers. This is something Owen's father might say. Reasonable yet impossible.

"Vocab books!" Mr. Gabriel barks. "Now!"

Owen has forgotten to bring any of his schoolbooks.

"You can look on with me," Tom says. Owen notices Jennifer Lemon, who sits next to Tom, give Jennifer Keyes, who sits next to Owen, a knowing look.

"Never mind," Owen says, slouching in his seat. "I don't give a shit."

"Suit yourself," Tom says, shrugging. His voice has that ridiculous, snooty mature tone again that makes Owen want to smack him.

He looks at the clock. It is only nine-twenty.

Since it's a Tuesday, at eleven A.M. Mr. Gabriel dismisses them to Woodworking. Owen can barely breathe; the unchaperoned pilgrimage

down one flight and two long hallways is the perfect opportunity for
Danny and his thugs to make their move. But Tom latches on to
Owen's side and spends the whole long trudge downstairs chattering in his ear. Owen can barely focus on what he is saying, but nods
every few seconds, when it seems appropriate. He doesn't remember
Tom being so talkative. Danny walks somewhere in the group behind them, so by the time they get to the safety of the Woodworking room, Owen's back is slicked with sweat, the skin between his
shoulder blades rippling with anticipation.

The students go to their cubbies to retrieve their current projects,
spreading out among the six large wooden worktables, a metal vise
at every corner. Mr. Mac—well over six feet tall and clad in a heavy
apron and goggles, sawdust showered over his salt-and-pepper
hair—stands by the electric saw and sander to supervise. During
Owen's absence, the class seems to have advanced; the Schroepfer
twins are sanding the edges of their bookcases, Marcia Flemming is
nailing planks on the top of a folding step stool. Tom, who stakes out
a high stool next to Owen, is painting the individual pieces of his
coffee table art—a dolphin that dives and spins when set on its
curved ocean base. Tom's piece is much more polished and artistic
than anyone else's; Owen finds it flashy and irritating. He can't understand why Tom didn't just make a piece of furniture like everyone else.

Owen has no project waiting for him. He goes to the sample table
where students pick what they want to build from the weathered,
dusty creations of Mr. Mac, who has been supervising the same projects for twenty years. None of the student projects ends up looking
as good as Mr. Mac's samples; the careful sanding of wood and time's
patina make his look like antiques. There is a full wooden train set,
cars connected by tiny magnets, various pieces of small furniture,

puzzles painted first then cut into complicated amoebas with the detail saw. While the process of picking a new project once excited him, now it seems there is nothing Owen wants to make. Mr. Mac comes over with a small plank of wood under his arm.

"We'll be starting string puppets next time," he says to Owen. "Why don't you work on this today?" He has penciled Owen's name onto the plank, in the fat, perfectly formed bubble letters that all the girls try to replicate on their notebooks. Owen is supposed to trace the outlines of the letters with a hammer and fat nail, settling his name permanently into the wood. A few coats of stain and two drilled holes for a string and it will be ready to hang on his bedroom door. Lena made one of these once, as did Hugh. Everyone in the school makes one at some point. Owen already has two himself. It's a babyish project, meant for third-graders, more popular with girls, and Owen's throat tightens at the offering. Perhaps even sweet, un-assuming Mr. Mac, whose layoff has been rumored ever since Propo-sition 2½ but never happens, has heard that Owen is a fag. He doesn't trust himself to speak, so he just nods and takes the plank.

"Do you want a picture on it?" Mr. Mac asks. They're allowed to request a favorite object or hobby next to their name: a kitten, a soc-cer ball, a rainbow, a racecar. Owen once admired Mr. Mac's ability to render a simple cartoon of almost anything, but now he merely shakes his head. His hobbies these days are not the type you put on a bedroom sign. Angels are for girls, and he can't ask for a grave-stone, or a glass thermometer.

Owen spends the rest of the hour hunched over his name, bang-ing the nail at close intervals to create a channel of pressed wood in the penciled curves and angles, while Tom tells him about role-playing games. Owen accidentally smashes the hammer onto his fingertip, cracking the nail and drawing blood. Molly Wood and Rachel Krauss, sitting across from him, scream about his blood being contagious and move to another table. Mr. Mac, looking confused, gives Owen a Band-Aid.

At lunchtime, Tom follows him toward the cafeteria, but Owen veers off with the excuse of the bathroom and goes to the nurse's office instead. He has come prepared, so when the nurse turns her back, he replaces her glass thermometer with one of his own. She clucks when she reads his fever. She calls home and has a brief conversation with his mother, who does most of the talking. When she hangs up, she looks at him, and Owen can't decide if it is with pity or suspicion.

"You can lie down for a while," she says. "But your mother wants you to stay until two. Your father will pick you up after school."

Owen lies on the cot behind the standing screen, staring at a poster about scoliosis. He wonders if the nurse has a chart of AIDS symptoms, hidden away but memorized. When the bell signaling the end of recess rings, he tells her he's feeling better and goes back upstairs.

By the time he gets there, the classroom has already been rearranged for math time tests, and Tom has made sure their desks are next to each other.

"Where'd you go?" he whispers, but Mr. Gabriel barks for quiet, handing out test papers facedown. Owen does worse than ever, finishing only half the page in the allotted four minutes. He's stumbling over sixes and sevens now, doesn't even attempt the eights and nines. Tom is not one of the fastest, but he still finishes in under four minutes. After they hand in their papers and they're putting their desks back, Tom gives Owen a sympathetic pat on the shoulder. Owen freezes, looking around to see if anyone has witnessed this.

"Don't worry," Tom says. "I'll lend you my flash cards."

"I don't want your stupid flash cards," Owen hisses. Tom, who seems incapable of taking a hint, shrugs nonchalantly. For the rest of the afternoon, Owen tries to ignore him, but Tom is oblivious. He keeps chatting at every opportunity, not noticing that Owen never responds, that he merely sits, curled into himself and blushing with rage and disappointment, glancing hopefully over at the only boy in the room who matters.

Owen has returned to school just one day before February break. He is buoyed by the knowledge that he won't have to come back for a week and a half. Mr. Gabriel keeps Danny and Brian Dowd after class, under the vague accusation of disrupting curriculum, giving Owen a head start. Owen says nothing when Tom asks him to wait while he uses the boy's room, then runs away as soon as the door swings shut. He is relieved to see his father already in the queue of cars at the front pick-up area. He climbs in the passenger side, refusing to answer when his father asks about his day. As they wait in traffic held up by the crossing guard, Owen scans the front of the school for Danny, who will soon be let loose from Mr. Gabriel's clutches. He imagines Danny sliding a cigarette from behind his ear and lighting it in the middle of a throng of children unwrapping pieces of Bubble Yum. He wants to see Danny now, wants Danny to look at him, even if it is with the hatred he's afraid of. Anything would be better, he thinks, than not existing in his best friend's eyes.

Instead, he sees Tom, looking befuddled and pathetically eager, his T-shirt tucked hastily and unevenly, scanning the crowd for a glimpse of him. Owen slinks down on the bench seat to below window level. His father taps the turn signal on and drives away.

———

At home, things have deteriorated. His mother's clothes are limp, her nose and chin greasy, her eyelids so swollen from crying they're dimpled. When they come in, she leaves Owen's father in charge of the phone and goes to lie down in her bedroom. Owen looks at his father.

"She didn't get much sleep last night," he says. No suggestion that this could be the beginning of more years spent in bed.

The phone rings and Owen's father picks it up before the first ring is done. He says, "Hello?" eagerly, then his shoulders drop with disappointment.

"She's not available right now. May I ask who's calling?" He listens, looking annoyed. Owen thinks it must be for Lena, until his father speaks again.

"She's fine, David," he says. "It's sort of a family emergency. She'll be back to work soon. I'll tell her you called."

"Isn't that the guy with AIDS?" Owen says, after his father hangs up.

"I think so."

"What did *he* want?"

Owen's father is not looking at him, but at the bulletin board next to the phone where they tack school notices, calendars, and photos of other people's children that come in the mail.

"He was just wondering why she wasn't around," his father says. "Don't you have homework?" he adds.

Owen goes to his room. He sits on his bed, tries to concentrate on the fractions homework, the first in a large stack of sheets he still has to make up. He falls asleep before he finishes it.

He wakes to his father shaking him, in dim light that could be dusk or dawn of the next day. His father's voice sounds distant, not as if he is far away, but as if Owen is going deaf.

"Owen," his father says again, translating what he didn't catch the first time. "Your friend is here."

"Danny?" Owen asks, sitting up in alarm.

"No, the other one. Tom."

Owen is seized by disappointment and relieved of fear all in one instant, and what comes out of the combination is a boiling up of unexpected rage.

"He's not my friend," Owen spits out, angry at his father for being so quick to believe what people tell him. *They'll never find her,* he wants to say, but this would make no sense; they are talking about Tom.

"Owen!" his father scolds. Owen looks up to see Tom standing in the doorway, Owen's forgotten nameplate in his hand. Owen's denial of him has not quite registered enough to wipe all the eagerness from his face. It's the same expression he's had all day, the desperate, overly willing, easily compromised demeanor particular to a child with no friends. Owen despises him.

"He's not my friend," he repeats, glaring at Tom's half-smiling face. This time, it registers. Owen feels an initial jolt of satisfaction, but loses his nerve and looks away before Tom's face can completely fall. He doesn't want to see it as much as he thought. He stays in bed while his father follows behind their guest, offering apologies as Tom runs for the front door.

15. lipstick

In the morning, when I stumble into the kitchen in a flannel shirt and boxer shorts, Lionel is there making pancakes. He's made a huge stack like he's feeding an army, but there's no one else up.

"I made too much mix," Lionel says to me, trying to flip a pancake. He's not very good at it; half gets folded under. He has the burner on too high—and the butter in the pan is turning brown.

"Want one?" he says. I shrug. I'm not sure why he's being so nice all of a sudden, but I don't want to jinx it. I take a plate and he glops butter on and hands me the Aunt Jemima, whose syrup-filled breasts used to embarrass me as a girl.

He sits down at the table with me, lighting a cigarette. I take a bite. The outside of the pancake is burned, but the inside is still raw. I'm trying not to look at it, which means I have to look at Lionel.

"You my brother's girlfriend?" he says. I shrug, trying not to blush at the memory of last night. Sebastian and I rolled around kissing for a while. Nothing serious, but my hip bones are a little sore.

"How old are you?"

"Fifteen."

"Run away?"

I shrug again.

"I just want to know if someone's going to come looking for you."

"Not here," I say.

"Good," he says. He takes a drag of his cigarette and blows the smoke out his nose. He glances at my chest again. He seems to be deciding something.

"You don't really think you'll *find* your brother, do you?" he says. I don't answer this. "I thought they decided he was dead," he says.

"No one decided anything," I say.

"Well, if I were you, I'd ask that slutty girlfriend he had."

"*Emily?*" I say, incredulous.

"Yeah. Emily."

"They broke up," I said. "Way before he disappeared. He was over her."

"Are you kidding? He was totally obsessed with that chick. He never got over her. Everyone knew that."

Something inside me goes very still. Like if I move, take another bite, look up at Lionel, breathe, I'll shatter into tiny pieces. All those pictures of Emily.

"You're just a kid," Lionel says, shaking his head like this is a shame. "How'd you get mixed up with my brother?"

When I don't answer him, he chuckles and goes back to flipping pancakes.

I keep checking the kitchen wall clock, feeling a jolt in my stomach every time I think of the clock in my own kitchen. Of my parents waking up, moving around in the pantry, pounding on my door, finally opening it when they get no answer. It's almost noon by the time Sebastian gets up.

One of Lionel's friends, Max, who I've seen in Hugh's pictures with more hair, wanders into the kitchen in underwear and sunglasses with a can of Coke and a bottle of Tylenol. Lionel asks him if he knows what happened to Emily Twickler.

"She stayed in western Mass," Max says. "After rehab. I think she goes to UMASS Amherst now."

"Let's go there," I say to Sebastian, while he smokes his wake-up joint.

"Why?" he says after an exaggerated exhale.

"She knows something about Hugh."

"Can't you just call her?"

"I need to go somewhere," I say. "It's too late to go home now." Sebastian smiles at this.

"I know the feeling," he says.

Lionel looks up then, from his coffee and *Mad* magazine at the breakfast table. He's wearing a fedora with acid papers and joints stuck along the brim. He squints at us and for a second I think he looks worried, but then he smiles.

"I'll drive you," he says.

"Thanks," I say. Sebastian just glares at him.

"It'll be good for business," Lionel explains. "Amherst kids will take anything."

Lionel's car is a beat-up gray-blue Chevy Impala, with such a big front end it looks like a cartoon version of a car. It sounds like a lawn mower when he starts it up.

"I thought drug dealers had Corvettes," I say to Sebastian, as he throws a duffel bag into the trunk.

"It's his car from high school," Sebastian says. "He's attached to it."

Sebastian pushes the passenger seat forward so I can climb in back. I have to shove aside cassette tapes, McDonald's bags, and what appears to be dirty underwear to sit down. The car smells like our old station wagon used to—like people have been smoking in it without rolling the windows down for about twenty years.

We stop in Harvard Square where I go to the bank and take out the rest of my savings—seventy-five dollars. Lionel and Sebastian talk to some people in the Pit, sell a few joints, smoke two, and generally act like they're in no hurry at all. By the time we get on the highway, it's six o'clock and already dark.

The Pixies are blaring from the tape player, and both Sebastian and Lionel are chain-smoking and sticking their finished Marlboros out the window cracks, letting the red embers fly away behind us. I'm cold and hungry and not interested in smoking for once. I eat a little stale Smartfood from a bag I find in the backseat, then stretch out, using Hugh's jacket as a pillow. His camera is in my backpack, on the floor of the car.

When the tape ends, Lionel asks Sebastian if I'm asleep and I close my eyes just as Sebastian turns around to check.

"What's your deal with this girl?" Lionel says. I can hear the creak of Sebastian's leather shoulders as he shrugs.

"No deal," Sebastian mutters.

"You should be careful with her," Lionel says. "She's still a kid."

"What am I, an old man?" Sebastian jokes.

"You're getting there," Lionel says. Then the sound of him spitting angrily out the window. "I've been talking to Mom and Dad," he adds.

Everything is so quiet for a minute I'd swear they are both holding their breath.

"Since when do you talk to them?" Sebastian says quietly.

"Since I think you should go home," Lionel says. He pushes the cigarette lighter in to heat up. They both wait an eternity for it to pop back out.

"Are you out of your fucking mind?" Sebastian finally squeaks. Lionel inhales on a new cigarette and puts the lighter back in.

"You should go back to school," he says. "You used to be good at it."

"But," Sebastian starts, his voice shaking, his hands fumbling for a cigarette. "But you *hate* them. You think they're the worst fucking parents in the world!"

"Yeah, well." Lionel sighs. "They're the only parents you've got." He says this without enthusiasm.

"Are you on X?" Sebastian says.

"No."

"Well, you're on something. There's no way I'm going back there. You can't make me." Sebastian sounds suddenly young, whining like Owen trying to get out of a day at school.

"I'm not supplying you anymore," Lionel says.

"So? You're not the only drug dealer in Cambridge."

"I want you out of the professor's house when we get back," Lionel adds.

"You're a fucking *pussy*," Sebastian says. I open my eyes just in time to see him rub angrily at his wet cheeks. "You're the biggest fucking pussy I know. Everyone thinks so. And I don't need shit from you."

"Whatever," Lionel says, flicking his turn signal on. He pulls off the highway into a rest stop with a McDonald's and a gas station.

"Hey, Boy George," he calls back to me. "Gotta pee?"

Lionel lets me out on his side and starts pumping gas. I go inside and use the ladies' room. When I come back out with fries for everyone, Lionel thanks me, but Sebastian just stares out his window, refusing to look at either one of us.

After two years my father was the only one still searching for Hugh. Organizations that were committed in the beginning fell off one by one, some out of lost hope, others because of confrontations I wasn't supposed to hear about but did anyway. The police officially filed Hugh's disappearance as unsolved. The Catholic church gave up after my father freaked out over what the CCD teacher said to Owen. Kids who had been my father's students at the time of Hugh's disappearance graduated and the new ones didn't volunteer to help. The calling room at the PBS station was taken away after three months because they needed it for their annual fund-raiser. The only official agency keeping an eye out for Hugh was the National Center for Missing Children. They still printed his face on milk cartons and accidentally sent us the donation appeal meant for families with children safe at home. I learned on a television news special that the pictures of kids who go missing when they are babies and toddlers had to be updated by an artist every year, to adjust for who they might have grown into. These altered photos looked slightly wrong, alien, like children in Halloween masks. No one did this for Hugh. He was old enough when he left, I guess, to have his permanent face.

I wasn't sure exactly how my father was looking for him. Sometimes he went to New York or D.C., I guess to walk around with the fliers, hoping to run into someone who had seen Hugh. He made a lot of phone calls, but the phone rarely rang back. He spent all the time he was not in class downstairs in his office, poring over old police reports. He didn't come upstairs for my amateur attempts at dinner. I did all the cooking by then. Even the neighbors stopped bringing casseroles.

I only knew how to make three things: tacos, creamed tuna and peas, and Shake 'n Bake chicken. Sometimes Owen and I ate Ellio's pizza or cereal. I would make up plates for my parents, even though they never ate them. My father ate on campus, came home smelling of fries and cole slaw. My mother ate ice cream late at night when she thought no one else was up. This was the only time she left the bedroom, despite a number of doctors' visits and a bedside table covered with prescription bottles. She occasionally made an effort to act motherly, inviting Owen in to watch cartoons on her small TV, or asking me to sit on the bed for girl talk.

She tried to talk to me about puberty. Even though my chest was as flat as a boy's, and I didn't have even one pubic hair, my mother seemed to think that because I was twelve I would explode any day. She gave me a book, *Changing Bodies, Changing Lives,* and told me to come back with any questions. I hid the book behind the *Little House on the Prairie* series on my bookcase, mortified by the idea that, since she rarely left the house, it was probably my father who'd actually bought it. I'd already learned all about that stuff in Human Development in the fifth grade.

My mother's puberty talks always took a turn—she'd go from chatting about pads versus tampons, to collapsing against the pillows as if she'd been pressed by an invisible weight. Tears leaked from her eyes, her nose flooded, and she started apologizing.

"I'm such a burden to you," she'd say. Or, "You have more on your plate than a normal twelve-year-old girl. Don't think I don't know that." Worst of all, "I wouldn't blame you if you hated me."

I couldn't stand it. This was nothing like the way my mother used to be. Now I was the one who never cried, who clenched her teeth and didn't complain. I stroked my mother's back as she sobbed and said the same thing over and over, even though I was pretty sure she didn't hear it.

"Daddy's going to find him."

When we get to the town of Amherst, Lionel drives around the UMASS campus for a while, looking for parties to crash. While we're stopped behind a campus bus, Sebastian jumps out of the car and pushes the seat forward.

"Come on," he says to me. I scramble for my jacket and camera bag.

"Give it a rest, Sebastian," Lionel says. "How are you going to get home?" The bus pulls out and the car behind the Chevy honks.

"Who says I'm going home?" Sebastian says. "Have a nice life." He walks away, leaving me to slam the heavy door. I feel like I should say something to Lionel, so I lean down to look in the open window. But he waves me away.

"Have fun babysitting," he says, putting the car in gear. I straighten up and he peels away.

I have to jog after Sebastian, who has gone down a hill toward a frozen pond.

"Wait up," I call out, but he doesn't. It's freezing, and I struggle with the zipper on Hugh's jacket.

I catch up when Sebastian sits on a bench and rummages in his pockets for cigarettes.

"Do you have any weed?" he says to me. I shake my head. "Fuck," he says. "My stash is in that prick's trunk."

"I'm sorry," I say, meaning sorry for a number of things, but Sebastian brushes me off.

"Got a smoke?" he says, crumpling his empty pack. We sit quietly smoking for a moment, our breath billowing with cold long after the smoke is out of our lungs.

"How will we find Emily?" I say. "This place is huge."

"We have to score first," Sebastian says. "Don't you want to get stoned?"

The answer to that is *not really*, but technically he isn't asking me anyway. He is rarely not at least a little stoned. It took me a while to figure this out. That he doesn't just do drugs because he feels like it, but because he needs them. Before Sebastian, I always thought drug addicts were dangerous lunatics. I didn't know they could be regular people who got needy and annoying when sober.

We walk back to the center of town where there are more people. Sebastian goes over to talk to a group of college kids outside a bar while I wait in front of a bulletin board. There's an ad for the movie *Ferris Bueller's Day Off* tacked next to notices offering babysitting. I watch Sebastian whisper into the ear of a tall girl with dyed black hair and a dog collar around her skinny neck. She takes him around the corner and out of sight. Suddenly, I don't want to do any of this: find Emily, wait for Sebastian, run away from home. I'd like to be back in my bedroom, warm and dry in my bed, before my life became irreversible. The problem is, that would be when I was about ten.

Sebastian comes back in twenty minutes, stoned and himself again. Before I can get mad at him, he walks right up close and moves a piece of frozen hair away from my forehead.

"Hey, gorgeous," he whispers, his mouth really close to mine. "Want to go to a party?"

And all that matters is the possibility that he might kiss me again.

On the walk to the party he offers me a pill, and though I have no idea what it is, I swallow it with a sip from the beer he must have gotten from that girl. I have surprised him. I usually ask what things are before I toss them down.

It starts to snow, the kind of snow that glints off everything, which when I was little Hugh called "sparkly snow." We pass a line of pay phones and it occurs to me that I should call my parents just to tell them I'm not dead. But I sail past the phones like something in a dream I can't reach. I try to tell Sebastian to slow down, but my tongue is stuck in my mouth like a sliver of old soap to a soap dish. I'm convinced that if I could move my tongue I'd make more sense than I ever have in my life.

We get to a house that is away from town on a quiet residential street. All the overhead light bulbs have been replaced with blue or red, so it's like moving through a darkroom or a horror movie. Some people in a corner of the living room wave Sebastian over, and he takes my hand to lead me through the crowd. Each conversation we pass leaves me with just a few words, but I think I'd understand it all if I could pause and concentrate.

We sit down on floor pillows at a round glass-topped coffee table.

There are two long-haired, heavy-lidded guys and the girl who got Sebastian stoned. She is anorexic-skinny, her collarbone popping out between her skimpy camisole top and the dog collar. She has short hair she has combed back to look wet and a lot of eye makeup that has started to smudge. She doesn't say hello to me, just Sebastian, and it looks like it's been a really long time since she smiled. She leans over the glass table and snorts a line of coke through a piece of straw cut short for this purpose. She wipes her nose, sniffling loudly, and passes all the equipment—little mirror, credit card, and straw—along to the guy next to her. He has been staring at her breasts, which are barely more than nipples. She sees me staring at her, too. She reminds me of someone and I'm staring because I'm trying to figure out who. I look away when she glares a challenge at me.

Sebastian doesn't bother to introduce me to anyone. I look around the room while they concentrate on their coke. Though it looks the same as a party at Lionel's, it's not. The girls here seem less giggly and don't cluster together, all of them bold enough to wander around and walk straight into conversations. It's like the difference between sophomores and seniors in the Quad. I wonder if these girls found themselves by going to college, or if they were the type who knew who they were and what they wanted all along.

Sebastian interrupts my watching by passing me the coke. I've never done it before. It burns the back of my throat, and my nose immediately starts running. I wipe it on a cocktail napkin and do another line. I light a cigarette and wait to feel different.

Sebastian hands me a plastic cup of purple drink. It's cold and sweet and easy to swallow. After two drinks and a few turns at the mirror, I'm starting to miss what everyone else is saying. I feel like my head is trying to walk off on its own, maybe somewhere quiet where it can think and remember. But I'm not moving. I have that calm fear somewhere in the middle of my chest that always tells me when I've had too much of something, but I don't care this time so I have another drink and another two lines. For whole long minutes linked together I forget everything—where we are, who I'm supposed to be, the location of my mouth, which hand holds my drink, the image of them waiting at home for me. And then I remember again, all of it at once, and it's too much, and the whole process, which keeps repeating itself, is pretty exhausting. I'd like to just keep remembering, either that or stay in the fog where I can't even figure out how to grab my drink. One or the other. It's the moving between them that hurts too much.

"Stop fidgeting," Sebastian says in my ear, and it takes me a minute to even realize what he means. I've been bouncing my knees under the table, vibrating the whole top without even knowing I was doing it. My mother used to get exasperated by this when we were little. She'd put out milk glasses and they'd move across the table. My father always said it's fast minds who fidget to keep from overloading. Which made me feel stupid, because Hugh was the fidgeter. My knees always stayed where they were told.

Sebastian doesn't seem to care that Anorexia is tapping her maroon fingernails on the table in a frenzy. I make myself stop my knees, but then Sebastian has to put his hand on them again. Apparently they keep going no matter what I do. Everyone at the table is looking at me.

"She's freaking," Anorexia says with a smile, and though I'm not, just having her say it makes me feel like I am. They all lean forward to check out my eyes, as if there are answers in my pupils. Sebastian must have told them that I'm a girl.

"Give her something," someone says, and Sebastian hands me a pill to swallow with my drink. I don't know why they're picking on me all of a sudden, when I've been sitting quietly without bothering anyone. It's Anorexia who started it. She probably wants to go back to being the only girl in a group of guys. I know, because it's what I always want. It's me she reminds me of.

"Take her outside or something," one of the guys says. Everyone is now looking like there's something grossly wrong with me, and I don't really appreciate it. It's like being told you have something between your teeth when you don't.

Sebastian helps me stand up and puts his arm around me to walk outside. I hope Anorexia sees this and reads into it, though his arm doesn't feel very sweet or boyfriendlike. It feels more like he's carting another guy away.

Outside he props me against a high wooden fence.

"Knock it off," I say when he grabs my shoulders and shakes. "What's your problem?" The snow must have turned to rain. It feels like every inch of me is being dripped upon by steady, relentless drops. They're getting into the collar of my shirt.

"Stop freaking on me," Sebastian says.

"What are you talking about? I haven't even said anything all night. Why does everyone think I'm freaking out?"

"Because you're crying," Sebastian says. "You've been crying for like an hour without stopping."

I laugh. I blink away drops and look behind his face. It is still snowing. My face is soaking wet, my nose running from the coke. "I don't cry," I say, but even as I say it I feel something. A familiar heaving sensation that I haven't felt since I was little, the one where you have to gasp like some sort of dying animal to catch your breath in between sobs.

The year after Hugh disappeared we ignored Christmas, no tree or presents except for what came in the mail from our grandmother. The next year, to make it up to us, my father decided we should all

go to the annual Theology Department party. My mother refused, so
he brought me and Owen. We had to wear jeans and sweaters since
we'd both outgrown our holiday clothes.

At the party Owen ran off with a group of kids playing hide-and-
seek in the upper sections of the Jesuit library. There was no one my
age, so I shadowed my father for a while, mumbling answers to professors' questions about school, my favorite books, whether I had a
boyfriend, what I wanted to be when I grew up. Once, when I was
five, I caused a stir by telling a Jesuit that I wanted to be a priest. But
it was usually Hugh who got attention at these parties. He was the
kind of kid who grown-ups actually liked to talk to.

I went to the ladies' room and watched a tall woman lean over
the sink to apply lipstick, her face close to the mirror. The plum-
colored lipstick transformed her, making her look brighter, more
there than she was with her naked mouth. She dabbed some beige
makeup on her nose and over a pimple on her chin, blending it in
with her fingers. She looked fuzzier, but pretty. Her hair was blond,
pulled back into a flawless bun, and rhinestones sparkled on the clip
that held it all together. She smiled at me on her way out. Girls in my
class wore Kissing Potion flavored lip gloss and strawberry blush, but
I didn't. I looked at myself in the mirror and wondered how I'd lived
twelve years without noticing how unremarkable I was.

When I got back to the party, I couldn't find my father. Owen had
been bullied by an older boy and was now wheezing, clinging to my
side and asking to go home. I asked Father Brian, who once came
regularly to our house for dinner, if he knew where my father was.

"Probably in his office, Pet," Father Brian said. "He's never been
one for the parties. Come, I've the key to upstairs."

I left Owen with a professor's wife and followed Father Brian up
a set of gloomy stone stairs. My father's office was at the end of a
long hall lined with stained-glass windows. We could see his light

shining through the frosted-glass transom. Father Brian put a finger to his lips and tried to make me laugh by tiptoeing down the hall. I didn't have the heart to tell him I'd outgrown this game years ago.

When we opened the door, my first impression was that there were too many limbs. My father, his tweed back to the door, was sprouting extra milky arms and legs like some sort of monster. Then I saw the long, white stockings and how my father was pressed between them, and the womanly arms, which clung to his back in a hug that was way too tight, the kind you gave when you were upset or excited. By the time I distinguished two heads they had moved apart.

It was the woman from the bathroom, a section of her hair yanked from its bun, her eyes having a hard time catching up to the interruption. Her plum lipstick was almost gone, only a light smear outlined her mouth. The majority of the color was on my father's mouth now, which looked like a bruise, hanging open, with nothing to say. Father Brian closed the door and walked me back down to the party, holding my arm with the same gentle pressure I had seen him use to guide people through funerals.

My father got fired. The plum woman turned out to be a theology student, one of his research assistants for the abandoned angel book. They had been letting him slide for a while, since Hugh's disappearance, out of charity. He hadn't published anything in years, and there were complaints from students about unprepared lectures and incomplete office hours. I overheard all this when Father Brian came by the house to talk to him. My father cried and begged, and Father Brian said he'd pray for him.

Later that night, my mother put on a robe and slippers and went downstairs to his office. She was down there for two hours, and only twice did I hear the pitch of her voice rise above a whisper. She came back up and, passing by my room, opened the door abruptly.

"Are you getting a divorce?" I said.

She reached out a thin pale arm and turned the switch on my clip-on lamp, dropping me into darkness.

"It's time you went to sleep," she said.

It takes almost an hour for Sebastian and I to trudge through the snow to a strip mall where we find a motel. I have to pay the guy at the desk $39.95 for the room. He gives us a key and we look for room 285 down a hallway of identical blue doors. Inside is a stale-smelling room with a huge bed covered in a floral polyester spread, a TV, and a tiny bathroom in the corner.

Sebastian decides I need a shower, though I am cleaner than he is. He takes my clothes off while I stand on the bathroom mat. This could be sexy except for the fact that I'm still crying and he's not looking as he does it, so it's more like babysitting. He turns on the water and slides open the frosted-glass door, holding my arm while I step over the tub lip. He sits on the toilet and smokes while I'm in there, as if he thinks I might drown. I hold my face under the stream of water that is stronger than my crying, hoping to wash it away. There is no soap or shampoo, so I just stand there for a while, letting the water pressure beat the gel and grease from my hair. When there's nothing left to do, I turn off the shower and Sebastian hands me a tiny towel before leaving the bathroom. Apparently he trusts me to dry off by myself. I put my T-shirt back on, which smells like Lionel's car, and abandon my underwear. I wish there was a razor to shave my legs.

When I come out Sebastian gives me a blue pill. He opens the bed for me and pulls the stiff covers up over my shoulders when I lie down.

"Aren't you getting in?" I say.

"I thought I'd sleep on the floor," he says.

"Why?" I say. "I'm not crying anymore."

"I don't want to confuse you," he says.

"You'll confuse me if you don't," I say.

So he gets into bed. I can't help feeling a little awful about it, like I begged him. Like maybe he's here because he feels sorry for me and he'd rather be back at the party with Anorexia. This makes me kiss him a little harder and faster than I really want to. And when he kisses back, when his breath gets ragged and he starts to look sort of distant and intensely focused at the same time, and a little mean, kind of like he doesn't recognize me even as he presses into me, at the same point at Lionel's where I got really scared and lonely and went limp so he would stop, this time I don't. This time I kiss him harder and make my own little demanding whimpers and press my hips up. Even though I don't mean any of it and want to stop and wish his eyes would go back to normal, still I let him take off my T-shirt and even help him undo his pants as though I'm proving something by doing this. Even at the last second, when his arms are shaking as he holds himself above me and he says *You sure?*, which is my chance to get out of it, I nod and even act like I'm a little impatient for him to hurry up. It's not until he pushes inside me and the pain makes me gasp out loud that I know I could have stopped him any time tonight, any time in the last few days, that I could still stop him now. But I didn't. I don't. I let him keep having sex with me even as I lie there wondering why I am letting him.

16. underoos

The door to Lena's room is wide open now, the walls lit starkly by a bare overhead bulb, a skeleton of hardware where there was once a milk-glass globe, broken in a game of indoor basketball when the room was still Hugh's. The contents of the room have been combed for evidence and tidied in the process, leaving behind an unnatural neatness that makes it look even more abandoned. As if, now that it has been cleaned up, Lena is never coming back. Like Hugh's room after he was gone, which Owen can't remember as anything but tidy and waiting, the bed made up, top sheet folded down in expectation.

She has only been missing for two days, but there are rumors sprouting like mushrooms in the neighborhood. Owen overhears the theories of her disappearance from nine-year-old Jason Lank two houses down. A black van with tinted windows has been cruising the neighborhood, a former child molester out on parole moved next door to Mr. and Mrs. Stein, the elderly Holocaust survivors local children are afraid to speak to. Owen doesn't bother to correct Jason or tell him the things he hears reported in his own kitchen. The chief informing his parents, with the gravity of a man reporting the discovery of a body, how they have checked Lena's bank account. She has emptied the cash from her savings.

Owen's parents go back to making phone calls to every parent in the sophomore class. His mother has not retreated to bed this time, but Owen is sure she will. He stops Chief Brody on his way out.

"Someone could have made her take that money out," Owen says. The chief sighs.

"Possible, kiddo," he says. "But unlikely." He puts a hand on Owen's shoulder, heavy with pity, and looks as if he is about to let him in on something. Tell him that his sister has run away. And that this is different—not as deserving of his time as a real missing child.

"Aren't you the one who never found my brother?" Owen says.

The chief, like everyone else these days, seems more baffled than hurt by Owen's meanness. This makes Owen furious. No one takes him seriously.

On Friday, his parents are gone by the time he wakes up. No one has told him anything, so Owen hangs around for the morning. By noon, he is bored, so he sneaks out the back door to avoid the police car he assumes is still out front. He doesn't bother to leave a note. They are too worried about Lena to think about him. He learned this yesterday after wandering off to the corner store for a Snickers bar, then running back without even buying it, terrified that he had caused them worry. No one noticed him gone. No one has offered him a meal in days; he grazes in the refrigerator when he's hungry, like the rest of them.

He walks for twenty minutes up and then down St. Paul Street, turns right onto Aspinwall, then left into Brookline Village. St. Mary's Church commands a whole corner, the statue of the Virgin looking a bit more battered than he remembers her. The blue of her gown is chipped and mildew grows like eczema over her cheeks. It is a weekday, masses are long over, but the heavy carved doors at the top of the stone stairway are unlocked. Owen steps in and stops to let his eyes adjust. Though the hanging lantern fixtures are fitted with bulbs, the sanctuary is never more than dimly lit. He walks around to the left aisle because the center looks imposing and official, as if he needs more of a Catholic education to be allowed to stroll up it. There is something he is supposed to do before getting in a pew, something like a dip or a curtsy he remembers his parents performing, but he's not sure how it's done, so he merely hunches as he slides into a bench just before the altar.

Everything is the same. Each thing he sees makes him remember it, as though these objects and smells have been there all along, locked in a cubby of his brain, and now that they're out he can't imagine not remembering them. It scares him, the fact that things can hide in your own mind. Fool you into believing you don't remember them, then reappear and pretend they've been right in front of you all along.

The mahogany pews are the same: old scars trapped under new polish, slick with layers of polyurethane and the residue of countless gripping hands. The maroon cushions are worn to pink in places and smell musty. On the back of each pew, at two-foot intervals, are small brass clips to hold music sheets or missals. When they were still going to church, and his parents were up for communion or simply not paying attention, Lena and Owen competed to see who could hold their fingertip the longest beneath these clips. He does it now, automatically, the memory blooming along with his movements. The clip seems to grip harder the longer he holds his finger in there. He used to let his nail turn almost purple before giving up. Still, Lena was always tougher. Now he wonders if it was Hugh who taught her this game in the first place.

Owen looks up at the ceiling where fat babies with wings float on clouds in pockets of painted blue sky. Behind the altar is a complicated carving of white marble turrets he once imagined was the gate to an entire secret city. On either side of this centerpiece are two tall stained-glass windows. Two men in robes, strong wings rising from their backs. One is dark-haired and brooding, the other fair and innocent. They are labeled Saint Gabriel and Saint Michael. It is these angels he has come to see. After Hugh went missing, before his father took them out of church, Owen spent the long boring mass, much of which he barely understood, staring at these two. Lit by mid-morning sun, glowing in the rich purples and greens of stained glass, their faces amber, their wings folded behind them, they made him think, long before that fateful conversation with his CCD teacher, of his missing brother. Michael in his blond innocence and Gabriel with his dark suggestion of danger. Their features were similar, as though they were related, a good and a bad twin. They made Owen think of the transformation of his brother, from soft-haired ninth-grader to a punk he could barely remember. They reminded him that anyone, even someone you'd known your whole life, could become unrecognizable.

Even Owen's prayers have an edge now. They have lost the sweet, easygoing quality he has begun to associate with a former version of himself.

"You're the one who can find her," he says to the image of his brother set in broken glass. "And you know it."

When he leaves the church, the first thing he sees is the back of a green-and-white-striped rugby shirt, a boy hunched and shivering on the stone steps, who he assumes to be one of Danny's friends staking him out. He is relieved, and then annoyed, when he sees that it is Tom Fisher.

"What are *you* doing here?" Owen says. Tom stands up. He looks silly in casual clothing, as if he is trying to disguise himself as a normal child. Owen has never seen him in anything but a white oxford shirt and khakis, occasionally accessorized with a pilled wool sweater. When he transferred last year from a private school it was rumored that his mother refused to believe there was no uniform. Owen wonders where his coat is, but doesn't want Tom to think he cares.

"I need to talk to you," Tom says.

"Are you *following* me?"

"Yes," Tom says, as if this is completely reasonable. "As I just said, I need to talk to you."

"Maybe I don't want to talk to you," Owen says. He takes the stairs two at a time, passing by Tom in a huff. But Tom follows, matching Owen's quick pace.

"You had no right to treat me like that," Tom says. His voice wobbles but he speaks carefully, as if he's been practicing what to say. "I've never been anything but nice to you."

There are so many things about this speech that infuriate Owen that, for a moment, he can't respond. He's still recovering from the indignity of being followed, and now, the straightforwardness, the maturity of Tom's confrontation makes him so furious he accidentally bites down on the inside of his mouth. This is what has bothered him about Tom all along; this is why Tom has no friends. He speaks like a grown-up, addresses things directly, does not play by a kid's rules. He makes the normal comebacks of an eleven-year-old sound ridiculous.

Owen tries one anyway. "Queer," he scoffs, under his breath, a dismissive snort in his throat.

"I bet you can't look at me and say that," Tom says. Owen has no response to this. He has never, not for as long as he can remember, spoken his mind the way that Tom does. No one else he knows does so, either. People are cruel to one another and never say a word about it. Bad things happen and are never mentioned again. Why is Tom allowed to fight back when Owen is required to keep everything inside? And why does he refuse to be driven away?

Owen trudges on, barely watching where he's going, hoping only that his pace and refusal to look will make Tom give up before he reaches home.

He doesn't notice that he's leading them by the shortcut he avoided on the way here, until they come upon the main gates of the graveyard. Owen pauses, scanning the landscape, and Tom, who has been trailing him with blind determination, almost runs into him.

"Is there a problem?" Tom asks, when Owen continues to stand there.

"*Is there a problem?*" Owen mimics, his voice high-pitched and prissy. He can't see the whole graveyard from this gate. If he continues by the road and goes around it, it will be far out of the way and obvious to Tom that he's avoiding something.

"That was unnecessary," Tom quips, and Owen stomps ahead into the graveyard without answering.

They are well inside the grounds and have turned left past the Civil War monument before he sees Danny. He is sitting up high, on top of a tomb, his long, stained jean legs swinging in boredom beneath him. He raises a brown-bagged bottle to his full lips. He appears to be alone. Danny spies them, lowers the bottle, and in the delay while he swallows, Owen dares to believe that it will be all right. He takes three more steps forward, large, enthusiastic steps, as if he is walking toward his best friend rather than his doom.

Danny swallows hard and lets out a delighted whoop.

"Hey, boys," he bellows. "Look who's decided to make this our lucky day."

Owen stops walking when he sees Brian Dowd and Mark Flint stepping out from behind the monument. He looks behind him, calculating the chances of running for it. Tom Fisher stands there, hands on his hips, looking disapproving and powerless, like an old lady trying to reason with bank robbers. He's not going to run, Owen realizes with a renewed surge of anger. He's going to try to talk to them. And Owen, even if he summons his meanest self, cannot leave him there alone. He turns back around.

Danny jumps from his perch and the three of them glide into a predatory circle, enclosing Owen and Tom in a small cluster of white granite graves. Danny is smiling, his gaze flashy but unfocused, and Owen can tell he is either stoned or drunk, possibly both.

"What do we have here?" he drawls in an imitation of a television bad guy, which would be laughable if it weren't for the glint of raw rage Owen can detect behind his toothy smile.

"You look a little pale, Furey," Danny says. "I hear you're pretty sick." Owen opens his mouth to protest, then decides against it. It doesn't matter what he says now.

"Who's your boyfriend?" Danny asks. His cronies smile on cue.

"Haven't you guys always wondered what fags do when they're alone together?" Danny says. Brian takes the bait and guffaws, nodding in agreement. Mark, who seems to have taken the question literally, looks unsure.

"I bet Owen and Tommy will give us a little show, if we ask nice," Danny adds. Brian laughs again, fidgeting with delight and grunting, like a dog about to be given a treat.

"You've never made sense to me, Danny Gray," Tom says calmly.

"Oh, no?" Danny laughs, seeming delighted that Tom has decided to help things along.

"No. I thought you were too smart to be a thug. Apparently I was wrong."

Danny's smile evaporates. He nods, as if considering something, and steps forward, putting one hand on Tom's shoulder. Tom looks quizzically at the hand while Danny brings his other fist slamming into his stomach. Tom drops to his knees in the terrified silent paralysis of someone who's had the wind knocked out of him. His face grows red and desperate, and he looks up at Owen for help. Part of Owen wants to kneel down and explain the physics of it all, how his breath will come back if he waits, because Tom looks as though this has never happened to him before. But he doesn't want to give Danny any more bait. Another part of him is annoyed. What did he expect, insulting Danny to his face? It's not Owen's job to hold Tom's hand through this.

"Hold him down," Danny barks, and Brian and Mark dive for Tom, pushing him back so he's lying with a gravestone at his head. They each pin one of his arms to the ground, digging their knees into his shoulder sockets for extra security. Tom's face contorts in pain.

"Let me go, you morons," Tom wheezes as soon as his breath is back. They settle their grips and look to Danny for instruction.

Danny takes out a cigarette and a matchbook, lights it, inhales, and tosses the still-burning match at Tom. It lands on Tom's stomach, where the rugby shirt has ridden up in his struggles, sticking for a brief second before Tom's thrusting flicks it off. A small, red welt is left in the spot where it briefly smoldered.

Owen is not sure how things have gotten out of control so fast. If this were one of Danny's games, his role now would be to push it further. But what rules apply if it's real? He wonders suddenly if the games themselves were supposed to be real all along.

Owen glances at Tom again. He looks terrified now, and loyalty rises in Owen like a rush of adrenaline.

"Leave him alone," he says to Danny. "He's got nothing to do with this."

"He's your new boyfriend," Danny says simply. "He asked for this, just like you did."

Something occurs to Owen then, and he throws it out before wondering if it's wise.

"What's that make you, my *ex*-boyfriend?" Owen says, trying to keep his voice from shaking. He gestures to Brian and Mark, holding down the no longer struggling Tom. "They're going to think you're jealous."

Though he knows on one level what he has done, he is still surprised at the look that lowers over Danny's face. He actually changes color, his amber skin growing a deep russet, his eyes retreating under his brows with fury. For an instant, Owen thinks he looks hurt. Then he sees nothing but danger.

"Take his pants off," Danny says to Brian and Mark, who are eagerly awaiting a response to Owen's challenge. This seems to baffle them, though, and they continue to look up, waiting for an instruction that makes sense.

"Take his fucking pants off," Danny says, enraged at their hesitation. He reaches behind his back, under his army jacket, and pulls his father's gun out from the waistband of his jeans. Owen has been waiting to see it. They've been practicing for this all along.

Mark takes over, holding both of Tom's arms while Brian unbuttons and unzips his jeans, which Owen notices now have been ironed so there is a crease running down the front of each leg.

"Look," Brian calls out with delight, "Underoos!"

The briefs Tom is wearing are decorated like the uniform of Spider-Man. Despite what happens next, Owen will remember this later as the worst moment of all—that glimpse of Tom's underwear, a fashion meant for a seven-year-old, clearly a vestige from childhood he has held on to, the image of a superhero's belt stretched out of shape across his groin.

"Danny," Owen says in a low voice. "Please stop."

Danny, who has been holding the gun by his side, now points it at him.

"What did you say?" he says. He gestures with the gun and Owen flinches. He tries to remember whether Danny knows where his mother keeps the bullets.

"Show us how you do it, Furey," Danny says. "We want to see you suck dick."

Tom, whose jeans are now bunched at his ankles, makes a small, miserable noise, pressing his shaking thighs together and bending his knees up to cover himself. Owen just stares at Danny, still waiting for that moment where Danny laughs and calls it all off. But Danny doesn't budge.

"I can't," Owen says finally. What he wants to say is that he doesn't know how. But he can see this won't go over well.

"Take his underwear off," Danny says to Brian. Brian pins Tom's legs down with his knee, then hesitates, his fingers spread over the area, uncertain about going so far. As if he, too, is waiting for Danny to fold.

"Do it!" Danny yells. Brian sticks two fingers of each hand under the elastic band decorated to look like Spider-Man's belt and pulls. He has to fight, as Tom presses his butt into the ground to hold them on. Eventually, with a tearing noise, he succeeds, jostling Tom's pink, curled-up penis. Tom closes his eyes and averts his head, the tears he has been fighting run over the bridge of his nose.

Danny steps forward and presses the barrel of the gun against Owen's temple.

"Do it," he says. He presses hard, forcing Owen down to his knees. "Or you'll be as dead as your faggot of a brother."

Owen drops to his knees, the gun such a sharp pain in his head, he wonders if Danny has fired. His vision pops with silver swimming circles. Just before what he later learns is the moment he passes out, he sees a figure standing a few graves away, backlit by weak winter sun. It is the rescue he has been waiting for. His brother, wearing boots and a long black overcoat, his face, hair, expression, and everything Owen once knew about him shadowed by the full extension of his muscular wings.

When Owen comes to and sees his fifth-grade teacher, he thinks he has fallen asleep in class and wonders how much of the last winter has been a dream. But then he sees gray sky framing Mr. Gabriel, and feels the cold ground beneath his throbbing head.

"I think you hit it on the stone," Mr. Gabriel says, helping Owen sit up. Owen's skull feels like it has split in two, the pain escalating like an unbearable noise. He looks carefully around. Tom is sitting, fully dressed, against a nearby headstone, knees pulled to his chest.

He won't look at Owen and is trying very hard to stop crying, wiping angrily at the stubborn tears with his sleeve. There is a strange man behind him, sitting a few graves away as if waiting politely for an invitation to comfort him.

"Where . . ." Owen starts. Mr. Gabriel leans against a grave, half sitting so he is closer to Owen's level, putting his hands on his thighs.

"They ran off," he says. "Not before Danny took a shot at me, though."

"He *shot* you?" Owen shrieks.

"Missed, of course. He seems to know how to threaten with a gun, but not much about aiming it."

"But if he got away . . ." Owen hears the panic in his voice.

"Don't worry, he dropped it." Mr. Gabriel shows him the pistol, wrapped in a handkerchief and stowed in the pocket of his long wool coat. He jingles the leftover bullets in his deep pants pocket.

"As soon as we get you home, I'll call the police."

"The police are at my house," Owen mutters. Mr. Gabriel smiles, something he does so rarely in class that he looks like a different person. The lines around his mouth conform to this smile, suggesting that, in his private life, he does not wear the scowl he is famous for.

"I'm going home," Owen hears. Tom is standing now, his arms crossed, shivering from more than cold.

"I don't think you should go alone, Tom," Mr. Gabriel says. "Wait one minute and we'll leave together."

"No," Tom says firmly, glancing at Owen and then away. "I'm going now." Mr. Gabriel sighs.

"You might have to give a statement to the police later. I can help you explain things to your mother."

"I just want to go home," Tom repeats. Owen flinches at the sound of a sob held back in Tom's throat.

"Mike?" Mr. Gabriel calls. The strange man, who has turned his back to it all out of apparent respect for privacy, stands up and turns around. He is younger than Mr. Gabriel and handsome, with gel in his short blond hair, wearing a trendy leather jacket and Levi's. He has a glinting gold hoop in one ear.

"Walk Tom home, okay?" Mr. Gabriel says. "I'll call his mother later."

"C'mon, buddy," the guy says, smiling gently. He doesn't try to touch Tom, simply follows alongside him toward the exit.

"Can you walk?" Mr. Gabriel asks when they're out of sight. Owen nods. He braces himself on a white granite slab and stands up, the pain shooting anew from the back of his head down his neck. Mr. Gabriel takes hold of his arm to steady him, then lets go. They begin to walk the opposite direction from Mike and Tom, toward the back gate that lets out a street away from Owen's house.

As they walk, Owen starts to wonder how much Mr. Gabriel saw before Danny fired the gun. When Mr. Gabriel clears his throat, he is sure he is about to ask for an explanation. But what he says is unexpected.

"I had your brother in my class."

"I know," Owen says wearily. He has had teachers say this before, praise his brother's memory as if they expect Owen will not live up to it. If they didn't have Hugh, they had Lena. The worst teachers are the ones who had both. Owen can't hide from them.

"Smart kid," Mr. Gabriel says. "Couldn't do multiplication tables to save his life, though."

Owen looks up. "Really?" he says.

"Time tests." Mr. Gabriel smiles. "They were his worst subject."

"Huh," Owen says. He can't think of anything to say to this.

"You must miss him still," Mr. Gabriel says. Owen stiffens.

"I can't even remember him," he says, knowing and liking how cruel and dismissive this sounds.

"You were calling for him," Mr. Gabriel says. "When Danny had that gun to your head."

Owen shrugs and shows the face that never fails to make his mother give up in disgust. They have reached the stone wall. Mr. Gabriel stops, turning around, as if to confront him. Owen picks at the moss in the cracks of the wall, satisfied by even this little bit of destruction.

"C'mon, Owen," Mr. Gabriel says. "Don't expect me to fall for the mean-guy pose. It's unconvincing and a waste of your time. I know who you are. You should, too."

Owen is quiet for a moment, considering this little speech. The urge to insult Mr. Gabriel is huge, but he is tired, he realizes suddenly, of being angry. And of being quiet.

"Do you know anyone with AIDS?" he says quickly.

"Yes, Owen," Mr. Gabriel says. "I do."

"I think I might have it," Owen says. He holds his breath, waiting for the moment of shock and realization, his teacher backing away from him in confusion. Instead, Mr. Gabriel smiles.

"I think that's highly unlikely," he says.

"But you don't know—" Owen starts.

"You don't have AIDS, Owen," Mr. Gabriel says. "You're a perfectly healthy, normal young boy."

They are quiet for a minute, and as they turn down Owen's street, he dares to ask one more question.

"Do you believe in guardian angels?"

Mr. Gabriel sighs. "No, I don't," he says. "I believe it is the responsibility of human beings to watch out for one another."

Owen considers this quietly, the pain in his head moving down, feeding the heaviness in his chest. Like a slab of stone pressing there, making it almost impossible for him to get out what he says next.

"What happens if they don't?"

But his teacher has no answer for this.

17. fish tank

"You're not going to make a big thing out of this, right?" Sebastian says.

It's almost noon, I've been feeling awful ever since I woke up, not just hungover and sore but wrong, like everything is off somehow. Lights seem too bright, my mind can't stay on one thing without pinging off to another, and then I have trouble getting back to the first thing. I've been waiting a long time for Sebastian to wake up and say something and now my vision is screwed up. There's a blind spot floating in my left eye so that depending on where I focus, either his mouth or his nose or one of his eyes is simply not there. This makes it kind of hard to concentrate on him.

"What?" I say.

"Girls tend to make a big deal out of it. Especially virgins. I just wanted to make sure you're cool."

"Oh." I can't think of anything else to say. Or, I can think of things, but none of them stays still long enough for me to understand it.

"Nothing's changed, that's all I'm saying. We're still buddies."

"Oh," I say again. I swallow. "Sure." His eyes narrow, his nose disappears.

"Don't," he warns.

"Don't what?"

"Don't do that. That chick guilt thing."

"Sorry," I mumble. I immediately regret this. I'm always telling people sorry when I should say something else. Like *fuck you* in this case.

I'd really just rather he'd drop it. I'm not worried about what happened right now. I was worried last night after he passed out and I started thinking about how he hadn't used a condom, and then at four this morning, when I was so sore I could barely pee and I had to sit on the toilet for twenty minutes smelling him between my legs until it finally came out in a disappointing trickle. I was worried when I got dressed and my pants seemed tighter than yesterday, and I had an odd ache in my lower abdomen, one that still hasn't gone away, and I wondered if getting pregnant showed so fast. I'd been warned by my mother's gynecologist that I could get pregnant even though I hadn't had my period, because I wouldn't know if it was going to arrive the next month. I always thought that was kind of unfair but also that it didn't matter because I had no interest in having sex until I was older and in love. There goes that plan.

Right now all I really care about is this weird blind spot and the fact that the sun coming through the motel room's one window is making me feel raw, like it's closer than it should be. Like I'm looking directly into an eclipse or something, which they say can make you blind.

Sebastian doesn't believe me. He just keeps asking if I'm all right with "it" until I snap that I don't give a shit. Then he's mad at me. It's a long walk back to town. I walk a few paces behind Sebastian, concentrating on my feet. One of them keeps disappearing when it moves into my blind spot. Though this is disturbing, it is better than watching pedestrians vanish just when they're close enough to attack. There's snow on everything and the sun glinting off it is like needles in my eyeballs.

We go into a coffee shop when Sebastian sees Anorexia and her boys through the window. They look like they never went to bed. I don't really trust myself to talk to anyone so I go to a table and drink my coffee alone and try to calm down. I have this weird thing happening now where I keep imagining I can actually feel my blood running through my veins and I can tell it's going way too fast. I'm sure if I look at my wrists I will see it moving under the skin, but when I do the blind spot keeps getting in the way so I start to worry about that again.

Sebastian comes over in a few minutes, straddling the flimsy metal chair.

"There's a party at some farmhouse," he says.

"I want to find Emily," I say.

"We can do that later."

"It's okay," I say. "You go to the party." When I look up, his face is whole, my vision is normal again.

"Don't you want me to go with you?" He pouts. I can't help but laugh. "What?" he says, defensive now.

I'm wondering why I don't even care that he's being such an ass-hole. I guess I'm not surprised.

"I'll meet you later," I say.

"Back here?" he says. He reaches out and straightens the collar of Hugh's jacket. He can afford to be sweet now. I'm letting him off the hook.

"Sure," I say, and he grins that grin that's like a punch in my stomach and suddenly I don't feel so uncaring anymore. But before I can say anything, and really, what would I say, since he likes me best when I say nothing, he's loping off, Anorexia smiling triumphantly as he makes his way toward her. When the waitress comes by I order another coffee. She looks at me strangely, like she's about to ask what's wrong with me but decides against it. I wouldn't know where to begin.

Back at UMASS I ask a teacher where I can find out the location of a student's dorm. He looks at me suspiciously but points me to the administration building. He's not the only one looking at me weird. Everyone I pass by does a double take, until I wish I still had that blind spot so I couldn't see what they were really thinking.

It takes me a while to convince the lady in the office to give me Emily's room number. I tell her I'm Emily's younger brother, and I'm surprising her. She gives in and shows me the location of Emily's high-rise dorm on a map.

Emily isn't in her room. I try waiting in the lobby, but the furni-ture is stained and reeks of B.O. and old cigarettes and I'm still sick to my stomach. Plus the whole place is kind of lacking in personality and is depressing: navy furniture and industrial carpet and a half-empty vending machine with candy bars and little packages of pea-nut butter crackers.

I go outside and wait for her on the steps. Some guys are playing touch football in the snow. I wish I'd thought to buy sunglasses while I was still in town. The light is blinding. My head is hurting in this liquid way, the pain sloshing from one side of it to the other.

"Want to play?" one of the football guys asks me, when he's re-trieving the ball from a bush to my left.

"I'm a girl," I say snippily.

"I didn't think you were a rock," the guy says. He's smiling. He's blond and handsome and normal and miles away from everything I feel. If I talked to him, he'd think I was nuts.

"No, thanks," I say. He shrugs and jogs back into the game.

I don't recognize her at first. She's gotten kind of chubby and dresses like a hippie instead of a punk, in a long gauzy skirt and peasant shirt. She jingles with beads and bracelets. Her hair is really long now, dirty blond, kind of greasy. But she's got a distinctive laugh, kind of goofy like a seal. That's how I know it's her. I can still hear her laughing behind my brother's closed bedroom door.

She has no clue who I am. I say my first name and she looks dumbly at me, so I say Lena Furey and she still looks confused, though she's now staring at my jacket, so finally I have to swallow and squeak out: Hugh's sister. She puts a hand over her mouth and takes a step away. Then she steps forward and grabs my arm. She's one of those easy touchers.

"Sorry," she says. "It's like seeing a ghost." Standing up to talk to her has left me kind of dizzy and my head is throbbing on one side.

"Why?" I say. I'm wondering if I look really pale or deadly or something. She smiles, avoiding my eyes.

"You're so tall," she says.

Then I feel stupid. She means I look like Hugh.

———

The first thing my mother did when she got out of bed was clean the house. She vacuumed up the hamsters of dust and skin and hair that crouched in every corner and wound themselves around the feet of tables and chairs. She attacked the crevices of the stove with a Brillo pad. She did load after load of laundry, piling the kitchen table with fluffy stacks of towels, sheets, and T-shirts, and single socks that had been missing for years. She took the blankets down from her windows, revealing nicotine stains on the lamp shades and the wall behind the bed. She threw out her cigarettes and chewed nicotine gum all day. She took phone calls from her friends again, stretching the phone cord to the stove while cooking dinner. Sometimes her friends made her laugh, in a croaking, unpracticed way I was jealous of. She still wasn't laughing with us.

I'd wanted my mother to get out of bed for three years, but once she was out, she annoyed me. She nagged at me to pick up after myself, asked about homework, restricted TV to half an hour a day. I was afraid arguing might send her back to bed, so I fumed silently. Owen rebelled for both of us.

He refused to do anything she told him to and sometimes did the exact opposite. He wouldn't eat what she cooked, wear what she washed, or answer when she asked him a question. This confused everyone, since Owen had always been the easy one. He stopped listening to me, too. For two weeks he survived on crackers and cereal and dirty underwear. Then my father, who had been hiding in his office, drinking Scotch and reading the Help Wanted section but never calling any of the numbers he circled, took over. He made Owen an egg and cheese sandwich and poured him a glass of milk and sat by while Owen wolfed it all down. He started driving Owen to baseball practice, washing his uniform, making the two of them a separate dinner of sandwiches and pickles. I thought about telling Owen the truth about my father's affair. I could tell that their bonding pissed off my mother, too. Owen had always been her baby. At night, I did my homework in the kitchen while my mother cleaned up, and Owen sat in the living room with my father. We had switched teams.

One night while I was reading in bed beneath the clip-on lamp, Owen snoring on the other side of the room, my father, on his way to the bathroom, pushed open the door.

"It's after eleven," he said. "Lights out."

I ignored him. I gripped the edges of my book hard, wishing I had the nerve to throw it at him.

"Lena," my father said in his warning voice. I said nothing, not even looking at him.

He turned off the light himself, leaning over me to do it. He paused a second, like he was thinking of kissing me good night or saying something else, then left and shut the door.

He didn't come back when I turned the lamp back on, and read until I could barely see the words, daring him, over and over in my mind, to try to tell me what to do ever again.

My father got a job at a publishing house downtown, where he was the editor of books on theology and religion. These were books for regular people, self-help books with titles like *Find God in Grief* and *What Heaven Is Like: Interviews with Children.* The publisher also made angel-themed greeting cards and tchotchkes. Their newest product was inspirational cards the size of fortune cookie slips, with cartoon angels and one word on each, like *Serenity, Doubt,* or *Abundance.* There were instructions about how to use them to guide you every day. My father brought a set home for me, because they were popular with teenagers. I never opened them.

Then my mother decided to go to medical school. She said she'd planned to do so out of college but was stopped by something she wouldn't name. I figured this was getting pregnant with Hugh, but didn't ask. I was kind of annoyed I had never heard about this before. I had sort of assumed that my mother had no career ambitions. The thing was, it also made me feel guilty, like I'd held her back or something. My father made this little speech about how we'd all have to pitch in around the house now that Mom wouldn't be there to do everything for us. Who are you kidding? I wanted to say.

"Can I have my own key?" Owen said, excited.

Then they gave me Hugh's room. I came home from shopping for back-to-school clothes with Owen and all of Hugh's stuff was cleaned out and replaced by mine. My books in the bookcase, my desk, Hugh's double mattress made up with new red flannel sheets and a purple comforter.

"Do you like it?" my mother said. I couldn't answer. I felt like I was going to throw up. Finally I managed to squeak out a complaint about the purple.

"You've always wanted your own room," my mother said, defending herself.

No one talked about Hugh. No one mentioned my father's girl-friend, or my mother's time in bed. It was like we had all been stuck in the same horrible nightmare, but now that we'd woken up, I was the only one who remembered it.

In Emily's dorm room, where she has a refrigerator and microwave and a sink like a tiny kitchen, she pours me a glass of water, saying I look dehydrated. Just hearing this makes me thirsty so I try to drink it, but it's too hard. It feels like someone is pressing a thumb into my throat. I keep pulling my T-shirt collar away, thinking it's choking me, but really it's so stretched it barely touches my neck.

Emily chats as she boils a small electric kettle and makes tea that smells suspiciously herbal. She asks about my parents, about Owen, a few of Hugh's friends who have gone off to college. She asks if we still live in Brookline and says her parents moved to New York so she's never been back.

"I was so jealous of you," she says, setting a mug of strong-smelling tea on the desk in front of me.

"What?" I say, trying to turn my nose from the tea. "Why?"

"It was more like I was jealous of your family. I wanted to be in it. You guys seemed so normal. My house was so fucked up in comparison."

"We're not normal," I say. She nods. She thinks I mean now, or since Hugh. But I can't remember us ever being normal.

Emily jumps up then, her largish bottom jiggling freely in her gauzy skirt. "Are you hungry? I can make you something in the microwave. Tofu stir-fry. I'm a vegetarian. Or my roommate has Pop-Tarts if you want something sweet, but you look like you could use something wholesome."

"That's okay," I say. I yank at the neck of my T-shirt again. The fluorescent light bulb above us is making everything look sort of green.

She sits on one of the beds. "I was a drug addict, you know," she says. I shake my head. "Hugh tried to get me to stop, but I was out of control. I'd try anything, and never knew my limits. My parents had to send me away, I know that now. But after what happened to Hugh . . . well, I wish I hadn't let it go that far. I hated myself after that."

"What are you talking about?" I say. My head is going so fast I'm sure everything else about me is speeded up, too.

"I don't know." She shrugs, looking uncomfortable. "It wasn't easy being the last person who ever saw him."

At first I think she's saying this to me. Like she's known my secret all along. Then I hear her again, like an echo in my head, and I realize she's talking about herself.

I have to run in the hall to find the bathroom because the thumb at my throat finally pushes me to the point of gagging.

Hugh went after her. She was at that rehab boarding school in western Mass, and wasn't allowed any phone calls or letters. She had written once to tell him to forget her. But he came anyway. Hitchhiked all night in a snowstorm to show up the morning of Valentine's Day. The staff tried to turn him away, but he made some sort of scene. She was pulled from jewelry-making class to calm him down. They spoke in the social worker's office, while the social worker and two security guards waited outside.

She was cold. Cruel. She told him she had a new boyfriend, which was only half true. She was trying to make him get over her, but she was also mad at him. For not running away with her when she asked. Because she had cold, distrusting parents and he didn't. Because she'd never really felt good enough for him. She said things she didn't mean. He brought her every picture he'd ever taken, but she refused to look at them. This made him cry and then she cried herself. She let him take her into one of their old hugs, where she tucked her arms in against his chest and he folded himself around her. And then she wrestled her way out of it and told him not to come back and left him in that office and went back to class to finish her earrings.

For a while she thought she'd succeeded in driving him away. Until she found out he never made it home.

———

"You have to tell someone," I say when she's done with this story. "We have to call my parents, the police. They were searching in all the wrong places."

Emily looks at me strangely. My eye has that blind spot again and my head and stomach hurt so bad it's actually difficult to talk. I never realized how many muscles you used just to form a sentence. She's already asked me if I want to lie down at least twice.

"Lena," she says. "They know. The police came and interviewed me and the staff. Your father came, too. I thought he was going to strangle me. They figured Hugh hitchhiked back, and got picked up by . . . well, you know."

"I don't know," I say. "I don't know any of this." Emily looks away.

"They had a hard time accepting that he was gone. Maybe they were trying to protect you," she says.

"Whatever," I say. My blood is doing that rushing thing again.

"Or they just couldn't mention my name. I don't blame them. I hated myself for a long time. I wasn't very nice to your brother. If it hadn't been for me he never would have disappeared."

"It wasn't your fault," I say.

"Oh, I know. I know it wasn't really anybody's fault."

"Not exactly," I say. "But it wasn't yours."

"Lena, you're really pale."

"I think I will lie down," I say. "I can't really see anymore."

She gives me Tylenol and a cold washcloth for my head, and I lie down on her narrow dorm bed with the shades drawn, my mind moving so fast nothing stays in it long enough to be true.

———

When I finished grammar school, I had no friends. Hugh had been missing for almost four years, and at some point I must have stopped making them. It wasn't like I could bring anybody to my house. I'd once only had boy friends. Girls didn't really like me. I could've made friends at the high school, the way every other freshman seemed to be doing, but I didn't really have the energy.

Once I got to high school I got kind of obnoxious at home. I talked back all the time, rolled my eyes, called everything annoying or stupid. Once, after my dad tried to help me pick out classes for my second semester and I said I didn't care for the hundredth time, he threw down the paper and pencil in disgust.

"You didn't use to be like this," he said. He left the room, pretending not to hear me mumble after him.

"How would you know?"

I had secrets. No one knew that I came home every day after school and went straight to sleep, getting up long enough to eat my father's latest attempt from *The Joy of Cooking,* then going back to bed until morning. I slept in classes, too, learning how to open my eyes and raise my head every few minutes to look like I was listening.

When I got behind in school, I'd stay up for days at a time, finishing papers I'd had months to do or cramming for tests. I took No-Doz at five times the recommended dose until I gagged if I moved too fast and my hands trembled. I stayed awake until I started to hear things—voices calling my name, television programs that hadn't been on for years—until the world moved so fast and I moved so slow I started to think it was leaving me behind. Once, during an algebra midterm, I swore under my breath because I couldn't get the variables to stay still on the page. When I saw the other kids and the teacher staring at me, I knew I'd said it really loud.

After my study binges I would sleep whole weekends away, leaving my radio tuned to the Top 40 countdown and candles burning to fool my parents into thinking I was awake. I told them they couldn't come into my new room without knocking, and I was so obnoxious when they did, they generally avoided it.

I experimented with myself. I stopped eating for days, or made myself throw up by sticking the wrong end of a toothbrush down my throat. I drank half a bottle of vodka in one chug on the fire escape behind the Coolidge Corner Theater and spent the rest of the night talking to strangers who looked at me like I was nuts. I don't remember anything I said, so they could've been right. I took a razor blade from my father's drawer in the bathroom and sliced thin lines in the skin of my forearm. I saved the washcloth that I used to blot these cuts, including the time I carved too deep by accident, and had to use pressure to stop the blood. I smoked clove cigarettes I bought at the pipe store, though I didn't know how to inhale them, and couldn't finish a whole one without feeling sick to my stomach. I set little fires in my room, of shredded paper and rug lint, and let them get big enough to be dangerous before putting them out.

I didn't feel better. I didn't feel worse. Nothing made me feel anything but what I'd already known for years.

When I wake up my teeth are chattering and I'm sure I've just heard my mother call my name, in the aggravated tone she gets when I've overslept. It's dark at the edges of Emily's curtains. I don't feel the slightest bit better. It's possible I feel worse. When I sit up I'm sure my head has split down the middle and I've left half of it on the pillow.

While I run water in the sink I hear it again. My name, like it's being screamed across a playground, in Owen's voice this time. It doesn't sound like I'm imagining it, even though I know it must be in my head. But my head doesn't feel in charge right now. Like it might be letting in things besides my thoughts to run around.

Emily has left me a note on the desk that says she's gone to her evening class but I can stay as long as I want. I can't stand the thought of waiting here for Emily. Eventually she's going to think to ask me if my parents know I'm here. And I no longer have any urge left to call them.

It's snowing outside again, heavy wet snow mixed with sleet. I go downtown to look for Sebastian, but it's pretty deserted. When I'm passing by a coffee shop I see him through the window. He's sitting at a table with Anorexia, and they're kissing. I can't seem to stop watching this even though it's not exactly what I want to see right now. He looks up, spots me, and comes outside. His whole posture suggests a tiresome chore.

"Are you okay?" he says. I nod. I try to light a cigarette but the whole pack is wet and it breaks off at the filter. "I'm sorry about last night," he adds. Anorexia is smoking impatiently inside, waiting for him to come back.

"Me, too." I laugh. Sebastian looks angry.

"Everything isn't always about you," he says. He looks like he might cry, and I know that if I say the right thing, I can probably get him back. But it will only be for about five minutes.

"Clearly," I say.

"Fine," he spits. "Be that way." He goes inside and I walk away knowing he won't come after me.

I find a group of teenagers huddling on the small island of snow and trees in front of Town Hall. Someone offers me a can of Budweiser and a hit off of a joint. I am looking for the right girl. Not too pretty, but not so bad she'll be easy. Someone in between, lonely, looking pissed off, smoking a cigarette like if she inhales deep enough it might change something. Someone who needs to be told the obvious, because she has ceased believing in it herself. A lost girl.

I kiss her against a wet, rough tree, deep and slow and long and like I have nothing else planned for the rest of my life. I kiss her like my head isn't pounding, like my stomach feels just fine, like I hear nothing but her soft whimpering against my mouth. I press my bruised hips hard, bruising hers.

"You're so pretty," I whisper, when the truth is my head hurts so much I barely know what she looks like. "Where did you learn to kiss so great?" She's an inexperienced kisser, no control, tongue all over the place.

"My boyfriend," she says sharply. That's when I realize I've miscalculated. She's not lost or lonely. She's just bored. And her boyfriend has seen us leave.

He punches me twice, hard in the face, holding on to me to make it hurt more or keep me steady, I'm not sure. The girl squeals and stomps away, saying she's tired of his temper. He gives me one last kick before chasing after her. "Fucking punk," he hisses. I laugh. I consider telling him I'm a girl. I wonder if it will make him apologize or hit me even harder. I lie there until I'm too uncomfortable to stand being still anymore and have no choice but to get up.

My head feels like it has small explosions going on inside of it, I'm doubled over with stomach pain, and if I look anywhere near a streetlight I go blind. Out of habit, I reach behind me to tap the camera bag, but it's not there. It's not on the ground nearby, either. Something rises in me. I try to remember if that guy took it, but I don't think so. I've left it somewhere. But when I try to think back to when I last had it everything swells and pops in my head.

"Shit," I say out loud. Hugh's camera bag. The binder of negatives. Every picture I've developed. "Fuck!"

An older couple walking nearby look at me like I'm dangerous. I squat down and hold on to my knees and rock back and forth. I need to think. I reach for a cigarette, but the pack is soaked from slush and unsmokable. My head is killing me.

I get up. I'll concentrate on a place to buy cigarettes. They will help me remember. I find a Cumberland Farms and buy two packs of Marlboros. I can't even smoke one, it makes me gag and cough. Not being able to smoke seems almost worse than anything that's happened so far. Like proof that nothing will ever be reliable. I decide to find a phone and call Emily. Maybe I left the camera bag there.

But once I'm in the phone booth, I feed change in and dial 411. I ask for a number in Brookline. He answers after one ring.

"Is Jonah there?" I say, even though I know it's him, by that quick, suspicious voice, like he's expecting something to be wrong.

"Where are you?" he says. He sounds angry.

"I have to ask you something," I say. My teeth are chattering so hard I can't keep the phone receiver still.

"Your parents called," he says. "They're really worried."

"Why'd they call you?" I say.

"Tracy told them to," he says. "Are you okay? Are you with Sebastian?"

I laugh at this, but it hurts my head, so I stop and hold my breath until the throb passes.

"Did you want to die?" I say, leaning against the glass, fogged now from my breath.

Jonah pauses. I think he's going to tell me to mind my own business.

"I don't know," he says finally. "I wanted everything to stop."

I nod. I don't trust myself to agree out loud.

"Do you want me to come get you?" he says. But I hang up. I'm out of change and don't want to talk anymore.

I fell behind in Ancient Civilizations, and for the first time, at ten o'clock the night before the midterm, when I hadn't even started studying, it seemed like I might not catch up. There was just too much. I locked myself in the bathroom and looked through the medicine cabinet. My mother must have thrown out all the stuff she took before. All I could find were Owen's inhaler, Tylenol, Triaminic, Pepto-Bismol, and Actifed. I stuck the Actifed in my pajama sleeve and brought it to my room with a bottle of ginger ale left over from Owen's last cold.

I took one tiny white pill every few minutes, pushing them out of their little tinfoil nests, waiting to feel something. After ten I got drowsy and felt like the lining of my nose was cracked. At fifteen I fell asleep. I woke up at two in the morning with a headache and threw up. For the rest of the night I could barely move, gagging into a Tupperware bowl by the side of my bed. By morning I looked so bad my mother thought I was too sick to go to school. This was on a Friday. I spent the weekend cramming for my makeup test and ended up with a B plus.

Though nothing happened—no one even noticed the pills were gone until months later when my father got a cold and my mother looked through the cabinet saying *I could have sworn there was an entire package*—swallowing those pills did something to me. It was like diving into cold water. I started studying again, threw away the razor blades, ignored my occasional hiccup thoughts about jumping in front of cars or lighting things on fire. I think I scared myself enough to be careful again. Then I found Hugh's pictures, and I forgot everything for a while.

One of the first rolls was of the New England Aquarium. Hugh used to take me there. There was a path around this gigantic fish tank, where we watched sharks and sea turtles swimming past the windows. The top of the tank had no glass, and you could stand by the railing and look down. I hated the top. I used to stay by the stairs and refuse to go near it. I could never explain why. Hugh thought I was afraid of the sharks and made fun of me. But what scared me was not leaping fish or deep water or even falling. It was this idea that, if I went near it, I would not be able keep from throwing myself in.

When I knock on Emily's door, she lets me in without a word. Her roommate is spending the night at her boyfriend's. Emily gives me a towel and some flannel pajamas and says I should get ready for bed. She hasn't seen my camera bag.

In the ladies dorm bathroom, I wipe myself and the paper comes away slick with gelled blood. I wonder dumbly for a second if it's from losing my virginity. I keep wiping and wiping and it doesn't get any better, it seems to get worse, like whatever is broken has decided, now that I'm paying attention, to bleed me dry. I start crying again.

Emily comes in, knocks once on the stall door then opens it.

"Have your period?" she says.

"I think so," I say.

"Is it your first time?" I nod again.

"I won't insult you with congratulations." She smiles. "Your headache may be a migraine. I'll get you something for it that will help your cramps, too. There are communal tampons and pads in that container behind you. You might want a hot bath. They help me."

I nod, sniffle, wipe at my face with a wad of toilet paper.

"It's not the end of the world," she says nicely. I try to smile. She's pretty, Emily. She always was, but now she's grown-up pretty, like a woman instead of a cute blond girl. She seems tough and happy now, the way my mother used to be. She closes the stall and walks toward the door.

"You may not believe me," she calls back. "But you'll get used to it."

When I'm in her bed with a heating pad on my stomach and a pain-killer making my head feel almost normal, Emily, who has been waiting in the student lounge, comes in to say good night. I start crying as soon as I see her.

"Feeling better, I see," she says. I shake my head.

"Get some sleep," she says.

"It won't help," I say. She turns to leave, and I grab her hand as it swings by.

"I hated you," I say.

"I know," she says, giving my hand a reassuring squeeze. "Now you'll have another reason to."

"Why?" She lets go of my hand and walks to the door. She opens it at the same time as she turns the light off, so all I can see is her silhouette in the doorway.

"Because I just called your parents," she says. "They'll be here in the morning." She pushes the band of light with the door until it's gone.

18. pajamas

There is no longer a police car outside the Furey house. Owen drags his feet up the brick steps, Mr. Gabriel follows uncomfortably close behind. Owen's face burns at the thought of what his teacher will say. Surely he'll mention the gun, but will he tell them about Tom stripped from the waist down, Owen kneeling over him? He hesitates at the door.

"I'm not sure there's anyone for you to even

talk to," Owen says to Mr. Gabriel. They are in the outer entryway they share with the nurses who live upstairs, which has a brown carpet funneled to catch rain and snow, a limp ficus tree, and a purposeful lack of any personality or style. This used to disturb Owen when he was first a latchkey kid. It could be anybody's hallway.

"My parents are probably still out looking for Lena," Owen explains.

Mr. Gabriel nods impatiently and points at the door, indicating that Owen should open it. He seems to have returned to his familiar scowling self. Owen fishes his key on a string out from under his shirt, leaning forward to slide it in the knob without taking it off his neck.

The house is quiet, dark, no lamps turned on to fight the gloominess. He assumes no one is home, and leads Mr. Gabriel into the living room to wait.

On the sectional couch, as stiff as if they've been captured in granite, sits his entire family. His parents are on the short piece of the L, his sister, or some barely recognizable version of her, alone on the long piece. The silence in the room is thick, as if no one has spoken a word in hours. As if they have been sitting there, afraid to begin, the whole time Owen has been gone. For a moment, he imagines they have been waiting for him. Without looking up, keeping her furious eyes on Lena, Owen's mother corrects this misassumption.

"Owen," she says. "Please go to your room."

"Mr. and Mrs. Furey?" Mr. Gabriel says, stepping up to Owen's side. Even he seems freaked out by the scene, his voice tentative in a way that makes Owen feel completely alone.

"I'm sorry to interrupt," he says. "But something has happened that you need to know about."

This cracks the spell. Slowly, as if turning away from a wild animal likely to attack or bolt, both of his parents look away from Lena and try to focus on Mr. Gabriel. In the delay before they are able to respond, Lena, who doesn't move her eyes from her obsessive, almost murderous gaze at the coffee table, is the first to speak.

"Hey, Mr. Gabriel," she says simply, her voice weary but casual, as if she has run into him at the playground, as if she is not sporting a purple welt under one eye and dried blood on her chapped bottom lip, as if she does not look like she barely made it out, of wherever she was, alive. This nonchalant greeting seems like the most inappropriate thing his sister could say. No one can proceed for a moment; they're all waiting to see if she'll say something else. Finally, Mr. Gabriel clears his throat.

"All right, Lena?" he says, surliness aside, smiling gently.

But apparently she is done, her mouth now occupied with chewing the skin at the edge of her thumb. Her nails are grimy, thick bands of greasy dirt under each one, the skin around them either scabbed or wound-raw. This is worse than the evidence that she has been beaten up, Owen thinks; she has done this to herself. She doesn't look at Owen, or say hello to him, even after he uses his foolproof little-brother stare, which never fails to get her to yell *What?!,* even with her back turned and a whole room away.

"Mr. Gabriel," Owen's father says. "I know there are issues with Owen's absences."

"This isn't about—" Mr. Gabriel starts. But Owen's father plows through him, the only indication that he has heard being the raised volume of his voice.

"Right now is not a good time. Could I call you later? Or speak to you at school next week?"

Mr. Gabriel opens his mouth to protest, but closes it again. He looks around, from their parents, to Lena gnawing on her hand, to Owen, who is wishing he could sink directly between the cracks of the hardwood floor. He imagines that Mr. Gabriel can see everything about his family, that they are laid out in front of him like specimens, and that nothing he sees is good.

"I'll call in a few hours," Mr. Gabriel says. "It's too urgent to wait." He makes a polite nod with his head in their direction and backs his way toward the door. Owen tries to indicate with the widening of his eyes that he doesn't want to be left alone, but Mr. Gabriel is gone, the front door latching quietly behind him.

Owen stands in front of his family and waits. He waits to be told that Lena has been saved from near death, ransomed from a kidnapper in a black van. He waits to be asked why his fifth-grade teacher is walking him home when it's not a school day. He waits to be asked how he is feeling, something they ask every day but never really encourage an answer to.

He waits, at the very least, to be invited to sit down on the long piece of the couch, even if it means he must join in the silence, which he expects has more to do with relief than anger.

But after a long pause where no one looks at one another, he is told again: "Go to your room."

Eventually they start yelling. Owen has no urge to eavesdrop this time; he is so determined not to hear a word that he puts headphones on, plugging them into the record player that is a hand-me-down from his sister, who now has a boom box that plays tapes. He listens to all of *Thriller* and *Purple Rain* (also hand-me-downs), wishing for a Walkman so he can move around the room. Instead he has to crouch in the corner, between the low record table and the wall, marveling at the amount of dust that has accumulated beneath his bed. There are clumps as large as the lint blankets he peels from the filter in the clothes dryer.

Owen pulls one earphone aside and checks their progress. Still yelling. Sometimes all three at once. He listens for a minute.

"You're failing the tenth grade," his mother says. "Do you have any idea how serious that is?"

"I don't care," Lena says.

"Do you care that we thought you were lying dead in an alley somewhere?" his father says.

"Not really."

"What is *wrong* with you? What have we ever done to deserve such—" his mother starts.

"Everything!" Lena screams.

"Name something," her father says. "Name one thing we've done that wasn't expressly to make you and your brother safe and happy." His voice kind of cracks at the end, like even he knows this isn't the smartest thing to say. Owen holds his breath. There is a long silence.

"I hate you," Lena says finally. Not in anger, but coldly, pronouncing every word. "Both of you. Owen hates you. Hugh hated you, too."

Owen will never know which one of them slaps her. And whether it is for what she said, or simply for using Hugh's name.

He puts his headphones back on.

Later, he feels rather than hears the thundering footsteps and slam of doors that indicate the end of the confrontation, the dispersal to assigned, neutral corners. He takes the headphones off. He can hear the running of water and clank of dishes in the kitchen. If they are doing dishes, it is safe to come out. But Owen stays put, crawling into his unmade bed even though it is barely six o'clock. He expects that his father will come in eventually to see if he wants dinner, check his temperature out of habit. But it gets later and later and no one comes in, and Owen grows so thirsty his throat catches when he swallows, and eventually he falls asleep fully dressed. Sometime in the night, he jolts half-awake at the sound of the phone, which rings at least a dozen times before it stops, the noise fading away rather than being broken by an answer.

At five A.M., Owen wakes to the familiar sounds of his mother in the kitchen. She always empties the dishwasher while waiting for her coffee to brew, and is incapable of doing it quietly, even during delicate hours. She opens cabinets and lets them slam shut, claps dishes against one another with a force that threatens to crack. From another room, she gives the impression of fuming anger, but if Owen interrupts, he usually finds her mood neutral, preoccupied, not making noise for attention but lost in her own world.

This morning, however, she is angry. Owen can hear her clipped voice in between the rattle and slam of the utensil drawer. Occasionally, the murmured response of his father.

He gets out of bed, still in his clothes from the day before, the knees of his dungarees streaked with graveyard dirt. He pads in sock feet to the kitchen, walking quietly past his parents who are conferring so intently in the pantry that they don't notice him.

Lena's door is open. He pauses on the threshold, squinting; behind him is the overhead light and her lair is lit only by candles. He spies her head behind the desk arranged in front of her bed like a barricade. She is awake, sitting upright on her bed, gnawing at her finger and staring at the opposite wall. She turns her head at the interruption Owen causes in the light. She scrambles out of her cave and hurries toward the door. For an instant, he is not sure if she means to hit or hug him. She does neither, merely motions him out of the way.

"I'm closing my door," she calls out. Both their parents are quick to stick their heads out into the hall to investigate.

"Owen's with me," Lena says, her voice sharp with scorn. "You trust *him,* right?"

Owen is unable to look at any of them after this comment. They either agree or neglect to object, because Lena grabs him by the arm and pulls him inside, slamming the door with a flourish. She storms back to her bed, letting out a long, frustrated roar, opens the window, settles herself cross-legged in front of it, and lights a cigarette. She inhales like someone starving.

Owen hovers by the closed door, not sure if she wants him there or is simply using him as an alibi. She is wearing pajamas, white cotton ones with a pattern of tiny pink rosebuds and green vines. He hasn't seen these pajamas in more than a year—she started sleeping in an old flannel shirt and boxers—and they look ridiculous beneath her cropped, filthy hair, and her black eye, which is beginning to develop a yellow ring around the welted bruise. When she glances right, the corner of her eye socket is a plug of blood.

She sucks down half the cigarette in three deep drags.

"They made me sleep in their *room,*" she says. Owen's look of surprise is apparently encouraging. "On the *cot.*"

He nods in sympathy. The cot is a horrid wheeled metal contraption with a moldy mattress, taken out for sleepover parties and out-of-town guests, most of whom end up preferring the couch or a sleeping bag on the floor.

"They won't let me take a *shower.* Or close my door. I'm a fucking prisoner."

"Why didn't you—" Owen starts. She doesn't hear him.

"I mean, who the fuck do they think they are? They haven't noticed a thing we've done in five years. They never cared if we were even home on time. They lied about *everything.* And now they think they can *ground* me?"

"I don't get it," Owen says.

"Oh, *I* get it," Lena says, lighting a second cigarette from the glowing butt of her first. "They've decided to suddenly become our *parents*. They are so lame. And too late. Fuck them."

Owen is dizzy from secondhand smoke and Lena's making no sense. He rubs the sting from his eyes, moving closer to her bed.

"Why are you grounded?" he says. "Didn't you tell them about that guy?"

"It doesn't matter what I tell them—" Lena starts, then she blinks. "What guy?"

"That punk guy."

"Sebastian?" Lena's face changes when she says his name, going hard to cover up another layer going soft. "Why would I tell them about Sebastian?"

"Because he made you go," Owen says. Lena looks at him strangely.

"What are you talking about?" she says.

Fear is rising in Owen's throat like vomit.

"He kidnapped you." He barely squeaks this out. Lena stares at him, the red stain in the corner of her eye widening. And then she laughs. Loudly.

"Are you *mental*?" she says. "Honestly, Owen, I think you're spending too much time alone in the house."

"You wouldn't run away," Owen whispers.

Lena lights another cigarette, refusing to look at him. He isn't sure with the dim light, but her cheek seems to flush red under the yellow. Her hand moving the cigarette back and forth is shaking, like someone smoking outside in the cold.

"I didn't *run away*. I had some things I had to do. You wouldn't understand."

The sound of that phrase, coupled with her admission of the impossible, sets an avalanche of voices roiling in Owen's head. There are so many sentences clamoring for release, it is as though a roomful of people are screaming them.

Danny almost killed me.

You're as bad as they are.

I thought you were dead.

You left me to be the only one.

I told on you.

But what he says instead is this: "No. I guess not."

At eight A.M. the phone starts to ring again, and this time Owen hears his father answer it. He sits paralyzed in his room, wheezing with fear. After about twenty minutes, his father walks down the hall and pushes open the door. Owen forces himself to look up and can't decide what he sees. His father's face gives nothing away. He comes over to Owen's bed and sits down next to him. His father's arm over his shoulders is awkward and heavy. Neither one of them wants it there.

"Are you okay?" his father says.

Owen shrugs. "I guess so," he says.

"I'm sorry, Owen," his father adds.

Owen nods. His father is always sorry.

Lena is furious.

"Why do I have to go? Owen's the one in trouble."

"He's not in trouble. He was bullied and needs to give a statement. And I'm not leaving you here alone."

"Jesus, this is so unfair. What, are you going to cart me around like a five-year-old now?"

"I am until you can act like someone old enough to be left home alone."

"I've been alone for *years*," Lena screams. Owen is sure this is not what she means to say. Doesn't she mean *home alone*? She slams her door hard enough to knock something off a surface in her room.

"Fine," his father says. "Let's just go." Like it's his decision.

At the police station, they are put into a room that looks just like the interrogation rooms on TV, with a long Formica table, hard metal chairs, and fluorescent lights, one of which is broken and hums in and out like a strobe. There is a corkboard on one wall with Wanted and Missing posters overlapping one another. On the opposite wall is a long mirror, presumably two-way. Owen is beginning to wonder if he may be in trouble after all.

But the officer who comes in for the interview is one he already knows, who worked a few shifts in the squad car outside their house, eating from a cardboard suitcase of Munchkins and sipping from a Styrofoam cup of Dunkin' Donuts coffee. He reminds Owen of a Smurf, short and round with a bald, slightly blue scalp. He is accompanied by Detective O'Brien, who seems harmless enough, thick Boston accent and mustard stained in a line on his white shirt.

The interview is easier than Owen expects. The detective simply asks him things he seems to already know the answers to—Danny's and Brian's and Mark's full names, who held the gun, had Owen ever seen it before. He doesn't ask why it happened, or what Danny wanted him to do. He doesn't seem to think this is important, or else he already knows and is sparing Owen embarrassment. The whole thing takes less than ten minutes, and Owen signs his name at the bottom of Detective O'Brien's clipboard, where the statement typed in a corner by the Smurf is secured.

"What's going to happen to him?" Owen asks, as Detective O'Brien gets up to leave.

"That depends on the courts," the detective says. "He shot at your teacher, so it's pretty serious. Could end up in the Juvenile Detention Center. Probation if he gets a soft judge."

"Will he come back to school?" Owen says. His father snaps his head to stare at him curiously. The Smurf and the detective both smile.

"Not to your school," the detective says. "That I can guarantee." Owen smiles in relief. As they're ushered out of the room, the Smurf slips Owen a Tootsie Pop.

In the waiting room are Tom Fisher and a thin, nervous-looking woman who must be his mother.

"You can come in now, Mrs. Fisher, Tom," the detective says. They both stand up, and with Tom's mother leading the way, they pass by Owen and his father single file, the parents glancing with curious sympathy at each other, the boys, each with an image of the other turning his neck red, refusing to look at all.

In the car, Owen's father clears his throat a few times and then asks Owen if he wants to talk about it.

"Not right now, thanks," Owen says. His father opens his mouth like he's about to say something else, then just nods and turns on the engine.

At home, his father goes straight to Lena's door, knocking loudly. There is a pause, then she screams out, "Go away!" Owen's father, looking relieved, obliges her.

19. pills

I go to CVS while Owen and my father are at the police station. I watch the pharmacist's waiting line for a while, mostly old people collecting their prescriptions and bellowing questions about side effects and insurance. I think about getting in line. Getting to the front and asking the guy in the white coat what you take when you can't feel anything but bad anymore. Just the thought of myself actually doing this makes me laugh, out loud, and

I startle the nearest old lady. I go down the remedies aisle to find something myself.

I pass by cold medicine, slide a package of Actifed off its metal hook. Then I remember how sick it made me, so I put it back. I graze by laxatives and analgesics and mouth-sore relievers and Band-Aids and stop at sleep aids. There are a few different kinds. I pick the one I recognize from the commercial where an oblong white pill rocks back and forth and snores. The bottle has fifty. I take two just in case.

On the way up to the counter I start to get paranoid. Maybe there is an alarm system just for catching loony teenagers buying sleeping pills. I need to add something to distract the cashier. Something that makes me look younger, innocent, happy. I choose a huge bag of candy from a sales bin. They are Reese's Pieces, with a little picture of E.T. in the corner, claiming to be his favorite candy. At the counter I also ask for a pack of Marlboros. The clerk barely looks at me, but I figure if she stops to think, my purchases are too confusing to assume anything about.

Once I am safely outside with my plastic bag I feel great. Like I've accomplished something. Maybe I won't even need to go through with it. Maybe I'll go home, gorge myself on peanut butter candies, smoke a whole pack of cigarettes, and wait until tomorrow to decide the rest.

Then I hear my name. It is a boy's voice and my heart sort of stops, thinking it is Sebastian. But when I turn around I hear it again and know the voice isn't traveling through air. Though it sounds far away it's actually coming from inside my head.

"Leeeena." Then closer, abruptly: "Lena." Like my name is the worst thing it can accuse me of.

———

I don't come out when my parents ask if I want dinner. On my bed, candles lit, I open the packages and count the pills. I count them by twos, then again by ones. I separate them into piles of ten in a velvet-lined box meant for jewelry I don't have. Into the piles I put a few Reese's for color. I wait for my family to go to bed and I tell myself I still might not do it. But it's like something inside me has made the decision and taken it into a locked room. I can keep asking, but there's no way I'll get it back.

At midnight everything is quiet. I go out to the dining room and look in the corner cabinet where my parents keep the alcohol. There's a bottle of Cutty Sark, but the smell makes me gag. I choose vodka, which smells like nothing.

Back in my room I prop myself against the wall behind my bed and begin. Two pills, a sip of vodka, and three Reese's to wash it down. I've taken ten before I remember that I was going to think about not doing it again before actually starting. "Oh, well," I say out loud, making myself giggle.

Two pills, one sip, three candies. Two pills, one sip, three candies. A lot of burping.

At twenty the bed starts to breathe. Like a massive sleeping animal, swelling with the inhale, flattening to let it out.

At thirty I'm having trouble with my hands. Picking pills up between my fingertips suddenly requires intense concentration and long breaks where I breathe in time with the bed and the walls. Then I forget which step I'm on and have to start from the beginning.

At thirty-six I start to wonder if this will actually kill me, rather than just make people take me seriously. I decide that it's just as well if it does. At forty I realize I've forgotten to write a note. My orange notebook with clues and song lyrics and stupid convictions is on the bed already. I open it to a clean page and with difficulty I write:

DON'T TAKE MY PICTURE. This seems very clever, but my chest is too heavy to manage a laugh.

At forty-four I am quite sure I've thrown up into a Tupperware bowl next to my bed, which is not good news for the count. But a few minutes later I look around and there is no bowl and my blankets are clean. It is all still inside me.

Fifty is when people come to visit.

The first person to open my door is Sebastian. He's hyper and happy, obviously high, and demands I get up and go to Harvard Square with him.

"Are you kidding?" I slur. Speaking is more of an effort than I thought it would be.

"No," he says. He is rifling through the drawers of my desk, probably looking for a cigarette. I want him to stop. I suddenly imagine I have my whole life in there.

"First of all," I say. "I haven't seen you since you basically dumped me in Amherst."

"We can have sex again if it makes you feel better," he says, grinning.

"I'm also in the middle of trying to kill myself."

Sebastian has found a stray Marlboro and lights it.

"Do it tomorrow," he says. "Come have some fun."

I close my eyes and let my head fall a little too hard against the wall behind me.

"I'm tired of having fun," I say. This must be convincing because when I open my eyes he's gone. He's left his cigarette half-smoked and smoldering in the ashtray.

While I try to take a little nap my grandmother comes in and turns on the overhead light and begins to vacuum.

"Do you have to do that right now?" I say. She doesn't answer, just runs the hose along my carpet, sucking up things I've left on the floor, a shoe, dirty clothing, a plate full of toast crusts. I can see the shapes moving their way up the tube.

My mother comes in behind her, carrying a tray with a bowl of soup, saltines, and ginger ale. She shakes a thermometer down and slips it under my tongue. I wish she would sit on the bed, but she moves around, straightening, hopping out of the way of my grandmother's hose. She gathers up a bunch of Hugh's clothes, muttering that they must be Owen's. I try to protest, but she glares a warning—no talking while the thermometer's in.

"Normal," she pronounces when she slides it out. "Back to school tomorrow."

"I can't go to school like this," I say. With the walls and the floors breathing I'm not sure I can make it across the room.

"Well, you're going to," my mother says without sympathy.

"I never said you guys could come in my room," I whine.

The two of them roll their eyes. My grandmother tugs the cord and the vacuum reels it back in. My mother gathers up the tray and they disappear.

But they leave my door open and suddenly there's a parade. Kids from grammar school file in behind Mr. Gabriel, marching through the door like my room is some sort of field trip, pocketing change from my desk or tapes from my stereo table. Some of them have charcoals and rice paper and are looking for gravestones in my closet. Mr. Gabriel is telling them all that they should be very careful to get enough sleep and do their times tables or else they'll end up like me. Most of them are only pretending to listen to him. They are bored by me. Someone asks if they can go to McDonald's for lunch.

They file out and only Tracy stays behind. She stands by the foot of my bed, looking like she'd rather not be there, pulling on the edge of her horse T-shirt. I can smell the faint, pleasant odor of manure that never really goes away, that has always made her seem so healthy and, because of that, so foreign.

"Mr. Herman's going to fail you," she says.

"I know," I say. "It doesn't matter."

She looks angry. "Of course it matters," she says. I shrug, looking away. She never understood me then, and I'm far too gone now.

"You think I was friends with you 'cause I'm a loser and I couldn't find anyone else," she blurts out. "But that's not true. I thought you were cool."

"I'm sorry," I say. But I'm so sluggish, she has run away before I can get it out.

I wish people would stop coming in. I'm starting to feel really sick now and it's making it harder to keep taking the pills.

Jonah is next.

"What now?" I say.

"Charming as ever," he says.

"Are you going to save me?"

"Little late, I think. Besides, I tried. I've been calling for days."

"They took my phone away," I say.

"I tried to talk to your mom, but she thought I was Sebastian and hung up on me."

"Why don't you mind your own business?" I say. "You act like you know everything all the time."

"I know more than you," he says.

"How can you be so sure?"

"Because I *was* you," he says. He leans forward and kisses me gently on the mouth.

"I thought this was in my dream," I say.

"Mmm-hmmm," he says, kissing me again.

"Then how come you're getting away with that?"

"You must secretly want me to." He smiles.

"Could you stay for a while?" I say. I look away, not wanting him to see that I'm close to crying. "Everyone keeps leaving. Stay the night. Not to fool around. Just stay in a corner, until the morning. I have a sleeping bag."

"Sorry," he says. "I have to go home."

"But what if I die and you never see me again?" I whine.

"You expect everyone to rearrange their life around you," he says.

"I do not," I say. "I just want them to notice me." But he's gone.

After this I drift in and out of sleep for a while. At least I think I do. My neck keeps snapping up and waking me. I forget about the pills and when I remember they don't go down as easy as before. My tongue feels kind of swollen, my throat like it's protesting every swallow. I try to keep my eyes open and watch the door.

When he comes my eyes have fallen shut so I don't see him at first. He's standing in the open doorway, tall and gorgeous and smirking like he has some great secret to tell me. I start to cry. This time I feel every tear. He comes over and sits cross-legged at the foot of my bed.

"Wasn't this my bed?" he says.

I nod. I'm crying too hard to trust myself to speak. He bounces a little as if testing out how the mattress has survived. He reaches over and picks up my jewelry box, stirs a little section of pills with one long finger. He helps himself to a Reese's Piece, crunching thoughtfully. He doesn't look as old as I remember him. He's barely my age.

"How many did you get up to?" he says.

"Fifty-six," I croak.

He whistles, impressed.

"Do you think it's enough?" I say.

"I wouldn't know, buddy."

"I'm kind of tired of taking them."

"I'll bet."

"I looked for you. I followed the clues you left. I went all the way to Amherst."

"I know. Silly girl."

"Why is it silly?"

"Because I'm gone," Hugh says. "You know that."

This makes me cry even harder.

Hugh sighs and watches and waits for me to stop. Like he always did. I try. I sniffle and heave and breathe deep. I look away and blink my eyes dry.

"Why did you make me lie?" I say.

"I didn't want to get caught," Hugh says. "I didn't know you'd be so good at it."

"I should have stopped you," I say.

"You were ten," Hugh says, as if this explains everything.

"I could've woken up Mom and Dad."

"I would've gone the next night."

"You would've been picked up by a different driver," I say.

"You don't know that. No one knows what happened." I pause after this.

"You know," I say. He shrugs, as if the subject is boring him.

"Did it hurt?" I whisper.

"Not for long."

I'm having a hard time keeping my eyes open now. Hugh seems to be moving up and down with the breathing of the bed.

"They've been awful since you left," I say. "Like they have nothing to live for."

Hugh looks at me strangely. Cocking his head and curling his lip like I've just said something ridiculous. I forgot that look. Forgot that it ever existed even though he must have given it to me a thousand times.

"You're the one with the pill collection," he says.

I can't sit up straight anymore. I lean over and put my cheek on the pillow. It has the perfect coolness of your first few seconds in bed.

"I want you to come home," I say.

"I know, buddy," he says. "I can't do anything about that." He stands up and pulls the covers over my shoulders, tucking me in.

"Aren't you supposed to be saving me?" I say.

"I can't," Hugh says, very softly. "I'm not really here."

20. WINGS

Owen wakes to the sound of his name. It's breathy, close to his ear, but abrupt, urgent. It is accompanied by a noise, a flutter and snap, like a sheet flapping in the wind. He sits up quickly and then freezes, trying to understand. Something is different, wrong, like when you wake up in a strange room and it takes you an instant to accept that it's not the place you expected. Or you're in your own room but someone else is there. His eyes adjust and he looks around, searching for the difference. He waits to see the movement of something, a body, an arching wing. But there is nothing. It was a dream, he thinks, and he's ashamed, as if there is someone there to witness the eager look that must have passed across his face.

He lies back down, turns his pillow to the cool side. And then he feels it. A lifting. Not a lift into the air, but as though his insides are straining up against his skin. An urgency. Like being pulled. A smell that he can't identify but he knows comes from the past. And his name, once more lost in the rushing of blood to his ears. He is supposed to do something.

The house is dark. Sometimes his parents forget a corner lamp or a closet bulb, but tonight everything has been switched off and there's no moon, so he has to feel his way along the walls of the hallway. Into the kitchen, past the back door. To his sister's door, plastered with warnings. He doesn't knock this time.

She is sitting on her bed, slumped sideways against a mound of pillows, the candles on her desk burned down to wax pools. She raises her head when he closes the door.

"Hi, Owen," she says. "Come on in. Everyone else is." Her speech is slurred, like she's stoned or sleep-talking. He doesn't smell any pot in the air.

"Except Dad," she says. "I don't know where Dad is."

"He's still asleep," Owen tells her.

"I had a bad dream," she says.

Owen walks toward the bed. He remembers, like one of those Super 8 movies, his sister bending over him, soothing away his bad dreams, late at night after Hugh and then their parents disappeared.

Lena doesn't seem to be able to hold her head up for long from where it lolls against the wall. Even the smile she gives him seems like an effort. She gestures sloppily to the collection of items next to her. As always, the other half of her double bed holds pens and note-books and ashtrays and dishes, the way their mother's was once piled with magazines and unopened mail and cartons of Marlboro Lights. In the clutter he sees what she is referring to. A wooden jewelry box with red velvet compartments. They are filled with candy and oblong white pills.

"I lost count," Lena says.

Owen doesn't really stop to think about anything. He leans over her—she smells bitter, chalky—slams the jewelry box shut, tucks it under his arm and runs, flies, his feet barely grazing the linoleum and hardwood, toward the door of his parents' bedroom.

It's like when you've been working on a puzzle and someone comes along and insists on trying all the pieces in the spots you already know they don't fit. His parents take forever trying to get information out of Lena, who at first doesn't seem to believe they are really there.

"Did you take these pills?" their father asks, holding her shoulder to keep her from flopping over.

"Duh," Lena answers. With the overhead light switched on she looks gray-skinned and small in her bed, and she keeps slipping away unless someone is yelling right in her face. Which they are doing a lot.

Their mother is on the kitchen telephone, the cord dragged taut so it reaches the doorway of Lena's room. She is reading information off the back of a pill bottle to someone at her hospital.

"Almost sixty, we think. We don't know when she started. She's been in her room all day."

"Don't worry, Mom," Lena says. "I already threw up. I just need to stay home from school and sleep."

"She says she's vomited," their mother translates into the phone. "But I don't see any and the bathroom is next to my bedroom. I would have heard her." She pauses, listening. The next thing she says through gritted teeth. "Yes, I'm sure, Marty. Mothers hear when their kids throw up."

After what seems like hours, a decision is made to bring Lena to the emergency room. Lena is still dressed in army fatigues and a long underwear top, so her mother tries to get her shoes on. Lena is whiny about having to get out of bed. Owen and his father wait at the kitchen table, trying not to look at each other. The sky is dark blue and getting lighter with every new delay. Owen doesn't understand why they don't just pick her up and carry her out. Everyone is acting so stupid.

Finally his father goes to warm up the car. Owen runs and puts jeans on over his pajamas and sneakers without socks, then goes to the front hall, ready.

When their mother walks in holding Lena's arm, Lena looks at Owen and then back toward the kitchen, almost falling over in the process.

"Danny is waiting to walk you to school," Lena says.

"Uh, thanks," Owen says dumbly. His mother looks daggers at him, as if to say, *Don't encourage her.* She struggles to keep Lena upright and moving toward the door.

Owen follows, and it's not until they are on the porch, the white sky of early morning showering snow, that his mother thinks to tell him otherwise.

"Owen," she says. "You stay here. Lock the door and we'll call you in a couple of hours."

She bends to accommodate Lena, who is looking at the sky, mumbling about the snow. Her purse keeps falling from her shoulder, heavy with a stethoscope and notebooks and the overstuffed wallet she's had Owen's whole life.

"I'm coming," Owen says.

"Owen, please. I don't have time to fight you, too." Their father, who has pulled the car out front, filling the crisp air with a huge billow of exhaust, rolls the window down and calls to them.

"What's the matter?" he hisses, somewhere between a yell and a whisper. Mindful of the neighbors.

"I'm coming," Owen says again. Then, though it sounds lame even to him, "I found her."

His mother looks at him then. She opens her mouth to say something nicer, but he is sure it is still a no.

"Elizabeth," his father calls. "What are you waiting for?"

"Okay, Owen," his mother says instead. "Help me get your sister down the stairs."

Owen closes the door, makes sure it locks, then gets on the other side of Lena, putting her arm around his shoulder. She is heavier than she looks, and his knees buckle, but he rights himself and strains to hold his side.

"Are we going sledding?" Lena asks.

"We're going to the hospital," their mother says. "To get your stomach pumped."

Lena frowns. "How come I don't get an ambulance?" She makes a dismissive noise in the back of her throat. "*Owen* got an ambulance."

"Give me a break." Their mother sighs. They half walk, half trip her down the stairs. Lena looks at Owen and rolls her eyes with exaggeration.

The snow is falling heavily now, large, swift, silent flakes that linger on their faces for a second before they disappear.

———

At the emergency room, they leave Owen in the waiting area while the rest of them are ushered through swinging doors, already expected. Owen slouches and sulks in an uncomfortable mauve chair, watching an early-morning news show with jokey, clueless anchors. The only other people there are a guy holding a bloody towel around his elevated hand and a girl a couple of years younger than Owen and her mother. The girl has a roiling, impressive cough. She has been given crayons and a coloring book while they wait for a doctor and she uses them halfheartedly, the way Owen still does in the dentist's office, out of boredom. She stops every few minutes to cover her mouth and cough for a long time. When her mother gets up to speak to the receptionist, the girl moves over and sits next to Owen.

"I have pneumonia," she says proudly.

"How do you know?" he says. "You haven't even seen the doctor yet."

She gives him a scathing look.

"I know. I've had it before. I have asthma so I get sick a lot. How come you're here?"

"My sister tried to kill herself," he says. He's tired of lying, plus he wants to shock her. This girl seems to think she's fearless.

"Really? Wow. Why'd she do that?"

"I don't know," Owen says. He feels an overwhelming sense of doom at the thought that he hasn't asked himself this yet. He was only concentrating on getting her here.

"Maybe she did it for attention," the girl says. She lowers her voice to a whisper. "Sometimes I fake bad breathing to stay home from school or get a new stuffed animal."

"She's not *faking*," Owen says, angry. The girl's mother calls out for her to leave Owen alone. He's relieved when she moves away and resumes coloring. In a few minutes a nurse calls her inside.

An hour later his father comes out to check on him.

"What's happening?" Owen says.

"Doctor stuff. Your mother's in charge. Lena will be fine. She's pretty sick right now, though."

Owen has heard what he thinks is Lena yelling and crying whenever the swinging door has been propped open to wheel things in and out. He can't remember the last time he heard his sister cry.

"It sounds like they're torturing her," Owen says.

"Well, she's not having fun. They have to get the drugs out and the methods aren't pleasant." His father puts his head in his hands, then runs his fingers through his hair. They are shaking. "God," he says, covering his face. His back lurches once, like he's about to throw up. He stays still for a long minute, then sits up again, recovered.

"I'm going out for a smoke and to call in sick to work," he says. He pats Owen's knee and hoists himself out of the chair. Owen watches him get swallowed into the automatic revolving door and spit out the other side.

There's no one at the desk next to the swinging doors now, so Owen slips through without being noticed. Inside is a long corridor with numbered doors on either side and a huge nurse's station down at the far end. He sees his mother there, white coat on, conferring with two doctors. He slips quickly into the room that has FUREY written in erasable marker on the white door.

His sister is propped up on a gurney in the center of the room, an IV in one arm, monitor wires disappearing beneath her johnny. The worst thing is the thick tube in her nose, full of what looks like black sludge. He thinks at first that this lava is being pumped out of his sister, then he realizes the tube is pushing the stuff in. She's staring at one corner of the ceiling, but looks down when Owen says her name.

"How come you never understand the grownups on Charlie Brown?" she says, pointing up to where a TV would hang if this were a regular hospital room.

"There's no TV," Owen says, and Lena blinks and shakes her head. Her eyes focus, the glaze disappears like a film she has peeled away.

"Oh," she says simply.

"What's that black stuff?" Owen says. Lena sighs.

"Charcoal. They tried to get me to drink it. I puked it up all over Mom." She smiles at this, but Owen remains straight-faced.

"Are you going to die?" he says.

"No. But they're sending me somewhere. A loony bin, probably."

"I'll visit you," Owen says. Lena turns her head for a minute on the pillow. When she turns back she looks like she's been trying not to cry.

"Okay," she says. "Thanks." Owen nods. She pauses. "I went looking for Hugh," she says. "I thought I could find out something nobody knew."

"How come you didn't tell me?" he says. She shrugs.

"You're still a kid," she says.

"So are you," Owen says. He can hear the whine making him less convincing. But she takes it seriously.

"I don't feel like one," Lena says. She's quiet for a minute, looking back to where she thought the TV was.

"Think that's why they never tell us anything?" she asks. "Because we're just kids?"

"I don't know," Owen says. "Maybe it just makes them too sad to say stuff out loud." Lena shrugs, looking away. This answer does not satisfy her.

She stares into the corner and her eyes go fuzzy again.

"He's here, you know," she says.

"Who?" Owen says, in a careful voice, like he is talking to an imaginative child.

"Hugh. He says you did a good job," Lena says.

"Okay." Owen fidgets, uncomfortable, wanting her to snap back to reality. She yawns and closes her eyes.

"He's got that Halloween costume on," she mumbles. "The one Dad made him. With the wings."

After they take the tube out of Lena's nose, a social worker comes in to talk to them. For some reason, Owen's parents let him stay for this. The room is small, and everyone is crowded around Lena's gurney like curious medical students.

"We're going to send you to another hospital," the social worker says to Lena. She has very short dark hair, like she's too busy to be bothered with anything else, and wears a white lab coat like a doctor. "They have an adolescent psych ward. You'll have a psychiatrist to talk to. They'll want you all to come in for family meetings."

Owen can't imagine them all in a psychiatrist's office together. What would anyone say?

"Can't I just go home?" Lena asks. She still has black crusted around her nostrils and along the insides of her lips. Her tongue looks like it has gangrene.

"You tried to kill yourself," the woman says, kindly, but such bluntness makes them all flinch. "We can't send you home until we know why."

"I didn't *really*," Lena says, sounding resigned, as if she doesn't expect anyone to believe her.

"Sometimes people hurt themselves as a way to get others to pay attention," the social worker says. Lena tears up again, and shrugs.

"They're paying attention now," she says. Lena looks up. Her mother nods, reaching out to awkwardly clasp her hand. Their father moves closer, putting his arm across Lena's pillow. They both look like they're begging for something.

"I want to talk about stuff," Lena says, really crying now.

"About Hugh," her mother says. The room goes still at the sound of his name, their father closes his eyes. No one expected his mom to be the first one to say it.

"Who is Hugh?" the social worker says, making a note on her clipboard.

"My brother," Lena says, at the same time their father says: "Our son."

"He died," Owen volunteers. He says it quickly, without thinking. No one contradicts him. His mother just reaches over and pulls him in, so they are all huddled around Lena in the bed.

"Not about Hugh," Lena says, tears running through the black crust and turning it gray. "About us."

While his father and the social worker are filling out the necessary papers to have Lena transferred, Owen's mother brings him upstairs to meet the AIDS patient. He is going home today after four months in the hospital.

"David," she says. "This is Owen." David is so thin he looks about fourteen, though Owen's mother said he was twenty. He grins and holds out a hand to shake. Owen takes it and wonders immediately if he should have. Owen's mother says she'll be back a little later to pick him up.

"I've heard a lot about you," David says when she's gone. He's wearing a blue oxford shirt and loose jeans, packing extra clothing and toiletries into a red duffel bag on the bed.

"You have?" Owen says. Owen can't imagine what his mother would say about him.

"I heard you were an artist," David says.

Owen shrugs. "I just like to draw."

"I'm in art school."

"Is that like college?" Owen says.

David laughs. "Sort of. College for people who like to draw." He finishes packing his bag and lifts it with effort, letting it drop to the floor. He sits gingerly on the bed, looking like packing has made him so exhausted he is considering a nap.

"Are you better?" Owen asks. He is so used to people asking him this, he has come to believe it is the polite thing to say.

"Better enough to go home," David says. "Not cured yet."

"Did you get a bad blood transfusion?" Owen blurts out. "Like Ryan White?" He knows this is probably going too far. David doesn't seem mad. He just smiles weakly.

"No, Owen. I'm gay."

"Oh." Owen looks at the corkboard on the wall opposite the foot of the bed. There are still get-well cards tacked to it.

"That's what you wanted to know, right?" David says. He sounds a little mad now.

"Sorry," Owen mumbles.

David sighs. "Don't worry about it. Not much privacy left when you've been here for four months. It's not like it's a secret, anyway. Ask away, Curious George."

Owen pauses, thinking, as if in careful consideration after being granted one wish.

"When did you know?" Owen says.

David smiles again. "Goin' right for the big one, eh?" he says. He scoots up on the bed, lifts his feet up, and leans back against the pillows. "I was pretty young. Younger than you. It wasn't any big revelation. It seemed like I always knew."

"Did you tell your parents?"

David frowns. "Sure. They kicked me out when I was seventeen."

Owen catches his breath. He can't imagine his parents doing such a thing. They are the type who wait up all night for children to come back.

"What about my mom?" Owen says then.

"What about her?"

"Does she know?"

"Of course. We watch the soaps together and drool over the same guys. Your mom's cool. You know that."

"Not really," Owen says, looking away.

"You play Scrabble?" David says then.

They set the board up on the blue hospital blanket and play game after game, waiting for someone to come and tell them it is time to head home.

After David's friend comes to pick him up, Owen goes back downstairs to the ER. His father is with Lena, who is sleeping. They are still waiting for word from the other hospital.

"Where's Mom?" Owen says.

"She went to lie down in an empty room," his dad says. "She's on call later."

Owen asks for money and says he's going to the vending machines in the lobby.

He peeks through the glass top of every doorway in the hall. One window is covered with a curtain, the room dark behind it. He eases open the door. His mother is curled up in a hospital bed, a blanket pulled across her middle, her shoes still on. Not like she plans to sleep forever, but like she is ready to bolt on command. He walks quietly around the bed, and when he stops she opens her eyes. She pries her dry lips apart, intending to say something.

"I'm not going away," Owen says.

His mother looks confused, then nods sleepily. She scoots back, opens the blanket, and invites him in. He puts his back to her front, so they are like spoons. He remembers this from somewhere so far away it seems like another boy's life.

His mother nudges the backs of his sneakers with her clogs. "You're getting so tall," she says sadly.

"Do I look like him?" Owen says. He tenses, ready for her anger.

"You do," she says. "You all do."

His mother holds on to him so tightly he can barely breathe. He doesn't dare tell her to let go.

epilogue
the fureys, 1986

On the days that they have family therapy, Lena comes by to pick her brother up. Most days Owen meets her outside, but there are some, when it's raining or cold or he's lingering by his cubby, when she has to walk through her life to get to him. She lopes—tall, lanky, and severe, with close-cropped hair and a look she thinks is adult weariness, but is not—past the carpeted pit of the kindergarten, the tiny water fountains and open classrooms of the first through third grades, the cafeteria and the nurse's office and the gym, up the stairs and past Mr. Gabriel's sex ed class, the World War II timeline, and the auditorium that hosts band practice, school plays, and dances for seventh and eighth grades. Boys and girls half her size part their ranks to let her by. The ones who have siblings just like her at home barely look up, but the other children stare back in awe, because to them the concept of a teenager is still shrouded in mystery.

Sometimes she brings Jonah with her, which makes everything easier. Owen has been hard. Her parents are nervous and careful and suddenly eager to talk, but Owen, after her eight weeks away, and a summer of close supervision, is suspicious. As if the person they sent back is not the sister he remembers. He likes Jonah and laughs more easily with him around. Jonah tells her it will take time. The same thing happened with his family. Owen has to recover from the thought of losing her.

They walk to the T station, shuffling combat boots and sneakers through orange and red leaves, stirring up smells that make them remember. They take the train downtown, exiting at Longwood Medical. Jonah stays aboard, heading to Kenmore Square to shop for records. Lena and Owen walk past flower shops, cafés, and doctor's offices, past whole hospitals devoted to cancer, diabetes, or women. Their parents, coming from the med school and an office building at Copley, meet them in the lobby of Children's Hospital, by the gift shop. For the first instant, when they are pushing through the revolving door and their parents are stepping forward to meet them, Lena always feels as if they are about to be introduced. As though one of the white-coated men or women speed-walking by will stop, point with a pen, and announce: *This is your family.* But then her father will ask about school, and her mother will use two fingers of each hand to swiftly tuck Owen's shirt in, and Lena will remember exactly who they are.

After the meetings—which are hard because Lena keeps rediscovering, every week, like a secret that has outgrown its hiding place, how angry she really is, and worse, how angry they are at her—the Fureys go home. They do homework, take baths and showers, do laundry, eat dinner, watch TV. Lena tries to make Owen laugh, because he's still in the habit of looking more serious and doomy than he actually feels. After dinner, their father will play cards or chess with Owen while Lena sits at the other end of the table looking at her negatives. She was given a camera for her birthday and takes pictures all the time, to make up for the ones she lost. She prefers taking pictures of objects, things and their shadows, because things do not pose or lie or try too hard to smile. But she also takes pictures of her parents, and Owen, and the family reunions at her grandmother's house. Somebody has to.

They go to bed early now, lights out, doors cracked open to let in the air. Occasionally, one will meet another prowling the halls, recovering from a dream, checking the beds, listening for breathing, relocking the back door. But mostly they sleep, saving their energy for everything they have to do during the day.

In the hallway, next to the print of a Byzantine seraph with dark eyes like pocks covering his six massive wings, is a small matted and framed quote. It is the epigraph to their father's book, which has been accepted by his publisher and is due to come out next Christmas.

Every visible thing in this world is put in the charge of an angel.

—SAINT AUGUSTINE, *EIGHT QUESTIONS*

Sometimes, when Lena stands there, under the wings and eyes, if she is very still, she can feel a hint of what Owen has told her about, a heaviness, a fluttering noise, a smell that has been gone for years. After it is over, she will think she imagined it. But while it is happening, she has the oddest sensation. She feels as if she is more than one soul occupying the same space. She can feel herself at every age, Owen alone in his room, her mother taking a stranger's pulse, her father trying to read a book on the train. She can see her entire family, not as if she is watching them from above, but as if she is all of them, looking out from within.

Even the one who is missing.